VIOLCA'S DRAGON

THE DRAGON RUBY SERIES

LEILANI LOVE

This book is dedicated to two of my favorite people, my mom and my oldest son Xavier. My mom, who always had time to read to me. Xavier, for being my biggest cheerleader.

This book is also in large thanks to Anissa, Ashley, Jen, and Rachelle. Without your encouragement I would've never finished this. Without you guys, I could've never done this. Love you all!

PRELUDE

Prelude

"Violca."

The name felt like a caress as the wind brushed the skin along her arms. Her hand came up as she pushed her hair back behind her ear. Looking around, she realized she was in the woods for some reason. The trees were sparse and the light from the moon was bright enough for her to see her surroundings. As she turned around, she noticed she wasn't wearing any shoes and the grass felt soft under her feet. She looked up the path and there stood the cabin her parents used to take them to, before they'd passed away. The light in the window drawing her forward.

The woods were quiet except for the sound of her dress gliding over the grass, and the occasional hoot of the white snow owl that sat in a tree watching her approach. As Violca got closer to the cabin, she noticed that the door was slightly ajar.

"Violca." This time the voice sounded familiar and again felt like a soft caress, like her name was a whisper carried on a breeze.

She paused as she reached the porch. Violca had a moment of doubt, but decided she needed to know why she was here. Violca hesitantly climbed the stairs. The owl hooted behind her as if he was trying to encourage her to go on, and she took the last few stairs a little faster. As she reached for the door it opened wider on its own, and Violca looked in to see the old cabin just as she remembered it. The brown couch and chairs in the living room were just as she remembered and folded over the back of the couch was the red blanket that she and her sisters would use when they would cuddle and listen to their mom read to them.

A flash of red caught her eye and she looked toward the fireplace. Standing near the hearth was a woman wearing a long red dress. She had long black hair that hung just past her waist. Violca's feet moved, as if on their own, into the living room. The woman turned and Violca stopped. "Mom," she gasped.

A slow smile spread across her mother's face as she held her arms open in invitation. Violca ran into her embrace. Looking at her face, Violca saw her own violet-colored eyes mirrored back at her and blinked back tears. "Mom, what are you doing here?"

Her mother lightly ran her fingers through Violca's hair. "I'm here to see you, sweetie." Kissing her lightly on the cheek, "It's time for you and your sisters to remember, and for you all to learn about your family. We started to tell you when you were younger, but when the hunters came and tried to kidnap you and Eva..."

Violca pulled back. "Mom, I don't understand. Remember what?"

"There are things that you'll remember shortly. Not all the memories will be yours, but they're all important."

Wrinkling her brow while chewing her bottom lip, she tried to think about what her mother was telling her. It made no sense. Of course, she had forgotten some things from when she was little, but she remembered a lot. What was she talking about, hunters? "I don't understand."

"You will sweetie, I promise." Violca's mother looked toward the door and then back at her, and Violca could see the worry on her face. "It's time to run." Her mother pushed her toward the door. "Whatever you do, don't let him catch you."

Violca looked over her shoulder as her mother seemed unable to look away from the door. The house started to shake and rumble under her *feet. "Run V! Run!" her mother yelled, practically shoving her to the door.*

Violca did not want to let her mother go. It had been so long since she'd seen her. Violca felt her mom give her one last shove as the house shook more violently than before, the floor boards splitting and the pictures falling from the walls. Violca ran outside and through the woods. The farther she got from the house, the darker the woods became. The light from the moon became less and less visible and the ground that had been so soft under her bare feet became rocky and full of roots from the trees that seemed to be growing closer together.

Looking over her shoulder, she suddenly became aware of a figure behind her. Whatever it was, it was huge and it was quickly catching up, growling like an animal but running on two feet like a man. With her focus on the monster approaching she stumbled as a rock stabbed the center of her foot.

The growling got louder, and she fought the urge to look over her shoulder. Suddenly, Violca tripped over a root landed at the base of a giant tree. Scrambling backwards, the figure loomed over her, and she found herself staring into a pair of blood-red eyes that not even the dark of night could hide. Unable to get to her feet, she let out a scream.

"Mine." The word came out like a growl as it opened its mouth and the little bit of light that was available shone on a pair of fangs. Violca let out another scream as it began to lower its head and growled at her again. Turning frantically, she tried to stay out of reach. She screamed in fear and frustration.

"Awake!" she heard her mother yell before everything went black.

CHAPTER 1

Shooting up in her bed, Violca reached for her throat, feeling for any cuts or bruises. She knew rationally that nothing would be there, even as her heart continued to pound and her breath came in short pants.

The soft squeak of the door drew Violca's attention. It had opened just enough for her youngest sister, Angyalka to peek her head in. Her sister's name was Hungarian for Angel. She was born with hair so pale blonde that it looked like she was born with a halo. Her mother had teased that she would either be an angel or the devil in disguise. Out of all the girls she was the one who looked most like their father. The rest of the sisters had dark hair, just like their mother. "Hey Angel, what're you doing up?" Violca asked, patting the bed next to her.

At ten, Angyalka still loved to cuddle with her. "I heard you scream," she announced as she quickly crawled into the bed.

Running her fingers through her little sister's hair, she saw her lip quiver as she made this little statement. Since their parents' death two years back, Violca had been raising her four sisters, in large part thanks to the life insurance policy their parents left. It helped that they owned a four-bedroom house which did not require too much upkeep.

Violca had dropped out of college and taken on a full-time job as a receptionist in a law office, just to make sure she would be home nights with her sisters. Angyalka, being so young, often clung to her, and she felt her heart tighten at the obvious fear in her sister's voice. "It was just a bad dream, sweetie. I'm okay, I promise." Feeling her sister curl up closer to her side she added, "Why don't you stay with me tonight and help keep the bad dreams away?"

"Okay," Angyalka mumbled while snuggling under the covers and putting her head down on the pillow.

Kissing her sister on the forehead, Violca lay down next to her and curled her arms around her. Angyalka quickly fell asleep. Listening to the slow rhythmic sound of her sister's breathing helped pull Violca back into sleep.

THE ALARM WENT off at 5:30 a.m. and she quickly turned it off, hoping not to wake up her sister as she got out of bed to hop in the shower. She still felt groggy, since her sleep had been interrupted, but she was thankful that after her sister had climbed into bed with her, the dreams had left her alone for the rest of the night.

Feeling the hot water run down her body, Violca couldn't help but think of her dream about her mother. While heading out for their 25th wedding anniversary, their parents were hit by a car that ran a red light. Last night was the first time she had dreamt of her mother in over a year, and even though she knew it was just a dream, she couldn't help but wish her mother could talk to her. Violca had at first felt so overwhelmed when she'd started taking care of her sisters, but they were a family and nothing was going to keep them apart.

Stepping out of the shower, Violca wrapped the towel around her body and blow dried her hair. While all the sisters, except Angyalka, had their mother's jet-black hair, Violca was the only one with their mother's violet eyes, giving her the name Violca, Hungarian for Violet. The other girls were all born with their dad's sparkling blue eyes. Finishing with her hair, Violca applied the bare minimum of makeup, lipstick, eye shadow, and mascara as she proceeded to finish her routine, so she could get the girls' breakfasts ready.

Walking into the kitchen, she saw that the girls were already up. Sari, the second youngest, was standing behind Angyalka, doing her hair in a light braid. They were the closest, being the youngest two, and they always seemed to be whispering to each other. Kati was washing fruit in the sink, and Eva was getting the bread out for sandwiches.

Taking out the pancake mix, Violca noticed one of her sisters had already turned on the griddle, and she started mixing. "Hey guys, you all got your homework done. Right?"

"Of course, V. I've got a party this weekend, and I know you won't let me go if I slack off," Eva answered. Eva was seventeen and a senior this year. She was constantly being invited to parties. Since she was the second oldest, she helped the most. As soon as she was able to drive, she had taken their father's old Corolla and helped with transporting the kids, mainly taking them to school or running errands while Violca was still at work.

Angyalka and Sari both answered simultaneously, "Yes, we finished early so we could watch cartoons."

Violca looked over at Kati, who gave her a half smile and nodded, yes. Out of all the girls, Kati was the quietest, keeping to herself. She was fifteen years old, about to turn sixteen, and Violca knew this was a rough time for her. She had a quiet strength and her blue eyes showed wisdom beyond her years.

While passing out the pancakes, Violca couldn't help but wish her parents could see how the girls were turning out. All of them were doing well in school and excelling in their own areas. Sitting down, she listened to the girls talk about what they had planned and who needed to do what. Not much for talking in the morning, she enjoyed the sounds of their laughter and the chatter that just seemed to be a natural part of their lives.

CHAPTER 2

Chase woke up slowly. The beast within him was getting restless. Ever since the name "Violca Grey" had appeared on his computer screen with a picture of her and her beautiful violet eyes, his dragon had been wanting out more and more, scratching at the surface, pushing him to go out and find her. Whether she knew it or not, she and her sisters were important in the fight that was to come. Grabbing a pair of jeans, he slipped them on and ran his fingers through his spiky blond hair before heading downstairs to make a cup of coffee.

The back door squeaked as it opened and Kassandra walked in. Her long blonde hair was down, and she was wearing a pair of skin-tight black leather pants and a green fitted blouse that emphasized her green, cat-like eyes. The look she gave him made him smirk. "Coffee?"

Her only reply was an unlady-like snort. His lips curved in a half smile as he grabbed two cups. Kassandra Knight had the ability to blend into her environment so well she couldn't be detected. She had been spending her nights trying to get information on what Dmitri's men were up to. Handing her a cup of coffee, Chase sat on the chair, stretching out his long legs. "What were you able to find out?"

As he took a sip, Kassandra brought the coffee to her lips and inhaled deeply giving a contented sigh before taking her first sip. "Dmitri's sending someone. He needs to verify that this Violca girl and her sisters are the descendants of the original Earth Witch. We don't have much time."

Raising an eyebrow at that, he took another sip of his coffee. "What do they know about her?"

She shrugged. "Not a whole lot. They know about what we know. Their parents died a few years ago. They have no relatives, so the older sister Violca chose to keep them all together and take care of them."

Chase thought about that for a minute. From the little bit of information, they had gathered so far, by all accounts, these girls were living normal everyday lives. Who would have thought that between them, they had the power to find and unleash the power within the Dragon Ruby? The Dragon Ruby was a stone that the gods made when they agreed to spare the original dragons' lives after they helped kill the titans. If the power was released from the stone, they would go back to their former size and strength, which in turn would start a war with the humans. Dmitri was the younger brother of the Dragon King, Viktor, and had decided that the dragons' place was to rule the world. Humans were nothing but inferior to them and should bow before them.

Getting up, Chase went to the kitchen and put his cup away. "Since they seem pretty sure that the sisters are the ones, it won't be much longer until they try to take them."

Before he even turned around Chase could feel Kassandra watching him, a small smile playing on her lips. He narrowed his eyes. She had been teasing him ever since his strange reaction to Violca's pictures. "Dmitri knows he has to win them to his side. He can't threaten to kill one of them. He needs all five. Plus, he fears that if he angers them, they'll turn their power against him."

"It's funny to think Dmitri's scared of a ten-year-old girl," Chase said with a bit of a laugh as he tried to picture the big dragon cowering before a child.

Shaking her head, Kassandra laughed too. "Well, you know what they say about small packages."

Raising an eyebrow, Chase said, "Small packages huh, I don't think your current lover would appreciate that statement."

Rolling her eyes, Kassandra checked her email on her phone. "I think it's time one of us goes to join Scott and Eryk. Those girls seem innocent so far, and alone. They're going to need our help when Dmitri's men show up."

Chase nodded. "I'll go. You're needed here. I can't sneak in and out of Dmitri's as easily as you can."

The look Kassandra shot him let him know she didn't believe him. "I'm gonna go shower and pack some stuff. Would you mind letting Scott and Eryk know I'm coming?"

For the past few weeks, Chase had been itching to do something. He was not a man who enjoyed sitting around for very long. Gathering intelligence was an important part of any mission, but the beast within him was ready to come out and fight.

LANDING AT THE AIRFIELD, Chase slowly descended from the Cessna Citation Bravo. He missed the days when he could just shift into a dragon and fly from place to place, but he did enjoy the little luxuries their king gave them to do their jobs.

As he walked out of the plane, a black SUV pull up. The driver's side door opened and out stepped Scott Tanner. Chase was tall, at over six feet, with wide shoulders. Scott was slightly taller, but leaner. The Tanner brothers were sent to watch after the Grey sisters when they first found out who they were almost two months ago. Scott had dark brown hair that was cut into a buzz cut. His emerald green eyes stood out against his olive complexion.

"Where's Eryk?" Chase asked when he noticed Scott was alone.

"He gets out of school in ten minutes. We enrolled him in the high school that the two older girls go to so he could keep an eye on them."

Chase nodded as he took his suitcase to the trunk. "Are you enjoying your job as a security guard?"

Chuckling, Scott got into the SUV and waited for Chase to get in before he started the engine. "My desk isn't too far from the reception desk, so I'm able to watch the oldest."

Scott backed up and left the small airport.

"What have you found out about her?"

"She seems nice, keeps to herself at work, but is friendly." Chase noticed Scott smiling. "One of the lawyers has the hots for her, but she doesn't seem to be interested in him. There's one guy who comes around, but from what I can tell, they're just old friends."

Chase felt the dragon under his skin scratching to get out. The Earth Witch was important, and his dragon wasn't pleased about the idea of some stupid human sniffing around her. Even hearing that they were old friends didn't ease his dragon. "Are there any signs that they've come into their powers yet?"

"Not that I can tell. No scent of magic or anything. Her scent is almost undetectable. If her mother cast a spell to make the girls undetectable, she did a great job. You can't even smell any residual from the spell."

Chase sat back and thought about that. Magic left a scent. If she wasn't using it, there was a possibility they were chasing after the wrong girls. The sound of his dragon snorting in his head almost made him smile. His dragon knew she was the one the moment he saw her picture.

Scott took a left turn down a long driveway. The property

was big, built back from the road to give them some privacy. The house was a light green with dark green trim and a white door. "So, what's the plan?" Scott asked as Chase grabbed his suitcase from the trunk.

"Keep an eye on them. Try to get close and keep an eye out for whoever Dmitri sends."

CHAPTER 3

Violca smiled politely as the attorneys came back from their lunch. Her lunch was later in the day, since she let most of the secretaries go before her. Usually, one of the secretaries who'd been at the company long enough to know the ropes took over her position for an hour or so. When Linda showed up, Violca smiled happily. "Hey, how was lunch?"

Linda had been with the company for about four years, as the secretary to one of the senior partners. She was older than Violca and sometimes treated her like a younger sister. "Too short as always," Linda walked behind the desk, pushing her toward the door. "Your handsome friend is outside waiting for you. Can you tell me why exactly you haven't slept with him yet?"

Violca rolled her eyes and laughed as she grabbed her purse. "Because he's like my brother, and that's just gross."

Linda laughed. "Okay, but if you don't want him, why don't you see how he feels about sleeping with a woman a few years older than him?"

Violca shook her head as she walked out the front sliding glass door. Stepping outside, she instantly saw her friend Brandon. He was leaning against one of the pillars wearing his policeman uniform, his sandy blond hair blowing in the breeze. Brandon and AnnaBelle were her two best friends. She had met them both shortly after her family moved to their new home in the East Bay. The three of them were inseparable as kids, and both had helped her when her parents died. Once a week Brandon met with her for lunch at a small diner nearby. Anna-Belle's schedule made it harder to get together, but they still saw each other as often as possible.

Brandon smiled when he saw her. His blue eyes sparkled with laughter. "It's about time," he said before bending down to kiss her cheek. He placed his hand on her back as he led her to his squad car.

"I still can't believe you choose to pick me up in a police car. You know these people are wondering why a girl who just left a law firm is getting into a police cruiser."

Chuckling, Brandon opened the passenger door for her before going over to the driver's side. "I let you sit in the front, so if they're paying attention, they'll notice you're not in the back, and I've never put handcuffs on you."

Shaking her head, she laughed, imagining Linda's reaction if Brandon were to pull out handcuffs.

Brandon had been busily working on moving up from being a beat cop to a detective. He read people better than most and his instincts were almost always spot on. He tried to make it to the house for dinner on the weekends, to visit with her sisters, but he had missed the last few weekends because of a case.

Waving at their usual waitress, Rebekah, as they walked into the diner, they headed to the booth toward the back. Rebekah came to the table with two glasses of sweet tea. In her early sixties, she had soft laugh lines around her mouth and her dark hair was peppered with gray. She was a fixture at the diner. "You two are here a little later than usual."

Brandon smiled, winking up at Rebekah. "Sorry, but that one over there kept me waiting. I almost left her at the office."

Rebekah rolled her eyes. "Please, we both know you'll always wait for her."

Sticking her tongue out at Brandon, Violca laughed. "Thank you, Rebekah. I think a grilled cheese with bacon, and tomato soup sounds perfect."

Brandon grinned, "Two please."

Rebekah winked over at him before she turned, heading back to the kitchen to put in their order.

"So, how're your sisters?"

Violca leaned back in her seat. "Pretty good, I think. Eva is the exact opposite of Kati and me. She's a little social butterfly and always has some party or something to go to. Sari is, of course, top of her class, and then there's Angel who is...well, she's one of a kind." Thinking for a minute, she added, "Kati reminds me so much of me in high school, she has Samantha but..."

Brandon reached across the table and squeezed her hand. "She'll be okay, just like you. Besides, she has you, and you being there for her probably helps more than you think."

Rebekah dropped off their plates and they ate in silence, both enjoying their sandwiches. Violca thought about the dream she had experienced that morning. The few dreams she'd had of her mother since the accident were memories. This was the first time that it felt like her mother was trying to tell her something. She reached up to rub her neck as she remembered the thing that was chasing her. What was it? She didn't watch a lot of horror shows, so it wasn't like it was some monster coming out to get her.

"Earth to V. You all right over there?"

Hearing Brandon, Violca jumped in response. "Sorry, just got lost in thought."

"Anything you wanna share?" Brandon asked while watching her.

She shook her head. "No, just had this weird dream about my mom and I don't know, it sort of lingered in my mind."

Brandon nodded sympathetically. It hit him hard when her

parents had died. They treated him more like a son than his own parents had, and she knew their death had hit him as hard as it had her.

Rebekah brought them the check when they finished eating and Brandon paid. "What? You got it last time, it's my turn."

With his hand on her back, he led her to his car, calling out to Rebekah that they would see her next week. The drive back to her office was mostly quiet, both of them were lost in their own thoughts. When they got to her office, Brandon looked over at her. "So far, it looks like I should be off this weekend, how about I stop by and visit?"

She leaned over and kissed his cheek. "That would be great. I'll tell the girls that if you aren't working, you'll be over."

Getting out, she waved to him before heading back into the office.

Inside Linda looked up and smiled. "How was lunch?"

"Good. I forgot to ask if he liked to sleep with women slightly older than him, but I'll definitely ask next time I see him."

Linda laughed as she stepped out from behind the receptionist's desk. "When you ask him, don't forget to ask if he can wear that uniform," she dropped her voice to a whisper as she leaned in close to Violca, "and bring those handcuffs."

Laughing as Linda walked away, Violca stepped behind her desk and picked up her headset to answer the call that was coming in. "Wilson, Wilson, and Associates, this is Violca. How may I direct your call?"

CHAPTER 4

Chase looked over the pictures that Scott and Eryk had taken. Most of the photos Scott had taken showed Violca at work. One was of her smiling up at a guy who Scott said was her friend, Brandon. He apparently took her out to lunch once a week. There was also a girl who looked to be about the same age as Violca named AnnaBelle. The background check on them showed they had no past connection to Dmitri, although AnnaBelle's job as a freelancer made it a little harder to keep tabs on her.

Eryk had taken a few pictures of Eva at school. Eva, the second oldest, always seemed to have a smile on her face and was usually surrounded by people. Kati, the middle child, seemed to rarely smile. Chase had a funny feeling she was trying to hide a curvy figure under the loose clothes she wore. Her blue eyes showed a wealth of wisdom that went beyond her years.

Eryk came into the room and Chase put the pictures down and smiled at him. "So how does it feel to go to a regular high school?"

Eryk chuckled. "Wasn't quite what I was expecting." Eryk was almost eighteen and just shy of six feet tall. Chase figured he would probably grow another couple of inches before he was done. Eryk closely resembled his brother. He let his dark brown hair grow out so that it hung just past his collar, and his warm smile showed off his dimples. He was excited to be able to help on a mission. Normally, Chase wouldn't let him, but since they needed someone who was able to get close and hang out at the high school, Eryk was the right age. His only assignment was to help keep an eye on the girls and to find out what he could.

Chase looked down at a picture of Kati again. "Scott was saying he couldn't smell any magic on Violca. What about her sisters?"

"Magic, no, but there's something about them." Eryk looked at the picture of Kati that Chase was looking at. "Something happened with her last year. I can't get anyone to talk about it. Whatever it is, her sister tries to protect her as best she can but her classes keep her on the other side of the school most the day."

Chase smirked. "You can't get the girls to tell you, Eryk?"

Eryk grinned, showing his dimples. "I know that whatever happened started with the cheerleaders. When I ask them, they ask me why I want to know about *that* girl. I tried asking her best friend Samantha, but she glared at me and told me to go back to playing with the bitchy cheerleaders and leave her friend alone."

Frowning over some of the pictures, Chase noticed Kati hunched over. Scrolling through, he found one where her face was relaxed, her attention fixed on something "What's she doing here?"

"She was drawing, and I managed to take that photo when she stopped to look at her picture."

Chase closed the folder with Kati's info so that he could focus on those of Eva. Kati and Eva had a lot of the same features, but Eva carried herself differently than her sister. She stood up straight, and in almost every picture, she was smiling and laughing. The only ones where she wasn't, were the ones where it looked like she was defending her sister. Most of the pictures where she looked the angriest have two boys who looked like jocks. "Who're these guys?"

Eryk glanced at the picture. "Those are the two who seem to torture Kati the most. They're both on the football team, total pricks from the few encounters I've had with them."

"Do me a favor and keep on her. Make sure these guys stay away from her."

Eryk nodded. "Not a problem." The grin he gave Chase was a little mischievous. "I would love a reason to knock them both down a peg or two."

Scott came in from the shower. "Who're we knocking down a peg or two?"

Chase interrupted before Eryk could answer. "I want him to keep an eye on these guys and keep Kati safe."

Scott nodded. "Good idea, although try not to get in a fight at school. We don't need to draw any attention to ourselves."

Eryk grinned. "Better head upstairs and finish the homework they gave me."

Both guys nodded before Chase went back to looking at pictures. Opening Violca's folder again, he found himself looking at some of the pictures with her and Brandon. He fought the urge to growl. For some reason, the pictures bothered him, even though Scott had said they were just friends. Looking up from the computer he saw Scott watching him. "What?"

Scott raised an eyebrow. "Everything okay?"

"Yeah, why?"

Scott chuckled as he grabbed two beers from the fridge. Handing him one, Chase noticed him trying not to smile. "You just have this look on your face like you're going to rip someone's head off."

"Whatever, man," Chase mumbled before opening the beer he'd taken from Scott.

Taking a swig of his beer, Scott smiled. "You wanna come by the office and check her out for yourself?"

Thinking about it for a second, Chase nodded. "Yeah. I messaged Viktor earlier, and he wants me to get to know her and see what I think. I told him you can't smell magic on her, but by the picture you sent of Violca, he's pretty sure she's the right one."

Scott leaned against the counter. "There aren't that many girls with truly violet eyes, so that alone puts her and her sisters in the running. She's really sweet, so a part of me hopes she's not the one, and we can leave her out of this mess, but I have a funny feeling she is."

Chase looked over her picture. His dragon's reaction to her also made him think she was the one. Most of the night, he looked over what they had found out about Violca, debating on the best course of action to get close to her. Scott's notes about her let him know she kept most men at arm's length. Chase admired how much research Scott had done. There was even a note about a boyfriend who had dumped her shortly after her parents had passed away. Because she had chosen to raise her sisters, instead of dumping them in foster care, he decided it was more than he was willing to sign up for. "Idiot," he mumbled to himself, thinking her decision to keep her family together and raise her sisters herself, told him more about her than anything else could.

CHAPTER 5

Violca jumped when the phone rang. "Wilson, Wilson, and Associates, this is Violca. How may I direct your call?" She heard someone rattle a name and knew the lawyer's assistant should be at her desk. "Hold one moment so I can transfer you to his assistant." Transferring the call, she sighed, leaning back in her seat.

The smell of coffee reached her and she inhaled deeply. Turning her head, she smiled when she saw Scott next to her with a cup.

"You looked like you were in need," he said.

Scott didn't look like their typical security officers. He looked more like a model, and Violca couldn't fault the girls around the office for trying to get his attention. "You're such a lifesaver." She took a sip and smiled. "It's like heaven."

"Let me know if you need anything." He chuckled and headed back to his desk.

"Thank you so much." A few of the younger assistants came in and gave her a look that let her know they didn't think she was worthy of his attention. Violca rolled her eyes, almost laughing out loud when both girls tried to get Scott's attention.

Since he had started working there, their skirts had gotten a lot shorter.

The rest of the morning went well. When Linda came to relieve her for lunch, Violca thanked her and headed out. The outside was calling to her today. The sun was shining and she had an urge to sit and enjoy it.

Taking a few steps, she bumped into what felt like a solid wall. Hearing a bunch of papers hit the ground she realized she must have bumped into someone. "Oh crap, I'm so sorry," Violca said as she bent down to help pick up the papers. A pair of masculine hands began helping her, and as she looked up at a warm pair of golden-brown eyes, her breath caught in her throat.

"No, it's my fault. I should've been paying more attention."

His voice was deep and sent a chill up her spine. With all the papers gathered, she felt his hand take hers in order to help her up. Standing, she bit down on her lower lip. "Here, these are yours."

"Thank you," he said, taking them from her.

Smiling, she continued walking until she heard him say, "I hate to bother you, but I was wondering if you could help me." Stopping, she turned and he smiled. "I was actually looking for a decent place to eat. Could you recommend something?"

"There are a few places within walking distance that are pretty good, depending on what you are in the mood for."

The man grinned. He had spiky blond hair. His eyes were brown with beautiful gold flecks. Dressed in a pair of slacks that hugged his muscular thighs nicely, and a shirt that clung to his chest, she was willing to bet the rest of his body was just as hard. "I'm sorry to bother you, if you're in a hurry."

Thinking he was way too sexy for his own good, she found her breath catching. "No, actually, I was just on my lunch break."

He ran his fingers through hair. "Would it be forward if I asked to join you? I'm new to town and eating alone again doesn't really appeal to me."

Violca tilted her head, thinking about it. "Actually, I was just going to grab a sandwich at this little sandwich shop around the corner and eat in the courtyard."

~

CHASE WATCHED her and had a funny feeling he was being more forward than she was used to and was surprised that she hadn't walked away. "Do you mind if I join you?"

He saw her thinking about it before she said, "Umm, okay."

He smiled, feeling she was a little nervous. "Great, my name's Chase, Chase Reed." He offered his hand.

"It's nice to meet you, I'm Violca Grey."

When she walked past him, he inhaled. Violca's scent was a mixture of lavender and a meadow after a rain. It was clean and earthy. His dragon was having a weird reaction to her, and he found himself fighting for control over it. His skin was getting itchy as his dragon let him know he wanted to get out. *I can't shift in public, and if I suddenly turn into a dragon, most likely the girl will be afraid. Relax.* He could hear his dragon huff before settling down, but it stayed close to the surface.

"Thanks again for letting me tag along," he said, pulling open the door to the little bistro and holding it for her.

She smiled. "This place has some great sandwiches. They make their bread fresh every morning. I can sometimes smell it when people open the office door."

He watched her as she smiled at the young guy behind the counter.

"Hey Violca, how's work today?"

"Good so far, but happy tomorrow's Saturday." She glanced at the menu. "Can I get a chicken cordon bleu sandwich, beer-battered fries and a Coke?"

Ordering a Philly cheesesteak sub, Chase also ordered the beer-battered fries and a Coke. Walking over to where she was waiting for her order, he smiled. "The food here smells wonderful."

Violca bit her bottom lip and he fought the sudden urge to kiss where she had bitten. "It's one of my favorite places."

Leaning against the wall, they waited in silence for their orders to be called. He watched her out of the corner of his eye. She smiled politely to a few of the employees and asked them questions about their lives. When their orders were finally ready, she led them back out to the courtyard.

CHAPTER 6

Chase could see Violca occasionally glancing at him. After taking a few bites of his sandwich he cleared his throat. "I'm going to assume you work around here?"

"Yeah, I work in those offices over there." She pointed to the law office building. "Right about where I bumped into you."

Chase raised an eyebrow. "You seem both too nice and too young to be a lawyer."

"That's because I'm the receptionist. As much as I love to argue, I don't think I could ever be a lawyer."

"You like to argue, huh?" When she blushed, he had a funny feeling she didn't realize how attractive she was. Her clothes were fashionable and fit her well but weren't meant to draw attention to her.

"I'm the oldest of five, all girls. I not only like to argue, I'm also rather good at it when needed."

Chase laughed at that. "I guess you'd need to be. Does your dad have any sons to help balance out all the girls, help keep other boys at bay?"

He watched her face. He knew about the accident that had killed her parents, but had to pretend he didn't. Seeing pain flash in Violca's eyes, he heard his dragon growl at him in response. "Nope, my poor dad just had us girls. I used to think there were so many of us because he was trying for a boy, but then one day he confessed that he loved having daughters. He said there was a special relationship between a father and his daughters and he wouldn't trade that for a boy."

Chase grinned. "I could see that until the girls become teenagers. Then I think I would get a head full of gray hair worrying over them."

Violca smiled and they finished their sandwiches. Looking at her watch, she stood. "I better get back to work."

Standing up, Chase walked with her back to her office. "Thank you for having lunch with me."

"You're welcome." Violca smiled up at him, pausing for a second. "It was really nice meeting you, Chase."

"Would it be too forward if I asked to see you again?"

Biting her lower lip, Violca looked up at him. "Um, I don't really know if that would be a good idea."

Frowning, Chase reached into his pocket. "Why don't I give you my number, and if you decide that you had a good time and would like to get together again, you can call me." Handing her his card, she took it and looked it over before putting it in her pocket.

"I promise to think about it," Violca told him, before saying goodbye again and heading into the building. He watched her walk to the receptionist's desk.

Chase turned and felt the hairs on the back of his neck stand up, and his dragon growled in his head. Looking across the street, his eyes locked onto a man who was leaning against the building. The man smiled, showing a pair of long fangs, just before his eyes flashed red. At six and a half feet tall, his eyes went from red to brown. His body was muscular. The only thing suggesting he might be older was his shoulder length silver hair. He nodded to Chase before walking away, whistling softly.

Despite the noise of the street Chase's dragon could easily pick up the sound.

Grabbing his cell phone, he called Scott. "Hey, do you guys have videos that face outside the building?"

He could hear Scott chuckle on the other end. "Why, were you hoping to get a video of your lunch? I can tell you what happened, she said no."

Chase growled. "Very funny. There's a guy across the street. He has shoulder-length silver hair. See if you can get him on the tape and print off a picture. I've never seen him before but…"

He could hear Scott typing on the other end. "Got him, sending the pic to our phones. I get off in a few hours. Will you be at the house?"

"Yep, see you there." Chase hung up his cell. Putting it in his pocket, he glanced back at Violca's office door before leaving reluctantly.

VIOLCA SMILED as Eva and Kati cleaned up the kitchen. Having finished popping the popcorn, she put it in three separate bowls. "Eva, you sure you want to go to a party and not watch the new Barbie movie with me and the girls?"

Eva snorted. "I would V, honestly, but I know you have been looking forward to this night all week, plus, you didn't make me any popcorn."

Kati laughed and Violca smiled in her direction. Her sister didn't laugh that often and when she did, her whole face lit up. "Please tell me you're joining us?"

Kati shook her head. "If you don't mind, I was thinking I could go to Samantha's."

"Sure. Are you going to the stay the night?"

"I don't think so, but I'll call you and let you know."

Sighing, Violca grabbed two handfuls of popcorn and threw

them at both of her sisters. "Fine, you two go out and have a great time. I'm going to watch Barbie."

Both girls laughed as she headed back into the living room. Setting the bowls down on the coffee table, she smiled when she saw Sari and Angyalka already drinking the root beer floats she had made them. Before she sat down, she reached into her back pocket and pulled out Chase Reed's card. It was simple, with just his name, email, and cell phone number. It didn't give her a clue about what he did for a living. Sighing, she put the card on the table. She had a hard time picturing a guy who was practically built for sin wanting to hook up with a girl who was raising four girls.

"V, let's start the movie," Angyalka said, pulling her from her thoughts.

Picking up her own root beer float, she sat on the couch beside her sisters, tucking her feet under her. "All right, all right," she replied, pushing play on the remote.

CHAPTER 7

Chase paced back and forth in the living room, his dragon furious that he had left Violca there, even though he knew Scott would keep her safe. His dragon had never reacted so strongly to another person. When Eryk had told him about her sister, Kati, his natural protective instinct had kicked in, which was why he asked Eryk to watch her at school, but his reaction to Violca was even more intense. He knew Scott was capable of keeping her safe, but his dragon acted like he'd wanted out to protect her.

Hearing a beep on his computer, he turned back to look at what Kassandra had sent him. Scanning through the email, he swore softly. From what she was able to find out, Dmitri hadn't sent any of the dragon shifters. Instead, the information that Kassandra gathered mentioned that he had been seen talking to a demon, and had sent him to get the girls. Demons always had a thirst for power.

The different races of supernaturals seemed to be split among themselves. Demons, however, as a group, thought that everything was beneath them. Especially humans. Chase couldn't believe Dmitri would be so stupid as to send a demon to fetch the

Grey sisters. If it turned out they were wrong and these were the wrong girls, the demon would kill them all without batting an eyelash. Since the demon's eyes had flashed red, Kassandra should be able to narrow down who it possibly could be.

Chase ran his fingers through his hair. Picking up the file, he tried to figure out what he could do to get close to the Grey sisters. How do you get close to a girl who is determined to keep you at arm's length?

Chase saw Eryk coming down the stairs dressed in a nice pair of jeans and a black button-down shirt. His hair was damp from his shower. "You heading out?"

"Yep, heard Eva was going to a party and thought I would show up and keep an eye on her."

"Is Kati going too?" Chase asked more out of curiosity than anything else.

"No, I heard she was going to her best friend Samantha's house tonight." Eryk tried to look offended when he continued, "I did ask if I could go over there, but Samantha's protective of her friend."

Raising an eyebrow, Chase said, "So I'm guessing you've been flirting with the females at that school pretty heavily if she's worried about you hurting her friend."

Eryk chuckled. "Tell Scott I won't be home too late."

Grabbing a beer from the fridge, Chase sat on the couch, glancing over the files, trying to figure out how he was supposed to get close to Violca after basically being shot down this afternoon. Hearing Scott pull up, he looked at the clock. "What're lawyers doing at this hour?"

Scott shrugged. "I think some of them have their dates show up so they can look important. Any luck on finding out who or what that guy was?"

Chase shook his head. "He's not one of the dragons who left with Dmitri. Kassandra said he's been trying to recruit from other species, but there's a rumor he might be a demon."

"Shit!" Scott said, rubbing the back of his neck. "There's only a few species that have red eyes and demons are the most common, and the most dangerous…"

His sentence trailed off, both of them thinking the same thing. *Nothing that has red eyes would be easy to guard witches against, especially if they don't know how to use their abilities.* "Oh, Eryk went to a party that Eva was going to so he could keep an eye on her."

Scott nodded and Chase grabbed his keys to the SUV. "I'm going to swing by the girls' place and see if there's any trace of our new friend over there."

When Chase got to the house, he parked around the corner. He got out of the SUV and took a short walk around the block. Letting his dragon come near the surface, he didn't detect anything other than humans in the area.

Once he checked out the neighborhood, he leaned against his SUV. Most of the lights were off at the house. With no one around Chase decided to use his dragon gift to look around inside the house. Chase's gift was the ability to turn himself into a dark mist, a shadow. Humans normally didn't notice him, but anything else could detect his scent and know he was there. Turning into a shadow, he slipped into the girls' house. It was quiet. Violca and the younger two girls were apparently in bed. Sliding down the hall, he followed Violca's scent to her room. Listening for a moment, he heard her steady heartbeat before he slowly let himself into the room.

Quietly gliding across the floor to her bed, he watched as the moonlight played on her dark hair. Violca was lying on her side, one leg poking out from the covers. Chase smiled and reached out to caress her cheek. She moaned softly and rolled onto her back.

At the sound of her moan, he felt his body react. His eyes traced the shape of her leg that was exposed to him. He decided it was best to leave before the other two girls came home. Sliding out of her room, he paused in the hall and found himself in front of the youngest sister, Angyalka, as she rubbed her eyes. She stopped.

Standing still, he knew her sense of smell wasn't strong enough to sense him. When she finished rubbing her eyes, she looked up at him, and Chase could swear she saw him.

She blinked her big blue eyes, before quietly whispering, "Why were you in my sister's room?"

Could she possibly see him?

"Will you get me a glass of water?" she asked, trying to reach for him. Her hand went through him and Chase realized that somehow, this little girl really could see him. He worried she might wake the others, so he materialized in front of her. Bringing his hand to his lips, telling her to be quiet, he took her hand and led her to the kitchen.

Chase wasn't sure what he found more surprising, the fact that she saw him when he was in his mist form, or that she wasn't scared to find a stranger in her house. Reaching into the cabinet, he grabbed a glass and poured her a glass of water from the sink.

Taking her back to her room, he found himself almost smiling at the girl when she pulled on his hand, making him look at her. "Yes?"

She smiled up at him. "Thank you, Shadow Man," she said before turning to go back to her room. Stopping at her door she turned and whispered, "My sister doesn't like people in her room, Shadow Man. She would be mad if she found you in there." With that she went into her room, closing the door behind her.

Chase returned to the living room and shifted back into mist form before sliding through the crack in the door. Slowly, he glided to his SUV and decided to hang out a little while. He stayed long enough to see Eva come home. She let herself in the house, and he saw a light come on in what must be her room. Once the light went off, he started the SUV to head back to the house.

CHAPTER 8

Smiling as Eva grumbled about how unfair it was that she had been coerced into taking the girls to sell cookies, Violca headed to the store. She was determined to get the shopping for the week done in one trip and enjoy her time away from everyone.

As Violca loaded up the cart, she shook her head thinking about how four girls who were all on the slender side, could put away so much food. She sighed when she saw the store manager come around the corner. A big smile crossed his face when he saw her, and she realized it was too late to turn around. Biting back a groan as he swaggered up to her, she tried to plaster a smile on her face.

"Violca." He smiled and his greasy hair fell over his brown eyes as he looked down at her. David stood at about five foot eight inches, which was just a little taller than she was, so even though he was trying to lean in and look impressive, Violca barely had to tilt her head to look at him. Watching him look over her body while licking his lips made her skin crawl, and she had to force herself to stand there. "David. How are you today?"

David's brown eyes lit up as he saw an opening. "Today's

looking better now that you're here." Reaching out he brushed her hair back. "My night would be perfect, if you would finally agree to go out with me."

Stepping back, she smiled politely. "Sorry David, can't. I promised the girls we would watch a Hannah Montana movie."

David frowned and leaned into Violca, stepping close enough that there was no longer any space between them. "You can't hide behind them forever and, eventually," he licked his lips as he looked at her breasts, "you're going to want a man to satisfy your lusty needs." Grinning, he stepped back before saying, "How many other guys do you know who would be willing to take a girl who's raising her four sisters and has enough money to support them? Even looking as good as you do, the list has got to be very short."

Standing up straighter, her eyes narrowed as she looked him over slowly. She started at his feet, pausing at his hint of a beer belly. Then she continued up to his brown eyes and brown greasy hair before answering, "I promise, it will be a cold day in hell before me and my… lusty needs, need to stoop as low as to agree to go out with you."

She saw his eyes flash in anger as he sputtered. Her back straight and head held high, she felt his eyes stay on her as she made her way up the aisle to the checkout.

Smiling politely at the cashier as she rang her up, and declining when a young man offered to help her with her bags, she headed out to the car. Loading everything into the trunk, she got in and drove out to see David standing outside leaning against the wall smoking a cigarette. Keeping her head straight, Violca glanced into the mirror and saw him watching her car as she pulled out into the street.

Listening to the radio as she drove home, Violca felt a little pain as another love song played on the radio. Realizing that the last time she'd gone on a date was just before her parents' death, she thought about how her life had changed that night. Not regretting her decision for a moment to take care of her sisters, she still sometimes wondered what it must be like to go out and date and have a social life. Violca's days were spent working, cleaning up after the girls, cooking, helping with homework, and driving them everywhere they needed to go. She wondered what it might be like to only worry about clothes, where to go, and which sexy guy she would go out with. Pulling up, Violca saw Eva getting out of her car, and Sari and Angel running in the front yard chasing each other. She smiled, thinking deep down she wouldn't change this for the world.

As the girls helped her unload the car, Kati came walking up the street. Smiling as she saw her, Violca started to call out until she saw that she had been crying. Telling the girls to take the bags inside, Violca walked up to her and brushed her hair back. "Hey Kati, are you ok?"

Looking her over for any physical signs of her being hurt, she saw Kati nod and bite her lip. Violca pulled her close and hugged her. "Kati, please tell me what happened. I want to be able to help you."

Feeling a few tears land on her shoulder, Violca rubbed Kati's back and her heart broke, knowing that her sister was hurting.

"I'm never going to fit in, am I?" Kati whispered.

Closing her eyes, knowing how hard it was to feel like the odd one out at this age, Violca pulled back and brushed the tears from Kati's cheek. "Sweetie, I'll never lie to you. High school sucks. I hated it, all four years of girls picking on me and guys making bets to see who could get into my pants." Seeing the look on Kati's face, Violca smiled at her, trying to be reassuring. "It was hard, but I got through it and you will too. I promise." Kissing her forehead, Violca led her back to the car. "Now, help me unload these groceries and let's make dinner. I have a bunch of ice cream and cookies we can eat later as we talk about how much some people suck." Kati smiled at that and Violca led her to the house, hoping that she could help her sister.

Violca took the girls to bed, and hearing Eva and Kati talking in Eva's room, she headed to her room to watch TV in bed. A *Sons of Anarchy* rerun on, she propped herself up on her pillows and got comfortable. Understanding the appeal, but not sure how a girl like the Doc ended up with a biker like Jax, she smiled at the fight scene. Okay, maybe she could see the appeal. Turning off the TV, she fell into a deep sleep.

VIOLCA TOOK ALL *the girls to the mall to buy clothes and have lunch together. When Sari and Angel asked if they could go to the pet store after they finished eating their burgers, Violca nodded. "Sure girls, when we're done, we can go look."*

Kati smiled. "Think you'll finally give in and let us get a cat, V?"

Eva shook her head. "Not a cat. How about a big dog?" She looked at Violca. "They're loyal and could guard the house when we're not home."

Violca, happy to see Kati smiling, felt a responding smile. "I'll think about it." Gathering the trash as everyone started to leave, V heard her Mom's voice yelling in her head, "Run V, run; he found you. Girls run now."

Looking up, she saw all her sisters were looking at her as if they had heard it too. Grabbing Angel and Sari's hands, V started to run toward the garage. Eva and Kati followed, bumping into people as they went.

"V, did you just hear Mom?" Eva asked worriedly.

"Eva, later. Let's get to the car okay?" Panting, almost tripping when Angyalka fell, Violca helped her and as they ran out the exit toward the garage, she heard an animalistic growl coming from it and looked in both directions. Feeling a pull to go to the right, she ran in that direction.

Pushing the girls in front of her to keep going, she looked over her shoulder and saw a familiar shadow running behind them. Sari looked over her shoulder, screaming before she fell. Eva and Violca helped her up and she yelled, "Whatever you do, look straight ahead; don't look back."

Turning up the sidewalk, not seeing any cars, they ran across the street. Hearing the pounding of feet coming closer and the growl getting nearer, Violca felt something hit her in the back and fell, crying out as the cement scraped her knees and she hit the side of her face. Hearing another growl and feeling something land on her back, she yelled, "Run, don't stop."

"Mine." The creature growled into her ear. Feeling its breath on her neck, she struggled to get away and screamed when she felt his mouth open to bite.

SITTING UP IN BED PANTING, Violca looked to the clock and realized that it was still the middle of night and that she didn't have to be up for a few more hours. She laid her head back down and sighed.

Wondering why her dreams were haunted by this strange creature, she closed her eyes. Feeling more tired now than when she originally went to bed, Violca found herself staring at the ceiling as her breathing evened out. Closing her eyes, she said a silent prayer to be allowed to sleep in peace before she drifted off again.

CHAPTER 9

Chase spent most of the day following Violca. Watching her at the grocery store, he found himself wanting to step in and tear the manager to shreds. He had to fight back a smile when she turned him down. When he finally walked by the guy, his dragon was practically fighting to come out, to let the greasy little man understand that Violca was not his bother.

Following from a safe distance, he watched the interaction between her and Kati. With his hearing, even at this distance he was still able to hear the conversation between the two. Messaging Eryk, he asked what happened to make Kati cry.

The girls stayed in that night, and Chase watched from his car until shortly after midnight. He circled the neighborhood, trying to detect anything out of place. Letting his dragon come up to the surface, heightening his senses, he reached out, trying to detect if there was anything out of the ordinary. Finally satisfied that the girls were safe, he headed home, hoping that Scott and Eryk were able to find something out about the man who was watching him and Violca.

When Sunday came, Violca spent it with the girls, taking them on a trip to the mall, as she had promised, and convincing them to spend the rest of the day at the Fountain Gardens.

Watching the younger girls run around and chase butterflies, she saw Eva in the corner with a few girls she knew from her school. Violca looked around and found Kati sitting by a red rose. Quietly walking up behind her, she looked over Kati's shoulder to see her drawing the rose in detail. Watching her for a moment, she was careful not to distract her as she started to draw one of the fountains behind the rose, drawing it lightly as a backdrop.

Walking around the garden, Violca saw a section that was dedicated to just orchids. Noticing the different kinds of orchids, she stopped and read a sign about how the number of species of orchids is double the number of bird species and four times as many as mammal species.

Stepping around the corner, she saw a small collection of delicate purple orchids that were slowly starting to wither. Reaching out and gently touching them, Violca caressed one of the withering flowers and the flower seemed to slowly open. Violca quickly jerked her hand back. She looked at the purple orchid and leaned in to touch the plant again. Seeing the plant's stalk slowly stretch up, and the flowers almost look like they were reaching for her, she looked around, wondering if anyone else had seen it, or if she had just imagined it.

Drawing in a deep breath, Violca was curious if she could make it happen again. Seeing a small withering plant, she walked over to touch it, just as Sari and Angie ran around the corner and right into her legs.

Almost falling over, she laughed and held them to her. "Hey, you two, where're you going?"

Giggling, Sari answered, "We were looking for you, V. We want money to throw in the fountain with the little princess."

Violca smiled as the two of them pulled her toward the middle of the gardens. "The little princess, huh?"

"Come on, V, we have to hurry, or our wishes won't come true," Angyalka said, yanking her arm.

Picking up the pace, and shaking her head, Violca whispered under her breath, "When did wishes get a time frame?"

When they got to the fountain, Violca laughed as she saw the princess they were referring to. It was a stone fountain that had a young girl in the middle sitting on a toadstool, holding a frog in her hands, kissing it. She smiled to herself as she reached into her purse and grabbed some change to give the girls.

Handing each of the girls' a quarter, Violca laughed as they ran to the fountain. Both girls closed their eyes and held the coin close to their chests before throwing it in.

Taking them both by the hand, they walked back to get the older girls. As they passed the orchids to go get Eva and Kati, Violca looked over and saw the purple orchids stretching up and thriving as if they had been healthy the entire time. Shaking her head, she saw Eva telling her friends goodbye and Kati gathering her drawings.

The rest of the day at the house went smoothly. The girls finished up any homework they had and helped with some of the housework before Brandon came over for dinner. The girls spent most of the evening telling him about everything that he had missed in the last few weeks.

Violca let the girls stay up a little later than usual to play games with Brandon, and she laughed when Sari beat him at Candy Land. Making plans to have lunch with him, as was usual, she locked the door behind him as he left. Tucking the girls in, Violca sighed before she headed to bed and silently prayed that her dreams would not be plagued by nightmares.

CHAPTER 10

After receiving an email from Kassandra saying that she had a lead on who and what was watching him and Violca, he found himself checking his messages while waiting in line for his breakfast order. Chase felt a little put out that Violca never called him over the weekend. Scott teased him, saying he was losing his touch with the ladies and offered to take his spot with getting close to the lovely Violca. The growl that Chase gave him made Scott smile in response, as if he knew something.

When the young girl finally handed him his order, he thanked her and headed outside. Violca was right, the smell of fresh baked bread was enticing, and he decided to see if he could make some headway by bringing her some. Not knowing how she took her coffee, he also put in some different creamers and sugar they had set out on the counter.

Using the revolving doors, he stepped into the law offices. Even though the firm was in a small suburb outside San Francisco, they obviously did well. The lobby was open and spacious. There were couches and chairs on the sides for people to sit on while they waited, and a walkway that led right to the receptionist desk. Behind that, to the side, he could see the security desk where Scott sat, next to the elevators.

Violca's head was down as she entered information into the computer, and he could hear her asking a few questions as he walked toward her. When she looked up her violet eyes met his, and when she recognized him, she smiled, although he could see a little confusion. Violca held up a finger to let him know she would be one minute as she finished asking the person on the line a few more questions.

While she was busy, he took the time to notice that she was wearing a dark purple blouse that made her violet eyes stand out even more. He liked the fact that her hair was down, looking silky and shiny. He found himself wanting to touch it, to see if it was as soft as it looked.

He heard her end the call before turning her head. "Hi, what're you doing here? Do you have a meeting with one of the lawyers?"

Chase grinned, realizing he was actually a little nervous. This was the first time he had ever had to make an excuse to talk to a woman. "No, actually I had business in the area this morning and when I smelled fresh baked bread I..." His voice trailed off as he handed her the bag and placed the coffee on her desk. She flashed him a smile that lit up her entire face. When he heard Scott coughing as if he was trying not to laugh, he cleared his throat. "Well, I thought you might like a muffin and some coffee this morning."

Chase saw Violca glance at two of the girls who were walking past them. Both girls gave her a look that spoke volumes about what they thought of her, until they noticed Chase looking in their direction. The girls looked to be about the same age as Violca, but where Violca was naturally beautiful to him, both these girls looked like they put a lot of time into getting ready. One was blonde, the other brunette. They had their hair perfectly done. The clothing they had chosen was meant to emphasize their curves and draw attention to them, down to their stiletto heels. The smiles they gave him were inviting, and let him know he could have them if he wanted.

They both turned slightly and walked toward Violca and him. "Hello Violca," the blonde purred, and he had to hide his smile when Violca raised an eyebrow.

Not to be outdone, the brunette said, "Violca, we were just talking about you."

He faintly detected Violca whisper, "I bet," before she smiled at them. "Hi Tiffany, Amber. I hope you both had a good weekend?" They glanced from him to her and he smiled when he saw Violca roll her eyes. "Tiffany, Amber this is Chase. Chase, this is Tiffany and Amber."

Tiffany, the blonde, extended her hand first. "It's nice to meet you, Chase."

Amber shook his hand. "It's a pleasure to meet you ladies," Chase said, wondering how long they would stay down here before continuing to wherever they had to go.

Amber smiled, "Chase, do you have business with one of the partners?"

Chase shook his head, his eyes going to Violca, who answered the phone as soon as it rang. "No, I actually just stopped by for a minute to tell Violca thank you while I was in the neighborhood."

A few gentlemen walked by and looked at Tiffany and Amber. Tiffany slowly licked her lips before smiling up at him. "Well those were our bosses. We'd better get to work, but I would love to talk to you later, if you want to have a drink." Looking at Violca, she smiled cattily. "I'm sure if you call the front desk, Violca will gladly transfer your call to me."

Both girls walked away. He noticed that they were swaying their hips, and he chuckled when he saw Violca roll her eyes again. "Thank you for this," she whispered, opening the little brown bag he gave her before the two girls came over. "If I knew bumping into someone would get me coffee and a blueberry muffin, I'd do it more often." She grabbed a few of the sugars and poured them into her coffee, winking at him when he laughed.

"Actually, I was thanking you for joining me for lunch, so I didn't have to eat alone."

"It was my pleasure."

"Could I talk you into joining me for dinner tonight?"

"I can't," she said before adding, "Besides, I think you might already have a date."

Chase looked her in the eye. "I'm not interested in them." When he saw her eyes widen and a faint blush form on her cheeks, he heard his dragon growl a very possessive *Mine* in his head. He stepped back and glanced at his watch. "I have to go, but I'm sure I'll see you later."

Turning, he headed back out, only to hear his phone go off. Looking down, he saw a text from Scott that simply read,

Smooth. Are you sure you don't want me to give it a go?

Realizing that from this angle Scott would still be able to see him, he raised his hand and his middle finger before walking off.

Parked in a spot that gave him a good view of the office's front door, Chase settled into his SUV. When he heard his email go off, he opened it up to see a message from Kassandra. She was able to identify the man in the picture as one of the praised demon warriors. His name was Micah, and he was known for being ruthless and willing to do anything to get what he wanted. It was rumored that he wanted to take over as the demon lord.

Chase scanned through the email, amazed at some of the stuff she was able to find out, and what Micah was rumored to do to get his way. His ability made him very dangerous. Micah's gift was to be able to take over another person and make him do whatever he wanted. Once he took over someone's mind, Micah could take it over whenever he wanted, whether the person was in his sight or not.

Chase swore when he finished reading the email. Realizing Micah had the ability to be anyone, anywhere, he needed to get

Violca and her sisters to safety, and fast. Demons were hard to kill and one that could hide in plain sight would make it that much harder to guard them. Their best bet at keeping them safe was getting the witches to trust them. Chase looked back toward where Violca was working and hoped that gaining her trust wouldn't prove to be too difficult.

CHAPTER 11

Violca sat in the courtyard, having finished her lunch. Her mind kept going to Chase's offer to join him for dinner. Before everything, she would have jumped at a chance to go out with him. He was handsome, polite, and every time he smiled at her, she felt beautiful. Since raising her sisters, she had found that most guys ran away when they found out she was raising four girls. They might be okay if she had one sister, but four… well, that scared them completely and the few it didn't, she noticed, thought that she should be grateful, and that she could be easily manipulated.

"Hey there, stranger." Startled Violca looks up and smiles to see her dear friend AnnaBelle. In a tight green blouse with a low scoop neck that emphasized her generous breast and drew attention to her sparkling green eyes. Her long, golden hair was pulled back in a ponytail. Her jeans were a pair of low riders that clung to her hips. She could have been a model with her natural beauty, but chose instead to become a freelance writer.

"What're you doing here?" Violca asked as she got up and hugged her tightly.

AnnaBelle sat next to her on the bench, and reached into her purse, pulling out a candy bar. "I missed you, so I thought I'd stop by on your break and bring you some dessert."

Smiling, she opened it. "Oh, see, I knew there was a reason you're my favorite."

AnnaBelle pulled out another bar, grinning. "And here I thought it was my dazzling personality that made us such good friends."

Swallowing a bite, Violca winked. "Well, that's a close second, but you bringing me candy randomly during the day has to be number one."

"What've you been up to?"

"I met a new guy," AnnaBelle answered cheerfully. "We've gone out a few times, and he seems very nice. Plus, he's sexy as hell. It's fun to watch girls stop and stare when he walks by."

"You finally found yourself some eye candy, huh?"

"Yep." AnnaBelle turned, looking at her. "So, what about you, have you met anyone interesting lately?" AnnaBelle laughed at Violca's red cheeks. "Oh, you have, who? Tell me all about him!"

Violca blushed more. "It's nothing serious, I..." Biting her lower lip, she smiled, "Well, we just met. I don't think anything's going to happen."

AnnaBelle smiled. "Well, with you blushing like that, he must really be something."

"He seems nice. I've just seen him around. We haven't been on a date or anything."

"Well you better get on it, if he got your attention, he must be something special and you deserve someone special."

Violca glanced at her phone. "Shit, I have to get back to work."

AnnaBelle stood up with her and gave her a hug.

"I'm glad you came by though. I've missed you."

AnnaBelle sighed. "I'm sorry, when I finish this article I'm working on, I promise we'll all have dinner, okay?"

"Sounds like a plan, thanks for the candy bar."

Violca hugged AnnaBelle one more time before heading back

to work. One of the other assistants had taken her place instead of Linda. This one being new, she looked annoyed and left the desk before Violca even got to it. Violca fought the urge to roll her eyes.

CHASE FOUND HIMSELF SMILING, watching Violca with her friend. He took a picture of the two of them together. His dragon senses came up to the surface as they talked. He loved the way she blushed when her friend asked if she had met anyone. He frowned, growling when she said it was nothing serious.

It wasn't, of course, she was just one of the girls he was sent to protect and to bring to their side. They'd just met, but he didn't like how she brushed him off as if he was just another man hitting on her. Chase was anything other than just another man. Violca would learn that quickly enough.

It was obvious to Chase that he would need to find a way to get close to her. He had never thought of himself as vain; women were just drawn to him. He knew most people thought he was handsome and considered him charming. He'd never had a problem before, and he found he didn't like being dismissed. Whether it was his own vanity or pride, he hated the fact that she still hadn't even called him.

Tapping his finger on his steering wheel, he started to think about how he was going to get Violca to spend more time with him. Smiling, he got out of the car. He was going to fix it so she didn't have a choice.

VIOLCA WALKED TO THE CAR, happy to be done with her day. Taking out her keys, she sighed when she noticed that the front driver's side tire was flat. Swearing softly, she pulled out her phone and looked up a tow truck. Finding one, she dialed the number, telling the driver what was wrong and where to find her. Hanging up, she leaned against her car, texting Eva, telling her she would be home as soon as she could.

Hearing a voice behind her, she turned around and saw Chase on his phone. When he spotted her, he told the person on the phone he would call back later. "Hey, I was going to swing by your work and see if you'd decided to have dinner…" His voice trailed off when he noticed her tire. "What happened?"

Biting her lip, she said, "I don't know, I'm thinking I ran over a nail or something."

"Do you need help changing it?"

"No, I just called for a tow, figured they could take it and have the tire changed for me."

Chase ran his fingers through his hair. "Why don't I wait with you and give you a ride home."

Shaking her head, she blushed. "No, that's okay, the tow truck's going to take about twenty or so minutes to get here. I'll just take a cab home."

He grinned at her. "It won't be a problem. Plus, my mother raised me not to leave a girl stranded."

Laughing, Violca sighed. "Thanks. I'd really appreciate a ride home."

He nodded his head, grinning. "It'll be my pleasure." Looking around, he nodded at the juice stand. "How about a smoothie while we wait?"

CHAPTER 12

Chase found himself disappointed that Violca didn't live farther from work. The tow truck showed up shortly after they'd received their smoothies. Not wanting her to have to pay for the tire, he gave the tow truck driver enough money to cover the cost. Chase made a point to tell the driver not to tell her he had paid for it. Just to tell her it was a repair, and that it was free.

The drive back to her house took only twenty minutes, since most of the traffic had died down already. Walking her to her door, he smiled down at her. "Do you need a ride to work in the morning? I have to drive back to that area of town tomorrow for a meeting."

She shook her head. "No, that's okay, I have a ride."

As she bit down on her lower lip, he resisted the urge to soothe it with a light kiss. Before he could ask if she was sure, the front door flew open and there stood Angyalka, who looked first at Violca, then at Chase, before giving them a big smile. Chase shook his head when she started to open her mouth, worried she would say she had seen him the other night. Her smile broadened. "You made it for dinner," she simply said before grabbing his hand and pulling him into the house.

Laughing, he let her lead him into the living room where he heard Violca behind him. "Angel, what're you doing?"

Stopping, Angyalka let go of his hand, and looked up at her sister before sticking out her lower lip. "I thought he was going to eat with us."

Violca took on a very scolding voice. "Angel, you can't grab strange people by the hand and drag them into the house."

Chase found himself smiling down at the little girl, who frowned for a moment before finally saying, "I'm sorry."

"Go and wash up, I'll be right there."

Angyalka started down the hall, then turned and ran back to him. "Are you staying for dinner?"

Chase winked at her. "I don't know. I was hoping your sister would ask me, it smells amazing."

Angyalka nodded. "My sisters made spaghetti." Turning, she looked at Violca. "Can he stay and eat with us?" She paused for a long moment before adding, "Please?"

Violca sighed, running her fingers through her hair. "Angel go… and maybe."

Angyalka beamed up at him before practically skipping back down the hall where he could hear her sisters. Chase turned, looking over at Violca, who looked surprised. "She's really cute."

"Thanks, she doesn't usually act that way," Violca smiled, "Well if you're interested, we're apparently having spaghetti for dinner. Would you like to stay and eat with us?"

Chase raised an eyebrow. "Are you asking because you can't think of a way to not ask me since…" he let his voice trail off and made a hand gesture pointing toward where Angyalka had just bounced off too.

"No, I'd like for you to join us for dinner," she said, and he noticed a slight flush on her cheeks.

"In that case, I'd love to."

Violca felt her cheeks heat up so much she wished that the floor would swallow her. She couldn't believe her sister had just done that. She did invite him to dinner because Angel had basically trapped her into it, but once he'd accepted, she was glad.

"Great." Smiling at him, she led him down the hall. "I hope you don't mind being in a room full of girls."

She heard him chuckle and when she got to the kitchen, Eva and Kati both stopped talking and stared at him. "Chase, this is Eva and Kati."

Before they could reply, Angyalka ran down the hallway with Sari and grabbed him by the hands. "Come on, the table's set already."

Smiling over his shoulder at them, he said, "Guess I'm going this way."

When he got out of ear shot Eva grinned. "Who the hell is that?"

Kati smiled, blushing. "You didn't tell us you were bringing a guy home tonight."

Violca grinned at her sister's reaction, feeling her cheeks heat up again, wondering what the hell was wrong with her. "He gave me a ride home after my flat tire, and Angel invited him to dinner."

Eva and Kati looked at each other and burst into laughter.

"Glad you find this funny." Shaking her head, she grabbed the bowl with the salad. "Come on, let's get the food on the table. It's time for dinner."

Kati grabbed the bowl of spaghetti and Eva grabbed the basket of garlic bread, following Violca into the dining room. Chase was sitting between the little girls, who both seemed to be trying to talk over each other. "Guys, it's time for dinner. If you two are going to talk his ears off, I'll move you."

Both girls pouted. Violca winked over their heads at Chase.

"Chase, have you met my youngest two sisters, Sari and Angyalka?" Sitting down, she pointed to the older two as they set down the food. "And like I was trying to introduce you to earlier, Eva and Kati. Guys this is my new friend Chase. He drove me home today."

Chase shook Sari's hand first, smiling at her before looking at Angyalka. "Angyalka, that's a pretty big name, for such a little girl."

"I'll be big one day like my sister, Violca," Angyalka said.

"I'm sure you will be," Chase agreed then looked at Kati and Eva. "It's nice to meet you both."

Eva grinned mischievously. "It's nice to meet you, Chase." She grabbed the bowl of spaghetti and everyone made themselves a plate as she continued, "It was really nice of you to drive Violca home today."

Kati smiled and Violca tried not to groan out loud while fixing her own plate of spaghetti.

"I was just in the right place at the right time."

The girls instantly started talking about their day, Angyalka and Sari being the loudest. In the middle of Angyalka's story about a boy who was mean to her, she looked up at Chase, "Violca says boys pull girls' hair when they like them. Is that true?"

Chase grinned and Violca saw his shoulders shaking as he tried not to laugh. "Yes, your sister's right, boys sometimes pull hair when they like a girl."

Sari frowned as if taking it in. "Did you pull my sister's hair before you drove her home?"

Eva and Kati coughed. "No, I haven't pulled your sister's hair."

Eva, not to be left out of the conversation, said, "Don't you like my sister?"

Chase smiled at both girls before looking at Violca. His eyes locked onto hers. She felt her cheeks heat up, and her breath caught as she waited for his answer. "I do like your sister, but I think your sister would get mad at me if I pulled her hair, so I thought I would try something different."

Sari nodded. "Good, I don't like when the boys pull my hair."

Eva and Kati, unable to hold back any longer, burst into laughter. Covering her face, Violca tried to think if there was ever a more embarrassing moment in her life and found she couldn't think of one. Counting to ten, she looked up to find Chase smiling at her. He winked before going back to talking with Sari and Angyalka.

Violca was happy when the rest of dinner went smoothly. She found herself a little surprised at how easily Chase adapted to sitting between two young girls who were determined to keep his attention during the meal. He smiled and asked all the right questions, making the appropriate noises when the girls took a breath during their stories. Eva and Kati asked him a few questions, which he answered easily. When dinner was over, Kati and Eva volunteered to clean up. Sari and Angyalka ran to their rooms to finish up the last of their homework.

Helping clear the table, Violca walked with Chase into the living room. "You were great with them."

Chase smiled. "Your sisters are sweet." He walked over to one of the family pictures. Picking up the frame, he studied it before looking at her. "You have a lot of your mom in you, but if you look carefully you can find just a few hints of your dad in your features too."

"Yeah." She paused to look at the picture. "I think Angyalka looks the most like our father with her coloring, but there are traces of both of them if you look close enough."

Carefully putting the picture down, he looked around for a moment. "Are your parents on vacation?"

Shaking her head, she looked away for a second before looking back at him. "No, they passed away a few years back. I'm raising my sisters."

There was a quick flash of sympathy on his face before he

stepped closer to her, tracing the line of her cheek down her jaw with the back of his hand. "I'm sorry to hear that."

Violca nodded, wanting to say thank you, but found herself swallowing a small lump in her throat. This was usually when most guys took off running, and she found herself a little sad at the thought that he might leave and not come back.

Their eyes locked and he slowly bent down, brushing his lips against hers. Her eyes closed and she thought she heard a growl coming from him. His hand slid around her neck, gently cupping the back of her head, pulling her up. When his lips brushed hers again, she sighed, parting them just a little and moaning when she felt his tongue come out and slide against hers. She jumped when she heard footsteps running down the hall. Blushing, she quickly took a step back as Angyalka ran into the living room.

"Violca, can you help me?" Angyalka asked, her math book in her hand.

"Sure, give me one moment, I'll be right there," Violca said and watched her walk back to her room.

"I should get going." Chase headed to the door.

Violca followed him, wondering if her cheeks were as red as they felt. When he got to the door, he opened it and turned to look at her.

"Thank you for the ride home."

He reached out and gently stroked her cheek, and her eyes closed enjoying his feather-light touch. "It was my pleasure. Are you sure I can't pick you up on my way downtown tomorrow?"

Violca started to tell him no, that she would take her sister's car, when Eva suddenly popped in the living room. "Hey V, I forgot to tell you, tomorrow I'm going to have to leave early with the girls. I have a study group for a test."

She realized that her sister was listening. "I, umm, guess I could use a ride."

Chase smiled and she saw him give Eva a thankful smile. "Great, I'll be here by eight, if that's okay with you?"

Nodding, she told him good night and locked the door behind him. Shaking her head at Eva, she headed down the hall to Angel's room to help her with her homework, her lips still tingling, and still tasting Chase's kiss. She tried to get her pulse to slow down as she concentrated on helping her sister.

CHAPTER 13

Chase found himself smiling as he got into his SUV. He hadn't planned on kissing her. There was something so vulnerable about her when she had told him that her parents had passed away. He wanted to pull her into his arms and hold her. If they hadn't heard her sister coming down the hallway, he didn't think he would have been able to end the kiss.

Driving around the block, he parked his vehicle and let his dragon come to the surface. Closing his eyes, he listened for anything out of place. He inhaled deeply, trying to detect any unnatural scents. Not sensing anything unusual, he started the SUV back up and headed toward Scott's place.

Pulling up to the house, he got out and headed up the few stairs of the porch to the door. Walking in, he was surprised to see Scott and Eryk sitting in front of the TV playing the latest *Call of Duty*. He heard Scott swear when a sniper picked him off. "I know these fuckers cheat."

Eryk laughed. "Well, glad you moved on from camping, mother fuckers."

Chase went into the kitchen, grabbing two beers, placing one in front of Scott before sitting on the chair. When the match ended, they turned it off and Scott took a pull on his beer, looking at Chase. "How was your night with the witch sisters?"

Chase felt a small smile play on his lips, his memory going to how Violca's lip tasted when they kissed. Scott chuckled. "Viktor's not going to be happy about you getting overly friendly with them. Violca's a nice girl, Chase. She's not one to play around with."

Chase fought the urge to tell his friend off and to back the hell away from Violca. His dragon, sitting just below the surface, growled. The word *Mine* played in his head. "I'm not getting that friendly with them. Besides, we're going to need to be close enough to protect them if we determine they're the sisters we're looking for."

Eryk shook his head, standing up. "I know we have no concrete proof, but I'm positive those girls are the ones we seek."

Scott nodded. "I agree. The original Earth Witch's eyes were supposed to be a rare shade of violet that was passed down to the first, and usually, only daughter of every generation. The rumor is that they only had one daughter though and the fact that they have five is truly unique. I don't smell magic on them, but Violca smells earthy, like…"

"Lavender and…"

Eryk laughed. "Man, I'm glad you're not getting *that* close to her." As Chase glared, he laughed harder. "I'm going to go up to my room and finish my homework while you two compare what you think the oldest sister smells like."

Eryk headed up the stairs and Scott grinned, shaking his head. "I better get up to bed, I have to work early."

Nodding, Chase told him good night while thinking about tomorrow. He didn't doubt he could win Violca over, but getting her to confess she was an Earth Witch probably would take more time than he had. Heading up to his room, he thought a good, long, hot shower would help clear his head and help him think of some way to get her to use her magic before Micah made his move.

~

THE NEXT MORNING, Violca gave her sister a dirty look. "I thought you were leaving early, Eva?"

Eva tried to look innocent as she finished putting her books in her backpack. "I was, but at the last minute, they backed out."

Rolling her eyes, knowing that Eva was lying to her, she heard a knock at the door. Looking at the clock, she saw it was a few minutes before eight. "How convenient," she mumbled, heading from Eva's room to the living room. Hearing voices, she shook her head, wondering how many times she was going to have to tell Angel to quit opening the door.

"Thank you for not telling on me," she heard Chase say quietly before stepping into the living room.

Angel giggled.

Violca frowned, wondering what he was talking about. "Angel, what're the rules about opening the door?"

Angel looked down, pretending to pout.

"Go finish getting your stuff for school. I think Eva's about ready to take you."

Angyalka headed to her room to grab her backpack, then looked over her shoulder at Chase. "Are you coming for dinner tonight?"

Chase winked at her. "If I can get your sister to ask me again, I'll gladly come."

"V, can Chase please come to dinner?" Angel asked, her hands on her hips.

"Maybe. Go get your backpack and jacket," Violca said, gently pushing her sister back down the hall, shaking her head. Running her fingers through her hair, she looked back at Chase, who was grinning at her as he leaned against the doorframe, his golden-brown eyes dancing. "She doesn't usually take to guys." Grabbing her purse and her black jacket, she followed him out the door.

Chase smiled down at her, putting his hand on the small of her back as he led her to his SUV. "She seems sweet. I hope she's not that friendly with everyone, but if it keeps getting me free dinners..."

She blushed as he opened the door for her. Violca found herself fidgeting with her slacks and her top. Her dad used to open the door for her mother when they were still alive, but the few boyfriends she'd had, never did that for her.

When he got in and started the car, she watched him from the corner of her eye. "So, what do you do? I don't believe you've ever mentioned it."

Chase glanced at her and smiled. "Nothing exciting, I'm a security consultant. I verify an object's value and then I see to the object's security when there's something worth protecting."

Violca tilted her head. "Can I ask what you were sent to protect?"

Chase grinned. "It's more than one this time and I'm researching them now. All I can say is that if they turn out to be what we think, then they're literally the last of their kind and worth more than their weight in gold."

Violca thought about it for a second. "I take it these items are a secret?"

They stopped at a light and Chase looked over at her. Violca saw his eyes linger on her lips for a moment, and her cheeks heated at the memory of his kiss.

"While I'm verifying if they're real or not, I must keep it a secret, but if you'd like, I'll make sure you're one of the first to know and maybe even get your input on helping me to secure them."

As they started to drive, Violca smiled at him. "I don't know what help I can be."

Chase pulled into an open garage near her work and got out

with her. Again, he put his hand on the small of her back, and she found the gesture oddly comforting. "I have a funny feeling you'll have some valuable advice for me."

When they reached her building, she paused outside. Turning to look up at him, she saw him glance at the door before looking down at her. His eyes darkened as he watched her licking her lips. "Thank you for bringing me to work today."

Chase reached up and brushed a strand of hair back behind her ear. "It was my pleasure. I'll call you later to see if you need a ride to your car, if that's okay with you?"

Violca blushed, still feeling the warmth from his light touch. "Sure, call me around lunch and I'll let you know."

He leaned down, brushing his lips against hers. "I'll call you around noon. Should I call the office number or would you like to give me your cell number?"

"Oh." Reaching into her purse, she grabbed one of the cards the office gave her when she started working there. "I never use these, but this has my work and my cell number. For some reason they order these for all the employees."

Chase tucked the card into his pocket, winking at her. "I'll call you later."

Nodding, she took a deep breath, gathering her courage before leaning up on her tippy toes and brushing her lips against his. "Thank you again, I'll talk to you later." Taking a quick step back, she took the sliding door into the office and headed to her desk, biting her lip as her cheeks heated up. Determined not to turn around and look back out the door, she busied herself with putting away her purse and jacket before finally glancing up. She saw him in the doorway, a small smile on his face, winking at her before he turned and walked out of view. Smiling to herself, she greeted the people as they came in, heading to their offices.

CHAPTER 14

Chase couldn't help but smile as he walked away from her office, back to where he had parked his vehicle. He found Violca's blush to be sweet, and when she took a few seconds to look back in his direction, he smiled even bigger. Rounding the corner, he bumped into Scott. "Hey."

Scott raised an eyebrow, looking at him. "Have you come up with a plan yet on how to verify if they're the right girls?"

Chase shook his head, feeling guilty. The last thing on his mind when he was near her, was proving she was an Earth Witch. "So far, she hasn't done anything." He shrugged. "I think I'm going to do some research and see if there's a way to get her to use her magic without putting her in harm's way."

Scott nodded. "Good idea. I know the quickest way to get a response would be to threaten one of her sisters, but she'd never talk to us again if we tried that."

Chase snorted at that.

"Okay, I've got to go to work, you try to stay out of trouble," Scott said with a small smirk.

"All right, I'll message you later if I come up with a good idea."

Chase headed to his car. His dragon huffed, not wanting to

leave Violca. He shook his head, reminding himself that Scott was there to protect her, and that he would not let her out of his sight with a demon lord roaming about.

Pulling up to the house, he headed to the dining room where his laptop sat along with all his paperwork. Putting on a new pot of coffee, he turned on the computer, logging into the database Kassandra had set up for them. Finding the tab pertaining to witches, he read through it, looking for information pertaining to Earth Witches. He read the story of the first original witch and the birth of her powers.

Earth Witches were known for having special gifts that presented themselves in different ways. One of the gifts was a healing ability that was the strongest among the direct line and extended not only to humans, but animals and plants as well. The rumor was that one of the witches developed skills so strong, grass practically grew under her feet when she stood still. It was thought that Earth Witches could have only one girl. The rest of their children would be boys. The boys might have abilities, but were not known for having the gift of magic. Their daughters would be considered demi-Earth Witches. Their power would never be as strong, but every few generations one was born with special gifts.

Chase thought about it for a moment. Just because there was no record of them having more than one daughter, didn't mean they couldn't. Based on that information, he wondered if he should hurt himself when she was with him, hoping she would heal him or if he should bring her a bunch of dying plants or grass. He smiled to himself, trying to picture the look on her face if he brought her a bunch of almost dead roses. She would be polite, but with a look that would clearly say, *'what the hell?'*

VIOLCA GLANCED at the clock again. She rolled her eyes when she saw it had only been five minutes since the last time she checked. Hearing someone chuckling, she turned her head and smiled at Scott. "Do you ever have one of those days that seems to drag on forever?"

The smile Scott gave her almost made her think he knew she wanted to leave to see a guy. "Hot date?"

"Don't I wish. I have to pick up my car from the shop. A friend's picking me up when I get off."

"Okay, getting your car does *not* sound fun. Any plans afterwards?" Scott asked, and she smiled at him. He was one of the friendlier guys who worked security. He often asked questions about her sisters and their lives. He mentioned he was raising his younger brother. They formed a sort of weird friendship, being in similar situations.

"Oh, you know, the usual, homework, dinner, helping the younger two get ready for bed. I know boys are different than girls and your brother is older, but are you able to go out during the week?"

Scott laughed. "Yeah he's probably less work. I don't have to make sure he takes a bath. Plus, I only have the one. You have a lot more on your plate. Maybe next year when he's in college I can start going to happy hour." Looking up over her shoulder, he grinned. "Isn't that the guy who came in the other day?"

Violca looked up and felt her cheeks heating up. Scott chuckled before saying, "See you tomorrow, Violca."

She blushed more when Chase walked up to her, his golden-brown eyes lighting up as he glanced between her and Scott. "Are you ready to go, or do you need a few minutes?"

Reaching into her desk, she grabbed her purse and then her jacket from the back of the chair. "No, I'm good. The phones will go to one of the secretaries' desks until they turn off the phone system."

Chase put his hand on the small of her back, leading her to the door. "So, should I ask what was making you blush when I walked in, or should I assume it's a private joke between you and your fellow coworker?"

"Oh, nothing serious." Violca let him lead her to his SUV, and she fought the urge to grin when he helped her in, closing the door for her after she was settled. Maybe chivalry isn't dead, she thought to herself. When he got in, she gave him directions to the shop the tow truck driver had taken her car to.

When they got to the shop, Violca headed in while Chase got out and stood in front of his vehicle. The older gentleman behind the counter explained that she must have gone through a construction zone because she had several nails in her tire. Thanking him for helping her, she went to pay him for the tire but was told it was already taken care of before handing her the keys. Violca held back a sigh of relief. She was pretty good at keeping a cushion for her and the girls for unseen emergencies and really hated it when she had to use it. She was grateful, but curious, since she was pretty sure her insurance didn't cover flat tires.

When Violca looked outside, she saw Chase leaning against his SUV. Taking a second to admire the view, she noticed how his jeans hugged his muscular thighs and how the dark green of his polo shirt made his eyes appear darker. Violca liked his short, spiky blond hair but wondered what it would look like if he grew it out just a little. He smiled at her and stepped forward, opening the front door of the shop for her.

"All fixed?" Chase asked.

"Yeah, he just said I went through a construction zone or something, ended up with a bunch of nails in my tire." Frowning, she remembered that Chase had talked to the tow truck driver when he picked up her car.

"Glad it went flat while you were at work and not driving around."

Violca smiled, glancing at the parked cars, spotting hers easily. "Yeah, that would have sucked." Violca bit her lower lip, thinking for a moment. "I don't know if you have plans tonight, but the girls and I were planning on having tacos, if you'd like to join us."

Chase smiled at her and she felt her pulse pick up. "I'd love to. Your sisters are interesting."

Violca snorted. "Most guys run from spending a night with five women."

Chase leaned forward, brushing her hair from her face, pushing it behind her ear. "I'm not most guys."

Licking her lips, she smiled at him. "Wanna follow me home?"

"I'd love to," Chase said, dropping his hand. Violca took a deep breath and headed to her vehicle. She could feel his eyes on her as she walked away and fought the urge to turn around and look. Mentally she shook her head, chiding herself for feeling like a teenager. She hadn't felt like this in a long time.

Chase followed her home and when she pulled into the driveway, she saw Angel and Sari run out of the house. Chase got out of his SUV and both girls made a beeline for him. Sari reached him first, jumping into his arms. Violca grinned when he ended up with both girls in his arms, twirling them around, making a growling noise.

"Chase, are you staying for dinner?" Angel asked after the girls got done laughing.

"I am. Your sister asked me earlier today." Both girls cheered loudly as Chase carried them back up to the house.

"Girls, you're too heavy, get down." Violca said and laughed when they both began to pout before sliding down to the ground.

When they stepped into the house, Eva and Kati came into the living room. Eva smiled a little too big. "It's good to see you Chase," she said leaning against the chair.

Chase winked at her. "Hi Eva, Kati. How was school today?"

Eva laughed. "Another typical day at high school."

Kati looked away, biting her bottom lip. Chase noticed that she and Violca had the same habit when they got nervous. When Violca did it, he had the urge to kiss it, but with Kati he found himself feeling protective. "It was okay," she replied quietly. Chase wondered what had happened to her today and made a mental note to ask Eryk and tell him to stick to her like glue.

Looking over at Violca, he saw she had taken a deep breath and was watching Kati. Violca glanced in his direction, giving him a fake smile before Sari and Angyalka started to ramble on about their days. Chase tried not to smile when Angyalka told a story about a boy who was picking on her and how she threatened to punch him in the nose if he ever pulled her hair again.

"Angel, you know if you punch a kid you'll get in trouble. Next time make sure you tell a teacher, okay?" Violca said. Chase saw that she was trying not to smile as Angyalka pouted.

Chase hung out with the two younger girls while Violca and the older sisters made tacos. He was surprised by how much he enjoyed dinner and how much fun he had watching the girls interact with each other. The girls were all very different and had their own distinctive personalities. Although Eva seemed to be more of the outgoing type, he had a funny feeling that when Angyalka became a teenager, she would probably give Violca the hardest time. Sari and Kati were a bit more serious than the rest, and he couldn't shake the feeling that Kati would smile more if he could figure out what was bothering her at school and fix it.

When everyone was finished, he followed Violca into the kitchen, carrying a few of the plates from the table.

She smiled at him. "Thank you, I can get these."

"I can help. After all, this is the second night in a row I had a home-cooked meal." The rest of the girls came in carrying more dishes. "How about this, I wash and you dry since I don't know where anything goes."

Eva came in with the last of the dishes and smiled brightly at him. "Wow, very sexy, Chase."

Violca blushed, giving Eva a look that caused her to bust out laughing. Chase winked at Eva. "I think I still need to get a 'Kiss the Cook' apron, but if you guys have those yellow rubber gloves…"

Laughing, Eva shook her head. "I'll make sure to put both on the grocery list if you promise to come back and eat with us again."

"Deal, just make sure you get a large."

Still blushing, but with a smile on her face, Violca said, "Eva go make sure Angel and Sari have their homework done."

Eva winked at Chase before heading down the hall. Shaking her head, Violca put away the leftover meat and cheese while he started the dishes. They worked together quietly to finish up and wipe down the counters. Violca leaned against the counter watching him for a moment. "Thank you for the help."

Violca grinned when he came over to her. She noticed his movements were almost predatory, his eyes narrowing, and she swore she could hear the faint sound of a growl as he approached her, putting his hands on either side of her, caging her in.

"Thank you for having me over for dinner."

Violca felt her breath catch, her eyes glancing down at his full lips before coming back up to meet his eyes that seemed to be more gold than brown. This close, she saw gold flecks in his eyes and she licked her lips nervously. His eyes darkened and he leaned forward, brushing his lips against hers, his hands sliding from the cabinet up her arms to cup her cheeks as he slowly deepened the kiss, his tongue coming out and slowly entering her mouth. She whimpered, her arms sliding up around his neck as their tongues dueled.

Hearing someone clearing her throat, Violca jumped away from Chase, who put his head against her shoulder. She could feel his shoulders shaking and she tried not to smile when she realized he was trying not to laugh out loud. Looking over his shoulder she saw Kati standing against the doorframe, her cheeks pink. Chase slowly stepped away and looked over at Kati and smiled at her.

"Should I go ahead and have Angel take her bath?"

Nodding, Violca felt the heat in her cheeks and knew she was again blushing. "Thanks that would be great."

Nodding, Kati turned and quickly walked back down the hall. Chase smiled down at her, brushing her hair from her face. "I actually think I should be heading home."

Biting her lower lip, she nodded at him. "Thanks for everything today."

Chase's lips came down and met hers one more time before straightening up. "It was my pleasure."

Licking her lips, Violca smiled as she walked him out. When they got to the door, he stopped and smiled at her. "I had a great time." He reached up and brushed the hair from her face, pushing a strand back behind her ear. "I hope we can do it again soon." He bent down and kissed her softly before whispering, "I also hope to one day soon finish that kiss without interruption."

Violca felt her cheeks heat up, swallowing before nodding. "I think I'd like that."

Chase winked at her before opening the door. "I'll try and call you tomorrow okay?"

Grinning she nodded. "Sure."

Chase stepped out, smiling at her before shutting the door. Violca took a deep breath, before releasing it slowly, and then walking down the hall to check on her sisters.

KATI DID her best during the day to stay invisible. She knew Violca didn't understand why she always bought such baggy clothes, but was grateful she never made a big deal out of it. Keeping her head down, she went to her math class but stopped when she heard familiar laughter behind her.

"If it isn't the beautiful Kati," she heard Rick as he walked up on her left. Feeling an arm go around her and pull her to the right, she sighed, pulling away, knowing that it must be Rick's best friend and ringleader, Alex.

"Let go of me," she hissed and felt him tighten his hold on her.

"Kati, we were hoping to run into you before class."

Kati finally wiggled out from under his arm. "Get away from me." She walked faster and heard Alex call after her, "I'll have you soon, Kati."

Kati found herself shaking in her math class. Last year, when she was in the shower after gym class, one of the cheerleaders took a picture of her in the shower. Like most of the girls in her family, she had developed early, but had hidden her breasts well with the shirts she wore. The girl who took the picture sent it out to all the cheerleaders and jocks. Eva found out and wanted to tell the principal and Violca, but Kati made her promise to keep quiet, hoping that it would just die down if she ignored it.

Kati managed to get through her math class and quickly headed to her gym class, ducking into the locker room. Changing in one of the bathroom stalls, she heard a few of the girls laughing as they talked about the fat girl who just tried out for the cheerleading squad. She sighed, trying to hide until the group left.

When the locker room was finally quiet, Kati stepped out of the stall to put her clothes away in her locker. Turning, she ran into Melissa, the head cheerleader, as well as the girl who had taken her picture and started all her torment. Melissa was almost Kati's opposite in every way. Her long, perfect blonde hair was pulled back into a ponytail. Kati hated her curves and envied Melissa for her small waist and hips. Kati was pushing into a D cup bra where Melissa probably barely fit into a B cup. Melissa never went outside without her hair and makeup done. Melissa smiled at Kati with a superior look. "Kati, you have got to quit hiding in the bathroom stalls." Her lips turned up as she looked her over. "You don't have anything that the rest of us haven't seen."

Kati looked down, trying to step around her only to have Melissa block her.

"Stay away from Alex."

Kati stepped to the side, Melissa finally letting her go. Walking to the door Kati sighed, "Not a problem."

Kati stayed as far away from them during class as she could. Once most of the girls cleared out of the locker room, Kati took her shower. Since she had lunch after gym, she was able to wait and take her shower last and avoid the other girls.

Wrapping the towel around herself, she headed over to the bench where her clothes were, when she suddenly saw movement out of the corner of her eye. Turning, she saw Alex and Rick standing between her and the doorway. Alex stood a little taller than Rick. Alex had sandy blond hair and brown eyes. His face was almost perfect, except for his nose that had a little bump in it from getting broken last year when he got sacked during the game. Rick had darker hair and hazel eyes. Rick's facial features were not as perfect as Alex's and the gap in his teeth was very noticeable when he smiled. Everyone knew Alex mainly kept Rick around because he was thicker, more muscular, and always willing to do exactly what Alex told him to do.

"Hello Kati." Alex smiled as he walked toward her.

Kati clutched the towel to her chest as she glanced at her clothes, then at the door behind them. "Unless you guys came to tell me I was right, and that you two are actually girls, I think you're in the wrong room."

Rick and Alex backed her up near a set of lockers and Rick winked at her. "We'll gladly show you that we're not girls."

Alex's grin made Kati shiver in response as he looked her over. His eyes paused when he got to her chest, and she tightened her hold on the towel. She tried to stand a little taller and look down her nose at them, trying to imitate the look she had seen

Violca give when some guy annoyed her. "You have nothing I want to see. Make sure the door doesn't hit your ass on the way out."

They both moved forward, and Kati felt her back hit the lockers behind her. Her eyes widened as she tried her best not to give into the panic that was starting to rise.

"I think it's time we prove to ourselves whether or not that picture was Photoshopped." With that, Alex reached out and yanked the towel from her grasp and dropped it behind him.

Squeaking, she tried to cover herself when she heard an unfamiliar voice, "Is this where the jocks hang out during lunch?"

Alex and Rick both turned to the voice and she noticed them tense. Glancing over their shoulders she saw Eryk. Kati had seen him around, but since she kept to herself, she had never talked to him.

"This is a private party, Eryk. You should leave."

Eryk glanced at Kati, and she thought she saw a note of sympathy in his green eyes. She blushed, wishing she could just melt into the floor. Her one arm crossed her chest as her other tried to cover herself. Her legs squeezed tight together. Kati was sure she could hear the sound of her knees banging together as her legs began to shake.

Eryk nodded. "I don't think you guys were invited either." He smiled at them, his eyes narrowing. "If you want, we can fight about it. Pretty sure I could kick your ass before the teacher hears us."

Rick and Alex glanced at each other before Alex turned his back to her. "Next time, Kati," he said before walking out, bumping Eryk along the way.

Eryk slowly walked to Kati. Picking up the towel and wrapping it around her, he kept his eyes on hers. "Are you okay?"

Kati nodded, swallowing past the lump in her throat. "I'm fine, thank you."

Eryk nodded, the look on his face saying he didn't quite

believe her. "Why don't you get dressed and I'll wait for you by the door to make sure no one comes back, okay?"

Nodding, Kati waited for Eryk to get to the door. Sitting on the bench she felt her body shake. Hearing Eryk shuffle, she took a deep breath and began to get dressed, determined not to break down in front of him.

CHAPTER 16

A sigh escaped Eryk as he leaned against the door. Picking up on her sorrow, he shifted a little. He should have entered sooner but had to wait until the teacher walked past so he wouldn't be seen. Running his fingers through his hair, he heard Kati walking toward him and turned, trying to smile reassuringly at her. "I was going to have lunch when I heard them. Would you like to join me?"

Kati nodded and walked in front of him, looking down. Following her out one of the side doors, he took the other side of a bench she chose. The smell of her nervousness filled the air. "I don't think we've officially met yet. My name's Eryk."

Kati looked over at him, smiling shyly. "I'm Kati."

"Nice to meet you, Kati." They both pulled out their lunches and ate quietly. When they were finished with their sandwiches, Eryk looked at her. "Can I ask what's up with those guys?"

Kati shook her head, and he could tell she didn't want to talk about it. "They're just jerks." He noticed she fidgeted with her fingers, playing with the side of her jeans. "Thanks for helping me out."

Eryk smiled at her. "It was my pleasure, trust me. Maybe next time, I'll get to punch that smug look off their faces."

Kati laughed and he grinned. He had never heard her laugh before, and he enjoyed watching how her face changed, relaxing, making her look more her age. Eryk had thought Kati and her sisters were pretty, but when Kati smiled, she was prettier than her sister Eva. Glancing at his watch, he smiled. "I guess we should go back to class."

Getting up, he swung his backpack over his shoulder and followed her to the door. "Hey, you have Mr. Reynolds for math, right?" Kati nodded and he smiled. "I don't suppose you'd like to hang out with me after school and help me with some of the problems?"

Ducking under his arm as she walked back into the school, she said, "I don't know how much help I could be."

He winked at her, stopping for a second. "Two heads are always better than one. What do you say, would you like to?"

Kati tilted her head before nodding. "Sure."

Eryk felt like he'd won a small battle. "Great, how about I meet you out in front when school gets out?"

Kati nodded, and they heard the bell that signaled the end of the period. "Okay." Eryk watched as she walked down the hall. He followed her to make sure she got to her class without incident before heading to his own class.

VIOLCA CHECKED HER PHONE, having a weird feeling that something was going on. Rubbing her chest for the third time in the past hour, she was sure something was hurting one of her sisters and she had a funny feeling it was Kati. She didn't believe in psychics, but sometimes she wondered if her mom was right about people having connections. Violca swore sometimes she could feel her sisters' pain or if something was bothering them.

The oddest thing was when one was sick or had a cut; it almost felt like she took some of the pain into her. AnnaBelle swore, when they met, Violca healed her scratch when she fell off her bike, and that was how they became close friends.

She knew Kati was going through something, but she had refused to talk to her about it. Violca didn't want to push her, but found it hard to see her sister hurting and not have any way to help her. Eva, lately, also seemed to have something on her mind, but Violca knew that Eva was more open than Kati. If she didn't come right out and say something, it wouldn't be long until she did. Eva for the most part, was an open book.

Seeing Linda, Violca smiled up at her and grabbed her purse from in her desk. Linda was wearing a red blouse today with a black skirt that hung just to her knees. Her hair was pulled back in a bun that was held together by chopsticks. A few loose hairs around her face helped her pull off the look. "Sorry I'm running late today, meeting ran late."

"I know how those meetings go, I knew you would be running late. I'm just glad I get to go have lunch. I'm starving."

Linda laughed as Violca headed to the door, smiling when she saw Brandon leaning against his cruiser, parked in front of the building in a tow away zone. He smiled, showing her the dimple on his left cheek, before opening her door. "Few more minutes and I'd have left without you."

Laughing, Violca slid into Brandon's car. "No, you wouldn't have."

Brandon chuckled, "Okay, you're right, I wouldn't have, but I'd have been grumpier."

Violca shook her head. She was glad Brandon had called her for lunch. She found herself often wondering what Chase was up to and she welcomed the distraction. He told her he would try and call her today, but so far, she hadn't heard from him. Shaking her head, she tried to focus on what Brandon was telling her as they headed to lunch.

~

HAVING MESSAGED Eva earlier that she would not need a ride after school, Kati stood outside the front, near the parking lot. She wasn't sure what kind of car Eryk drove or where he parked. Turning, she saw Melissa coming out of the school. When Melissa saw her, she smiled a snide smile before flipping her hair. Kati noticed a few of the girls from the cheer squad following her and bit back a groan.

"Well, if it isn't Kati. Got tired of hanging out in the bathroom stall?"

Kati heard the girls behind Melissa giggle and felt her cheeks heat up. Before she could even think of something to say, she heard Eryk. "Sorry I took so long Kati."

Melissa turned around, her brown eyes looking at Eryk, smiling coyly. "Eryk, I didn't know you knew our dear friend Kati."

Eryk glanced between the two before smiling at Melissa. "Actually, I know Kati very well." He winked at her before reaching past Melissa, taking her hand. "Are you ready to go, baby?"

Kati could feel her cheeks heat up as she let him lead. The surprised look on Melissa's face was priceless. Her mouth opened and closed before a superior look crossed her face. "Well when you want to upgrade, let me know," she said before turning and walking away with her friends.

Eryk rolled his eyes, keeping her hand in his. He led her to his car, a red Altima, and opened the door for her. Once she was in, he closed the door. When he slid in the driver's side, he shook his head. "I hope that was okay back there. That girl Melissa seems kind of…"

Kati found herself grinning, and finishing for him, "Bitchy?"

Eryk laughed, as he began backing out. "Exactly."

Most of the drive to his house was spent in light conversation,

Eryk mainly asking some questions about her family. When she told him, her parents were dead and that her sister was taking care of them, she was surprised to hear that he was also being raised by his brother and felt an instant kinship with him.

"Can I ask you how it is you became so popular with everyone?" When she didn't answer right away, he continued, "I know it's none of my business, but I think hearing your side of the story would be better than one of them telling me their side, and yours would probably be the true version."

Kati looked out the window and kept her eyes focused on what they were passing. "Last year Melissa thought it would be funny to take pictures of some of the girls younger than her in the shower. Once she took mine…"

Kati stopped, trying to figure out how to finish the story when Eryk replied, "Did she get in trouble?"

Kati shook her head. "No, I thought if I just let it go, they would get bored and leave me alone, but so far that hasn't happened."

They spent the rest of the drive in silence. When they pulled up, she followed him up the stairs. "My brother actually gets off early today. He should be home soon."

Kati smiled and he pointed toward the kitchen table. "Let's work in here. I think it has the most room." Eryk hurried over and moved a few papers and folders as she took out her book. Turning to the correct chapter, she pulled out a piece of paper and began to work on the current assignment.

CHAPTER 17

Scott pulled up to the house. He saw Eryk's Altima and remembered that Eryk had texted him earlier saying he was bringing the middle sister, Kati, over to do math homework. He had also told Chase to make sure that he did not randomly show up.

Scott walked up the stairs, catching the faint earthy smell that was similar to Violca, but instead of the faint lavender, he smelled honeysuckle. Scott's cat seemed to have an instant reaction to the scent and he followed it inside, wondering why his cat suddenly seemed to be so near the surface.

Stepping into the house, he walked through the living room, hearing Eryk's deep voice asking a question, followed by a softer feminine voice that caused him to almost purr at the sound. Scott shook his head before entering the kitchen next to the dining room where he saw Eryk and Kati, heads both down as they worked on their current math problem. Eryk glanced up, smiling at him. Kati's head slowly came up and looked right at him. When her blue eyes locked onto his, Scott felt all the air leave his body, like a punch in the gut. "Kati, this is my brother, Scott, who I was telling you about."

Kati smiled shyly.

He heard Eryk clear his throat and realized he was just staring at her. "Hi. It's nice to meet you, Kati."

Eryk gave him a weird look before going back to his homework. Scott ran his fingers through his hair, trying to figure out why he was having such a weird reaction to this young girl. Walking back out of the kitchen, Scott decided to head upstairs and take a shower, hoping that would wake him up.

Scott had been staying up late trying to help Chase research the girls' history. No matter what database they looked in, they couldn't find anything before their parents. It's like their family history was erased and whoever did it, sure as hell did a good job. No matter where he looked, the link to get more information was listed as under construction or had been moved. That same message came up no matter what they did.

After his shower, Scott put on a plain black T-shirt and a pair of blue jeans. Heading back downstairs, he again smelled Kati in the kitchen. He walked into the living room, determined to ignore them and tried to flip through the channels, hoping that the television would drown them out.

Despite his best intentions, he could hear his younger brother saying something about how he was glad she was able to come over and help him since he was having a hard time figuring out the homework on his own. Her soft reply made him smile. Listening intently to them, he frowned when he didn't hear any noise.

Getting up, he walked to the kitchen, his excuse being he needed a beer. Walking in, he saw Eryk leaning over Kati and growled loudly. Without thinking about it, he took the few steps to Eryk and grabbed him roughly by the collar, pulling him off her. "What're you doing?" he said between gritted teeth, feeling his cat right below the surface as his teeth lengthened.

Eryk's eyes widened and he could smell Kati's fear. Instantly he let go of Eryk. The thought of her being afraid of him caused him instant regret. Eryk rubbed the back of his neck where Scott grabbed him. "She was just showing me the steps she took to get the correct answer."

Scott looked at Kati and swore when he saw her big blue eyes rounded in fear. He looked back at Eryk, then at Kati, not knowing what had come over him or how to explain it, "I'm sorry, I…"

Kati bit her lower lip before whispering, "Eryk, can you please take me home?"

Eryk nodded and walked past Scott, not even looking at him. Fighting the urge to punch the wall and swear, Scott mumbled another apology before walking out of the kitchen, down the hall. Using the back door, he stepped out of the house and paced.

What the fuck had happened? His brother might have been a little closer than was appropriate, but he was not doing anything wrong. Besides, what if they were doing something? They were the same age. Growling low at the thought of his brother touching Kati, he heard the car start and kicked the wall. "God dammit," he said, fighting the urge to follow them.

KATI LOOKED out her window the entire ride back to her house, giving him directions when they came to a turn he needed to take. She was shaking, not sure what had happened between Eryk and his brother. Was Eryk the type of kid who took advantage of girls; was that why his brother was all over him? Or was his brother some weird psycho who beat on his brother?

When they got to her house, Kati reached to open the door and felt Eryk's hand on her arm, causing her to jump. "I'm sorry, Kati, about what happened."

Kati nodded, biting her lower lip before asking, "Does he do that a lot?"

Eryk shook his head. "No, he's never done it before, actually."

There was a pause as if he was trying to think of the right thing to say. "He's been working really hard lately and is under a lot of pressure, but that still gives him no reason to act like that."

Nodding, she opened the car door. "I, um, will see you at school tomorrow."

"Okay. Again, I'm really sorry for my brother."

Kati tried to give him a small smile before getting out of his car. Closing it, she practically ran to the front door. Violca would be home soon from work and Kati would prefer not to tell her she went to a guy's house she barely knew and that his brother pulled him off her even though nothing was going on. Walking in the house, she quickly headed to her room, avoiding Eva, who called after her from the kitchen.

CHASE PULLED up to the house and saw that Eryk's Altima wasn't there and wondered if he was still taking Kati home. Walking into the house, he noticed Scott sitting in the living room with a beer in his hand. "Where's Eryk?"

Scott looked up at him and by the look on his face, Chase could tell he was upset. "He's taking Kati home." Taking a big swig of his beer, he shook his head. "Man, I don't know what happened, but I think I fucked up."

Chase frowned. "How the hell could you have fucked up? Did you tell Violca something you shouldn't have?"

Scott shook his head. "No, when Kati was here, I almost punched Eryk for touching her."

Chase started to smile until he saw Scott's face and heard him growl, his eyes narrowing on him. "I don't understand, he's not the type of kid to take advantage of a girl. Why would you care if he was touching her? What happened?"

Scott stared at his beer, his thumb stroking the top. "I don't know, she smells like honeysuckle and I..."

His voice trailed off and Chase thought about it for a second before smiling at him. "Did you imprint on our very young witch?"

Scott growled, shaking his head. The idea had obviously never entered his mind. Chase tried not to smile as he saw his friend thinking about what he had just said. Suddenly Scott growled, "Shit!" The sudden outburst caused Chase to laugh.

"What the fuck am I supposed to do now? She's too young to claim and if Viktor finds out..."

Chase shook his head and walked to the kitchen. "I think you need another beer and I'm going to join you." Grabbing two beers from the fridge, he opened them both before walking back into the living room. Handing one to Scott, he smiled. "Think this is karma for you teasing me about getting too close to the older sister?"

Scott took a drink of his new beer. "Viktor's going to kill us both."

CHAPTER 18

Violca walked into the house and instantly felt the tension coming from inside. Walking down the hall, she saw Eva sitting in her room. "What's going on? Why's it so quiet?"

Eva shrugged. "Sari and Angel went next door to play, and Kati went right to her room after she got back from studying at Eryk's house."

"Who's Eryk? I don't think I've heard of him."

"He's new to the school, cute and seems nice so far. I didn't know he and Kati knew each other until she told me she was going to his house."

Nodding, Violca walked over to Kati's room. Standing outside, she took a deep breath. Violca really wished she and Kati were closer. She always felt like she was saying the wrong thing. Knocking on her door, she waited a second before letting herself in. Kati was sitting in her bed, sketchpad in her lap, her hair down, blocking Violca's view of her face. "Hey, how was school today?"

Kati nodded before answering in a shaky breath. "It was fine."

Violca closed the door and walked over to Kati, who was

sitting on the bed. She sat there for a moment, the silence stretching out. Violca could feel that something was bothering her. "Your sister told me you went to a kid named Eryk's house. Did something happen that I should know about? Did he hurt you or anything?"

Kati looked up, shaking her head. Violca could see that her eyes were red. Scooting closer to her on the bed, she reached out, pushing her hair back behind her ear. "What happened, Kati? Why are you crying?"

"No, Eryk didn't do anything. We were studying in his kitchen and I guess his brother thought he was doing something and got really mad at him. I got scared, thinking he was going to hurt him."

Violca bit her lower lip. "What was he doing that his brother overreacted?"

Kati sighed and played with the string on her bedspread. "He was leaning over, looking over my work, trying to see how I did one of the problems that he wasn't getting." Violca raised her eyebrow and Kati shook her head. "He wasn't touching me or anything, just leaning partly over me to look at my paper."

Violca trusted her sister so she smiled. "I believe you, Kati. Maybe it just looked different from the brother's angle."

Nodding, Kati looked at her drawing.

"Did your friend Eryk act like stuff like that happened a lot?"

Kati shook her head. "No, he seemed totally surprised."

Violca smiled. "I'm sure they talked. For now, why don't you invite Eryk over here so there are no misunderstandings?" Getting up she headed to the door, ready to change out of her work clothes for the day. "As long as he stays out of the bedrooms, you know I have no problem with boys coming over."

Violca saw her sister grin when their eyes met. Eva and Kati knew that she trusted them but believed in "not tempting the fates" as her mother used to tell them. Kati nodded at her and she nodded back before turning to leave the room. Feeling better,

Violca went to her room to change into a pair of jean shorts and a tank top. Walking back to the kitchen, she sighed, going through the fridge. "Eva, why don't you go get the girls? I was thinking we could do pizza tonight, I don't feel like cooking."

She heard Eva call back, "Sounds great, be right back," before she heard the door open and close.

Hearing her phone ring, Violca looked around. She found it in the living room and answered it without glancing at the caller ID. "Hello."

"Hi, Violca. This is Chase." Violca smiled at the sound of his voice. Throughout the day she had checked her phone and felt like a silly teenager.

"Hi there." She closed her eyes thinking about how she had already said that. "How was your day?"

"It was good, sorry I didn't have a chance to call you earlier. I wasn't quite sure how your work felt about you taking personal calls, and then I got absorbed in my research."

Violca smiled. "It's okay, my work is usually all right about it, as long as we aren't busy, but that's hard to predict most days." The door swung open and Sari and Angyalka ran in, both loudly yelling about what kind of pizza they wanted.

"There's a rumor going around that you guys are having pizza tonight." Chase teased and her heart skipped a small beat.

She saw Eva looking at her. Eva smiled a little too brightly, then ushered the girls from the room. "Yeah, I thought I would treat the girls, would you mind if I call you later, maybe after dinner?"

"Sounds good, I'll talk to you later tonight."

Saying her goodbye, she hung up the phone and turned to see Eva in the doorway smiling at her. "What?" she asked and grabbed her keys and purse, she walked down the hall to get Kati so they could head out to eat.

~

SCOTT PACED in the living room, waiting for Eryk to get back from taking Kati home. Glancing at the clock, he realized that Eryk must have stopped or something along the way since he should have been home a while ago. Once Chase pointed out that he had imprinted on Kati, he went upstairs so he could be alone with his own thoughts. He swore again. How the hell could he be imprinted on a girl who wasn't even out of high school, and worst of all, seemed to be scared of her own shadow? "Fuck!" he growled again.

Hearing a car drive up, Scott saw Eryk. When he walked in, his green eyes looked worried before he looked down and tried to walk past him. "Eryk, stop, we need to talk." Scott ran his fingers through his hair. "Please, I…I'm sorry."

Eryk stopped and looked at him. "Did you think I was trying to take advantage of her?"

Scott shook his head, his mouth opening then closing. "Sorry, when I saw you leaning over her…"

"You assumed what, I couldn't control myself?" Eryk asked and Scott flinched at the sound of hurt and anger in his voice.

"No." Scott fought the urge to swear again. "My cat took over and didn't want you to be that close to her."

Eryk frowned for a moment before putting it together. "You imprinted on Kati?" Scott nodded and Eryk slowly smiled. "Oh…"

Growling softly, he raised an eyebrow. "How'd you get her to come over today? I thought you two hadn't talked."

"Do you remember me telling you that she was getting harassed by some of the kids in school?" Scott nodded before Eryk continued, "Chase asked me to keep a closer eye on her, and today two of the guys at school…"

Scott growled, gripping the couch until he heard some of the fabric rip and realized that his claws had started to lengthen. "I got to her in time, and I was able to figure out why they're giving her such a hard time."

Scott looked at Eryk, trying to not yell at him.

"I need you to relax before I tell you what happened and to promise you won't go and kill a few stupid teenagers."

Scott growled, knowing he was not going to like what his brother was about to tell him. Walking into the kitchen, he grabbed two beers and handed one to Eryk before he sat down. Normally he wouldn't give his brother a beer, but after the day they'd had he figured they both deserved one or three. Taking a swig of his beer, he growled, "I won't kill anyone."

CHAPTER 19

Chase found himself sitting outside Violca's house, late at night, making sure everything was okay. Leaning back in his seat, he watched as the last light turned off. Violca had called him earlier, after she took the girls out for pizza. The conversation was light and he enjoyed hearing about her day. Inhaling deeply, Chase caught the scent of something different in the air. Getting out of the SUV, he walked closer to the girls' house, stopping when he saw a black wolf near the side. As Chase neared the wolf, it growled, low and threatening. Chase noticed its fur was standing up as it lowered its' head. The wolf's canines showed, and as it snarled, its eyes glowed an almost blood red.

Chase's dragon let out a low, long growl of its own, and he could feel the skin on his arms and legs itching to change. Fighting to keep control, he reminded his dragon of the damage they could do in this small neighborhood if he shifted. The smell of the wolf was off, and he knew it was a demon pet that could be taken over by the demon if it wanted. Enhanced by dark magic, they're taller than any wolf and twice as strong.

The wolf came out from the side of the house and they circled each other in the front yard. Between clenched teeth, Chase growled, *"What're you doing, demon spawn?"*

The wolf almost seemed to smile at him and he could hear his response telepathically, *"I'm here to check on what was promised to the master, dragon."*

Narrowing his eyes, Chase let out a large growl and lunged for the wolf, who jumped away, and the sound of laughter filled his head. *"I'm over 200 years old, dragon, and my master is much, much older. You'll leave the young witches alone; they're not your concern. "*

His dragon growled *MINE* and the fight to keep control over it got harder. *"The witch is mine, wolf, and I'll chew your hairy ass and spit you out before I let you close to them."* He heard the wolf laughing, before he finished. *"The witch is mine."*

The wolf lunged at him, then turned to mist and vanished. The smell of sulfur was the only thing left behind. Chase clenched his fist, wanting something to hit. Frustrated, he walked back to his SUV. Picking up his phone, he instantly called Scott. "We have a problem," he started when he heard Scott's voice.

"Are the girls all right?" Scott asked, and Chase could hear the growl stemming from the need to protect his mate.

"They're fine, but there was a wolf, a demon's wolf."

"What was he doing there?"

"I think he was here to tell me to leave the girls alone, but just in case..."

Before he could finish, Scott cut him off. "We need to confront Violca and move them into protection."

Chase swore, leaning his head back against the headrest. "What do you want me to say, 'Hey are you and your sisters' descendants from the original Earth Witch? There's a demon who's after you, and oh yeah, I'm a dragon and I need you to come with me. Our dragon prince decided you are needed so he can rule the world and restore us to our former glory."

Scott snorted, before mumbling, "Oh and by the way, a panther imprinted on your teenage sister."

Chase could feel the start of a smile on his lips at Scott's comment. "Look, during the day you watch Violca, I'll watch the younger two and Eryk can keep watch on the older two until I figure out what to do. Maybe Kassandra or Viktor can help us come up with an idea. We will have to take rotations to guard their house."

He heard Scott sigh in frustration before he said, "Fine, but you better come up with something soon. I'll not let a demon get his hands on them."

"I will, I'll take first watch tonight." Scott agreed to take the second watch, Eryk taking the last, following the girls as they go to school. Getting comfortable in his car, Chase watched Violca's house.

Violca looked around to find herself back in the woods by the cabin. She turned at the sound of the white snow owl behind her, then she turned back and slowly headed to the cabin. Walking hesitantly to the door she paused, placing her hand on the knob before turning it. Walking in, she saw her mother by the fireplace again, standing in the same long red dress.

Violca's mother turned to look at her. "Violca," she said, slowly coming toward her.

"Mom." Violca hugged her tight. "I know this is a dream, but I'm so happy to see you." She tried to blink back the tears that were threatening to form.

Her mother's smile was warm. "I have so many things I wish I would have told you when I had time, but now I really need you to listen to me."

Violca frowned at her mother's words.

"I need you to go to the cabin and find my book, sweetie. It will help you and your sisters with the things that are to come."

Violca tried to think of what book her mom could possibly be talking about. "I don't remember you having a book at the cabin other than the ones you read to us as kids."

The white snow owl hooted outside, and her mom shook her head. "Find the book, the owl will help. He guards over it, waiting for you and your sisters to return."

The flames in the fireplace flickered and her mother looked behind her, eyes narrowing. Turning back to Violca she whispered, "You must be careful. Danger is circling you and your sisters. Retrieve the book, my dear daughter, and trust your heart. It will help you figure out who to trust and who to be wary of."

The sound of the owl got louder and her mother brushed her lips against Violca's cheek. "It's time to leave, he tries to find a way in and my power grows weak. It's time to wake, Violca."

Sitting up at the sound of the alarm, Violca turned it off and leaned back on her pillow. With a sigh she thought of what her mother had told her in her dream. The rational part of her knew it was a dream, but another part felt that her mother was trying to reach out and talk to her.

It was a long drive to the cabin. Could she take her sisters out of school for a long weekend to look for a book that may or may not be there? Getting out of bed, she headed to the shower, wondering what her mother meant when she told her danger was circling her and her sisters.

CHAPTER 20

After Scott relieved Chase, he spent most of the night in his dragon form, flying. Chase's dragon had been itching to get out. After his flight, he slept a few hours and then was ready to watch the younger girls at school.

Eryk drove by him, following the older two girls to the high school. Nodding to him, he parked away from the building. Getting out, he walked toward the school, watching the people dropping off their kids or walking by the school.

Canvassing the school, he found an open window. Not seeing anybody, he misted and slid in, floating up the air vent. He wasn't sure which classroom the girls were in, so he used their scent to find them. Finding Angyalka first, he smiled when he heard her voice. Looking through the vent, he watched her for a few minutes before scanning the room, checking out the teacher, the aides, and even the students. The demon could possess anyone, which made his job of protecting them that much harder.

Noting everyone's face, he slid through the vents, looking for Sari. When he got to her classroom, he looked over everyone in her room too. He noticed a little boy pulling her hair and Sari glaring at him. Chase smiled.

Chase watched as Sari looked behind her at the teacher. When she noticed that the teacher was not paying attention, she reached back and touched him. The kid jumped like he was shocked and Sari smiled before turning back around. Chase frowned, having never seen any of the girls use magic, ever. It could have been static electricity but judging by the way the kid jumped, he doubted it.

Scott's panther was not happy that he was not the one guarding Kati. He understood that it was easier for his brother since he was already at the high school. He knew Eryk would protect them, guard them with his life. That was the only thing keeping him calm.

Since the death of their parents, he'd trained Eryk to protect himself. Eryk was a natural fighter, and when Scott joined with the dragons, they helped train him in ways Scott never could have.

He watched Violca, noticing that she had dark circles under her eyes. He saw her rubbing her eyes again and he walked over to the coffee machine in the back. He made her a cup, making sure to add plenty of cream and sugar, and took it to her. "I would ask if you had a late-night partying, but I know more than likely one of the girls kept you up."

Violca smiled at him, her eyes lighting up when she saw the cup of coffee in his hands. "No, just have a lot on my mind. Do I look that bad?"

"Nah, I just noticed you yawning and thought you could use a pick-me-up."

Tilting her head, she looked him over. Violca could tell he was muscular by the way his shirt hugged his body and she was willing to bet he had a six pack under there. The way his eyes lit up when he smiled gave him a cute boyish appeal. "Can I ask you a personal question?"

Scott nodded.

"How come you never go out with the girls that are always trying to get your attention?"

Scott blushed, fidgeting. "I guess I'm picky, plus like you, I'm picky about who I bring around my younger brother."

An image of Chase in her house with her sisters made her blush. Before Violca could reply, the phone rang and Scott winked at her, leaving her to answer it. "Wilson, Wilson, and Associates, this is Violca. How may I direct your call?"

The rest of the day went by rather quickly. Violca found herself thinking about her dream and her mother. Part of her thought she was going crazy, the other part wondered what would happen if she and the girls took a few days to go to the cabin.

When it was finally time to leave, Violca gathered her stuff and headed to her car. As she passed a guy, he bumped into her. Turning to apologize, she stopped when the guy turned to look at her, a cold smile on his face as he looked her over. His hair was cut short in a buzz cut and he had a prominent tattoo on the side of his neck, in the shape of a scorpion. He stood well over six feet tall, making her feel small. She fought the urge to shiver. "I'm sorry, excuse me."

"Sorry, Miss, I wasn't paying attention."

Nodding, trying not to be rude, Violca continued to her car. Looking over her shoulder, she saw him still there watching her and she walked faster. Maybe she should get away for a little while.

When she got to her car, she looked around one more time. The garage was empty and Violca shook her head, thinking she was getting wound up for no reason. The guy was a little creepy, but there was no reason for her to think he was following her. Starting up her car, she backed out and left the garage.

Violca looked both ways before she pulled out and noticed the guy leaning against one of the walls of the building across the street. Standing next to him was another man not quite as tall.

His head was also shaved and he also had the giant scorpion tattoo on his neck. The guy she'd bumped into earlier winked at her, and Violca drove away.

Was he what her mother was talking about? Were those dreams real? Shaking her head, Violca wondered if she was going crazy. On her way home, her phone went off and she saw Anna-Belle on the caller ID. Smiling, she answered and looked around. She noticed that there were no cops and decided she could spend a few minutes on the phone with her. "Hey sweetie, how are you?"

"I'm good. I just thought I'd better call you since I wasn't sure when I could make it over."

"Work keeping you busy or the new man in your life?"

AnnaBelle laughed. "A little of both, actually. But I promise when I can, we'll get together and I'll catch you up."

"You better. Brandon has been pretty busy with work and I miss you guys."

"I'm sorry, V, I promise soon I'll find time to come over and we'll have lunch and I'll catch you up."

"You better girl, I need to let you go. I'm driving."

"Okay V, I'll call you soon."

"Okay, talk to you later." Hanging up, Violca smiled, feeling better having talked to AnnaBelle. Brandon and AnnaBelle could always make her smile, even when it was something as simple as a phone call.

CHAPTER 21

Chase watched the girls for a little bit, smiling when he saw Violca pull up to the house. Waiting a few minutes before calling her, the sound of her voice instantly made him smile. "Hey Violca. It's Chase."

"Hey, Chase, how are you?"

"I'm good, I was just wondering if you and your sisters wanted to go out for dinner tonight? Italian, maybe?"

"That sounds good."

"Great, I was doing errands and should be there in about twenty minutes, if that's okay?"

After she agreed, they hung up and he looked at the clock on the phone. He saw Angyalka's white head bounce past one of the windows before popping up in her room. Waiting long enough, he started his vehicle and pulled up to her driveway. Getting out of the car, he saw the front door open and Sari ran out to greet him. As she jumped into his arms, he laughed. "Hey Sari, how was school today?"

She smiled, blushing. "It was okay." Chase wondered if her blush had anything to do with her possibly shocking that kid in class. He hadn't seen anything else the rest of the day but found he could not totally explain how she did what she did. It could have been static electricity, but with the look on her face, he thought it was intentional.

"Just okay, huh?" He grinned when she blushed more, nodding.

When he got to the door, Angyalka came running to him. "Chase!" she yelled, throwing her arms around his legs. Smiling, he bent down and picked her up too.

"Hey Angel, how's my other favorite girl?" Angyalka giggled, but before she answered Violca came down the hallway, wearing a pair of blue jeans that hugged her curves nicely and a black, scoop neck top. Chase loved that Violca had her hair down, and she smiled when she saw him.

"Girls, go get your shoes on." Chase released them and they both ran down the hall. Laughing, Violca smiled at him. "You spoil them, you know."

Chase winked at her and smiled when he saw a small blush covering her cheeks. Closing the door behind him, he walked over to her and brushed his lips against hers. "So, how was work today?"

Violca shrugged. "It was okay." When they heard the girls running back down the hall, Violca stepped away from Chase. Eva and Kati came out smiling and greeted him. "You mentioned Italian. Did you have a place in mind?"

Chase shook his head. "I saw a place not too far from here, unless you girls have somewhere else you prefer?"

"You might've seen Mama Mia's down the street. They're pretty good," Eva said.

"That should be good. Is everyone ready?" Violca asked. The girls nodded and they headed out. Chase offered to drive, since his SUV had enough room for all of them, and Violca gave him directions.

Chase knew Scott was sitting outside watching while they had dinner. Scott was having a hard time staying away from Kati and worried that his outburst the other day would make her scared of him. He also wanted Chase to talk to Violca, especially after what he'd told him about Sari in school.

They enjoyed their dinner, Angyalka and Sari keeping the conversation light and full of laughter. Chase enjoyed listening to them and watching the dynamics between them. Violca wasn't that much older than Eva and Kati, and the role Violca had with them was different than the one she had with Angyalka and Sari.

After dinner, Chase took them home and helped Violca get the younger two girls ready for bed. Eva and Kati smiled at him, saying they were going to their rooms. Eva winked at him before heading down the hall, and he smiled. He liked Eva. She was very outgoing and seemed to be encouraging Violca and him to be alone.

Violca came back from the kitchen with a beer, catching Eva's wink. "Subtle," Violca mumbled and Chase laughed.

"I don't think she even tries," Chase replied, smiling at her when she sat next to him, pulling her legs up under her.

"No, she doesn't. One of her many, many charms."

Chase slid his arm around her and couldn't help but chuckle.

"I think it's amazing how you take care of your sisters. Tell me about your parents. What did they do?"

Violca tilted her head, and he could see her thinking about it for a minute. "My parents were a very adorable couple who met when they were quite young, actually. My dad said he knew she was the one when he met my mom. He was just in the third grade but he said he knew that he was going to marry her."

"Your mom must've made quite an impression."

She nodded. "There was something about my mom that drew people to her. She went to school to be a teacher, but after I was born, they decided she would stay home. My dad was an accountant to several big companies that paid him very well because he was known for his honesty and ability to help people increase their bottom lines without layoffs."

Chase's finger slid up and down her neck, gently playing with her earlobe. "Your father sounds like a very smart man."

"He was. He worshiped my mother and adored us girls." She looked up at him and he could see her breath catch when he traced her ear. "He never seemed to mind having only daughters. He said he knew that we would be as wonderful and gifted as our mom and that no boy would compare."

Leaning down, he brushed his lips against hers. "Like I said, very smart man." Chase felt her lips curl up in a smile, and he used his hand on her neck to tilt her head up as he gently deepened the kiss. When she sighed, he gently coaxed her tongue into his mouth and sucked on it. Violca turned more toward him, and he moaned as he pulled her closer, his hand sliding up and down her back.

They continued to kiss, Chase slowly lowering her onto her back on the couch. His hips cradled between her thighs, he pulled up one leg, his hand continuing down until he cupped her firm butt, angling her up more as he gently moved against her.

Breaking the kiss, he put his forehead against hers, panting softly. Chase gently kissed her again, smiling as he tried to catch his breath. He pulled back, brushing her hair from her face. He noticed she was biting her bottom lip, indicating she was nervous. "What're you thinking about?"

"The last boyfriend I had was two years ago when my parents passed away. He dumped me when I moved back into the house and started raising my sisters." Taking a deep breath, she continued, "I haven't been with anyone since, and never in my parents' house."

Chase smiled and brushed his lips against hers before slowly sitting up, pulling her with him. "Your boyfriend was an idiot." Violca smiled at that comment and he looked into her violet eyes and could see her nervousness. His dragon wanted to reassure her, nuzzle her neck, letting her know that everything was okay.

"How about if I go home tonight and we take things slowly and see what happens?"

"Are you sure you don't mind?"

Chase grinned and kissed her on the nose. "Not at all." Standing up, he reached down and pulled her up. "Personally, I'm happy your ex was an idiot and easily scared off." He kissed her gently. "Can I call you tomorrow?"

Violca nodded.

"Make sure to lock the door when I leave." He pulled her to him one more time for a kiss. Her response made him hungry for more. He broke the kiss before he went too far. "Sweet dreams, Violca."

A light blush spread across her face. "Good night, Chase."

He walked out the door, smiling when he heard her lock it behind him. Looking at his watch, he got into his SUV and drove around the corner. His watch would not be over for a few more hours. He could still taste Violca on his lips, his cock was still hard so he squeezed himself trying to relieve some of the pressure, and thought to himself, this was going to be a long night.

CHAPTER 22

Violca woke up the next morning with the same feeling again, as if the dream of her mother had been her trying to talk to her. Wiping the sleep from her eyes, she heard the door open and turned to see Angyalka standing in her doorway in her pink nightgown, her pale hair flowing around her head like a halo. "Hey, Angel, what are you doing up?"

"Can we take the cat with us?" Angyalka said, rubbing her eyes until Violca patted the bed next to her. Angyalka climbed in, and Violca thought about what her sister had just said.

"Honey, what cat and where would we take it?"

"The big black cat that likes Kati. I don't think he would like it if we left him here while we went to go play at the lake," Angyalka said matter-of-factly.

Violca tried to think of any cat hanging around the house. Not remembering one, she smiled indulgently. "I think the cat will be okay if we leave it here for a few days." Thinking more about what Angel said, she tried to remember telling any of the girls about possibly going to the lake. "Angel, sweetie, what makes you think we're going to the lake?"

"We went in my dream." Violca brushed the hair back from

her sister's face. Occasionally, Angyalka said something about things she couldn't possibly have any idea about. At first, Violca, Eva, and Kati thought she'd overheard something and just repeated it, but other times they could not explain it and tried to ignore it.

"I was thinking about going to the lake. Would you like to go?" Violca asked, glancing at the clock, realizing that her alarm was going to be going off soon.

Angyalka nodded and Violca smiled at her. "I think we should go too. If you want, you can get a little more sleep while I take a shower, okay, munchkin?" Violca kissed her on the nose before getting out of bed and heading into the bathroom to take a shower.

When she was done, she stepped into the kitchen, happy to see everyone getting ready for school and having breakfast. "Hey, what would you guys think about us taking a long weekend to go to the lake?"

Sari immediately jumped up. "I want to go!"

Eva put the last sandwich in the bag, "Long weekend... does that mean we get to miss school?"

Violca tapped her fingers on the counter. "Does anyone have a test coming up?"

Both girls shook their heads no and Violca smiled. "If you're all okay with it, why don't we go tomorrow?"

Everyone agreed. Violca knew she had a ton of vacation and sick hours she never used so getting off wouldn't be a problem. After breakfast, she kissed Angyalka and Sari on the forehead and hugged Eva and Kati before running out the door.

At work, Violca parked her car and headed to the front door. When she got close, she saw Brandon standing there with a cup holder, holding two Starbucks cups and a bag in his hands. "What're you doing here?" she said, hugging him tight. "I thought you were busy on a case?"

Releasing her, Brandon looked down at her, his blue eyes

sparkling, his smile so bright she could see his dimple on his cheek. "I was. We caught him, V."

He hugged her again, using the arm holding the bag. When he released her, he held up a cup. "I bought you some coffee and a muffin."

Grinning, she grabbed the coffee and the bag. "We should celebrate later."

"How about this weekend? I actually have a few days off and thought I could come over and maybe BBQ at the house," Brandon said.

"Oh, we can't this weekend. I decided to take the girls to the lake to stay at the cabin for a long weekend." Violca took a sip of her coffee, sighing happily. She went through the glass doors, Brandon following her, "How about you come with us?"

She saw Brandon thinking about it as he walked her to her desk. "Stuck with you and the girls in a cabin by the lake?" Violca raised an eyebrow and Brandon laughed. "Sounds perfect, I've missed everyone. When do we leave?"

"Tomorrow morning, think you can have stuff packed by then?"

"Yep." Brandon leaned across the desk and kissed her on the nose. "I'll call you tonight, don't tell the girls, I want to surprise them."

"Okay."

Brandon laughed, then turned, practically running into Scott, who was standing close behind him. Scott frowned at him and Brandon smiled politely before leaving out the sliding glass doors. Taking her muffin out of the bag, Violca smiled at Scott. "You don't look very happy to be here today. Rough night?"

"No, more like a rough couple of nights."

Violca smiled politely, thinking he must be talking about his brother.

"You look happy. I take it your friend brought you breakfast."

Violca heard the slight emphasis on the word friend and smiled. Most people had a hard time believing she had a guy as a best friend. "He did. He was excited to finish a case and wanted to share the good news."

"Have you two ever..." Scott's voice trailed off and Violca smiled at him.

"No, we have not. I've known him since we were both little kids."

"Friends are important," he said before going back to his desk.

Violca took a few small bites of her muffin between phone calls, enjoying her coffee. Calling up to HR, she let them know that she would not be in for a few days.

Linda came down in the afternoon to relieve her for lunch. "Hey, I hear a rumor you're going to take a few days off."

Violca grabbed her purse. "Yeah, taking the girls to the cabin up at the lake."

"That should be fun. Are you bringing that guy who has been coming around here?"

Violca shook her head before saying, "No, he's not going."

Linda made a tsking sound. "That's too bad."

Laughing, Violca headed out the sliding glass door. Eva had packed a lunch for her that morning and she was going to enjoy it on the bench near the park. Eating her lunch, she noticed two squirrels playing in the trees above her head.

After a few minutes, one of them ran in front of her, stopped, and sat up on its hind legs, looking at her. Biting off a piece of her apple, she tossed it toward the squirrel. The small piece landed between her and the squirrel, who ran to take it. A little surprised that the squirrel didn't immediately run away, she bit off another small piece and tossed it in the squirrel's direction. The other squirrel ran over and took it, both watching her before someone walked past, scaring them away.

Finishing her lunch, she threw away her trash and walked

back to the office. Glancing past the door, she noticed that the guy she saw yesterday was standing there. His head was turned and she could see that the scorpion tattoo on his neck had writing around it. He looked in her direction, smiling at her, and again she felt a chill. Quickly walking through the sliding glass door, she hoped he was gone before she got off work.

CHAPTER 23

Chase received a text from Scott telling him he overheard Violca talking to her friend Brandon and that they were talking about going to a cabin near a lake for a long weekend. His dragon growled in the back of his head, not liking the fact that Violca had made plans with another male to go away for the weekend.

Kassandra listed a cabin that the family owned in northern California. The cabin was at the base of a mountain, near a lake. If they drove, he figured it would take about six to eight hours to get there, depending on how many stops they made. Kassandra was monitoring the girls' finances and since she didn't report any big purchases, he assumed that was where they would be going. He decided to call Violca after everyone got out of school, to see if she would tell him where she was going, and if possible, to get invited.

Chase followed the girls' home, meeting Eryk around the block. "Hey, how was school?"

"I managed to get a few classes switched so I could be in some of Eva's classes and managed to run into Kati between some of hers."

Chase nodded, wishing the younger girls' classes were closer together. "Have those guys been giving Kati a hard time?"

Eryk grinned, his eyes lighting up. "Not since we had our little chat the other day."

Nodding happily at that comment, Chase couldn't help but grin back. "Did Kati mention going to the cabin this weekend?"

Eryk nodded. "Yeah, said her sister woke up this morning and asked them. So, they're taking a long weekend to go to their family's cabin."

Picking up his phone, Chase debated about calling Violca now or waiting until she got off. Deciding to wait, he nodded to Eryk. "You should go home. I'll take over watching the girls for now."

Eryk nodded, getting into his car and driving off. Chase moved his vehicle, parking so he could still see the house and keep an eye on things. Scott was paying close attention to Violca and took some pictures of her at lunch feeding two squirrels. He also took a snap picture of a guy who seemed to scare Violca when she was coming back from lunch. The tattoo on the guy's neck looked just like something demons might use to mark their slaves. The picture was a little blurry so he couldn't make it all out, but Scott was going to try and see if he could get another picture and stay closer to Violca just in case he was right about the tattoo.

Viktor, their king, was not happy about how things were progressing. Kassandra had passed on a message wanting them to hurry up and prove that these were either the girls they're looking for, or not. If not, he wanted them to come back and get ready. His brother's army was growing and harassing dragons and other supernaturals, trying to get them to align with him.

With about thirty minutes left before Violca got off work, Chase decided to go ahead and call her. "Wilson, Wilson, and Associates, this is Violca. How may I direct your call?" The sound of her voice made him smile.

"Violca, hi, it's Chase." He asked how she was doing, and tried to keep the conversation light. "I was wondering what your plans are for the weekend?" he finally asked.

There was a pause before she spoke up. "I'm actually taking the girls to a cabin we have up north. It's near a lake and I thought a mini-vacation would be nice."

"That sounds fun, just you and the girls, or are they bringing friends with them?"

Violca laughed. "No, the four girls are enough. An old friend of mine is coming, but that's it." There was a pause for a second before she continued, "What about you, any plans this weekend?"

"Probably will work. My employer is getting impatient. I think I might have to go on a road trip though, not sure just yet."

He heard ringing in the background. "I have to go. End of the day and the phone's going off. I'll call you back later tonight."

Chase said goodbye and hung up. Seeing some movement from the front yard, he looked in that direction and smiled when he saw Angel and Sari running. The girls were chasing each other around and laughing. Kati came out, sitting on the porch with her sketchpad. He noticed that even though she was drawing intently she kept looking up to check on the girls. He could see a small smile on her lips when she looked over at them.

Chase smiled, thinking about how his friend had imprinted on this young girl and how well he'd handled it so far. Neither one of them had told Kassandra or Viktor yet. Kassandra, he knew, would get a good laugh, but Viktor, well that's a different story altogether.

If these girls were the ones they were looking for, Viktor could react in one of two ways. He might use Scott, since he knew that by being imprinted on the girl, he would give his life for her or he could get so pissed he'd skin him alive and hang his cat hide on his wall.

It had been so long since any of the dragons had found their mates, he had a funny feeling Viktor might be happy that his friend had imprinted. Shifters and Weres mated for life. Unlike his friend though, Chase wouldn't know he had found his mate until after he slept with her. That seemed like the much more fun way to find his mate.

Chase saw Violca pull up and his body instantly reacted when she got out of the car. Most days she wore slacks, but today she was in a gray pencil skirt and a white blouse that clung to her breasts nicely. He smiled when he noticed she was barefoot and carrying her heels in her hand. From the smile on Kati's face and the gesture of her hand, he could imagine her making a small joke by the way they both grinned and laughed.

Chase thought Kati was a pretty girl even though she seemed to be trying to hide herself most of the time. When she smiled and laughed, Chase knew without a doubt she would grow up to be beautiful. Poor Scott was going to have a hard time keeping the guys off her when she gained some confidence. That thought made him chuckle.

The girls followed Violca inside and he saw them occasionally walk by the window. He knew they were packing up for their trip tomorrow, since Scott and Eryk both confirmed the girls were leaving in the morning. Kassandra sent them satellite pictures of the area and selected a few spots where they could rent a cabin but they decided camping would be better, since the nearest cabin for rent was over twenty miles away. Tomorrow they would follow behind the girls and *Brandon*.

CHAPTER 24

Brandon pulled up to the house in a long white van. Violca walked outside to greet him, "Where'd you get this?" she asked, giving him a light kiss on the cheek.

"I rented it. I figured if I took my car you would make sure the youngest rides with me. This way we can drive together and you can help keep me awake."

She laughed, thinking Brandon knew her too well. It was a long drive and the girls had a hard time entertaining themselves. The look on Brandon's face told her he knew he had guessed right. "What? The girls miss you and want to tell you all about what's been going on at school."

The girls' bags were in the living room. They used their backpacks to bring something to do when they weren't outside. Hearing Brandon's voice, Angyalka and Sari ran into the living room, throwing themselves against his legs. Brandon picked up each girl and kissed them loudly on the cheek. Kati and Eva came in next, giving him a hug and a kiss on the cheek.

"Hey stranger, we missed you," Eva said with a wide grin.

Brandon shook his head looking over at Violca. "I see Eva hasn't changed." Eva stuck out her tongue at him and he laughed.

"Sorry, I actually landed a big case that just broke, and it looks like we got the guy."

Brandon looked over at Kati. "Can't wait to see what you've been working on." She smiled at him and he grabbed one of the heavier looking bags. "All right, girls, let's get the van loaded, head out, and get breakfast."

The younger girls cheered and they all grabbed something and headed out. Violca looked around, making sure they'd gotten everything before locking the door. When she got to the van, she heard Brandon telling them about the TV's that are hooked up and how they can watch different movies if they want. "Wow, you got a fancy van."

Brandon chuckled. "Nothing but the best for my girls."

Violca snorted, throwing the bag in the back. Closing it up, they all piled in. She heard the younger girls in the back debating about what movie to watch first.

Chase growled when Brandon led Violca into the house. His eyes narrowed at the guy's hand on her back. He heard Scott and Eryk both chuckle and he looked over and glared at them, which seemed to make them laugh harder. Ignoring them both, he went back to watching the house, glad to see they didn't linger.

They pulled out shortly after the girls, keeping a far enough distance that they hoped Brandon didn't notice them. Chase didn't think he'd be paying that much attention, but as a cop he might notice a car that stayed behind them for several hours.

Eryk brought plenty of food and Scott brought them all a thermos full of coffee. "What did Viktor say when you talked to him last night?" Scott asked, shortly after they get on the highway.

"He told me that I had until Sunday night to find out for sure and to secure the girls; otherwise he said he would be coming to take care of it for me. Said we've had plenty of time."

Scott turned slightly in his chair, looking at him. "Did he say anything else?"

Chase looked at Scott from the corner of his eye. He could feel that Scott was nervous. If Kati was one of the Earth Witches, Viktor would be unpredictable and even though the goal was to keep balance, there were some who thought locking the Earth Witches away would solve their problems. One mentioned killing them, but since they were the last of their kind and the key to getting the stone, no one knew what would happen if they all died. Would it release their abilities and anger the gods? Chase was happy Viktor was against killing them. Before he even met them, he knew killing the Earth Witches would not bring balance.

"Nope, just let me know that if I was not up to the task, he would either finish it for me or send someone else who would."

Scott nodded and everyone was silent for a bit. Eryk cleared his throat. "So, do we have a plan on what we're going to do when we get there? We not only have to show up at the cabin but find out if the girls are what we all think they are."

"Maybe we can show up with some cookies and tell them that the cabin just happened to be in our zone," Scott said, a small smile on his lips.

They all laughed, some of the tension leaving them. "I'll think of something," Chase said before they got quiet again, keeping an eye on the van several cars ahead of them.

They exited about an hour out of town, stopping at a small restaurant that they must have known about beforehand since it was not even on the signs when you exited. There was a gas station kitty-corner to the restaurant that gave them a good view and let them fill up the SUV and run inside and get what they needed.

"Why do I have a funny feeling that restaurant is really good and we're missing out on some good breakfast?" Eryk asked, getting back in the car with a bag full of junk food.

"'Cause we can smell it from here and it smells amazing," Scott grumbled, looking over at the restaurant again.

Chase chuckled at his friends. Chase's stomach had mainly been in knots since his talk with Viktor, and he had no desire for food no matter how good it smelled. He was not looking forward to confronting Violca. He was both scared that she might be the witch they were looking for and scared she might not be.

If it turns out they weren't witches, he would be ordered to leave and Chase would have to go. The future of his kind and that of other supernaturals depended on them finding the witches. If it turned out Violca and her sisters were who they were looking for, their lives would forever be changed.

Chase selfishly almost wanted her to be the one. He didn't want to leave her. Viktor might kill him if he got involved with her, but Chase thought he might be willing to make that sacrifice. The dragon did not speak to him directly, but he was always aware of him and always knew how his dragon felt and it wanted Violca. Chase had been attracted to other women before, but with Violca, his dragon was aware of her, knew her smell and above all else, it wanted to protect her.

Watching them all pile back into the van, Chase's eyes narrowed and he tried to stop the growl that rose in his chest when he saw Brandon whispering something into Violca's ear that caused her to laugh. The distance and the traffic made it impossible for even his dragon to hear and he gripped the steering wheel tightly. Following behind them again, he tried to remind himself that Violca might not appreciate him killing her friend.

CHAPTER 25

Violca stretched when they got out of the van. The drive was long and she was glad to be at the cabin. The girls ran out. With the TV screens, the girls were mostly entertained but were starting to get restless toward the end. Smiling, watching the girls bounce, she grabbed one of the bags before heading to the front door.

They had a caretaker who watched over the place. Unlocking the door, Sari and Angyalka ran inside. It had been almost two and a half years since they'd visited the cabin and she was not even sure if the two younger ones remembered it, except for what they saw in the pictures.

The cabin had four bedrooms. The one that Angyalka and Sari were staying in had two bunk beds, the other rooms had full size beds, and the other was her parents' room that had a nice queen size bed. Brandon agreed to sleep in that room, despite his earlier protest. There were two bathrooms, one in the master bedroom and the other one between the other girls' rooms and across the hall from hers. Her father talked about building a third one, saying that two bathrooms was not enough for that many girls, but he died before he could get it done.

Brandon came up behind her, smiling. "I'm glad we came. Some of my best memories are the summers we used to come up here."

Violca nodded, finally stepping over the threshold. "Mine too." She heard the girls laughing. "I should have brought them back here sooner."

Brandon touched her back and she saw understanding in his eyes. "Let's get the van unloaded. I have a cooler in the back with some burgers and charcoal. I'll grill while you help the girls unpack."

Smiling at him, Violca felt a little better. She put her bags in her room before going back out to help unload. Kati had taken the girls out to the back where their dad had built a big swing set and tree house for them.

Violca put the food items away before putting away Sari and Angyalka's bags. She could smell the grill going outside and the sound of the girls' laughter and she knew she was exactly where she should be. She could almost feel her mother's presence surrounding her.

With everything, for the most part, put away she headed outside to join her sisters. Violca smiled when she noticed Eva swinging beside Sari. Angyalka was in the tree house with Kati, looking down at them. Brandon looked over his shoulder, a big smile on his face. "Burgers are almost done."

"Good. They smell great and I'm getting hungry." Brandon helped her make the girls' plates and they called them over to the table on the patio.

"I forgot how beautiful it was out here," Kati said, looking around.

"Me too. It's colder here, but still nice," Eva smiled at Violca. "Good call, V, I think a mini-vacation is exactly what we all needed."

Brandon lifted his beer. "Hear, hear." The girls raised their glasses before they drank. During dinner they finished catching

Brandon up on what had been going on and they spent most of the night laughing and teasing each other.

When night fell, Violca put the younger two to bed, and headed outside with a glass of wine. Sitting on the stairs, she leaned back, looking up at the stars. She was wearing a jacket as the evening was cooling down.

Hearing the hoot of an owl, she looked up to see a snow owl in the biggest tree in front. It hooted again, looking at her, and Violca swore it was the same owl that had been in her dream. "Do you have something to tell me?"

The owl hooted again, turning its head and looking around. It began to flap its wings and she was surprised to see how large the wingspan was before it took off, heading in the direction of the river.

Violca headed back into the house. Everyone was in their own rooms and Violca rinsed off her glass before heading to her room. Tired from the drive, she crawled into bed, sighing happily when her head hit the pillow.

Violca knew she was in a dream the second this one started. *She was standing on the porch, wearing the same long, white dress that she was wearing in all the other ones. Hearing the door open behind her, she turned, smiling when she saw her mother come out, holding something tightly to her chest. Her mother was wearing the long, violet robe that her father had bought her. He had said the shade was almost a perfect match to her eyes.*

Her mother walked straight through her and headed down the stairs toward the giant tree in the front yard. She looked around before kneeling, caressing the item in her hand. Violca walked slowly behind her and saw that the item her mother was holding looked to be a very old book with weird gold symbols and writing. Her mother wrapped it up and began to dig a hole with the small shovel that was left out from when the girls were playing earlier.

Her mother looked up at the tree, smiling when she saw the snow owl above her head. "Make sure you guard this and the girls." Her mother wiped her eyes and Violca suddenly realized she had been holding back tears. The owl hooted in reply before gliding down from the branch, swooshing just above her mother's head and flying back up to one of the lower branches as if trying to get closer to her. "Thank you, my friend," her mother whispered.

Waking up suddenly, Violca looked around the room. Disoriented, it took a few minutes before she realized that she was in her room at the cabin. She reached up and realized that her cheeks were wet and that she had been crying in her sleep. Sliding out of bed, she looked out her window, which overlooked the front yard, giving her a perfect view of the tree in her dream. Up in the tree, she saw the owl in one of the high branches.

Biting her lip, she debated about what to do. She didn't think she would be able to get back to sleep any time soon. Grabbing her jeans, she slid them and her jacket on and headed outside. On the side of the house was a small shed her mother and the caretaker used to store items for the garden. Grabbing a shovel, she walked over to the tree. Before she dug, she looked up. "You would tell me if I was doing something stupid, right?"

The owl didn't reply, just tilted his head. "Yeah, that's what I thought," she mumbled before digging carefully. After a few minutes, Violca really began to question her sanity. What was she doing out here in the middle of the night? She'd had a dream. It was probably nothing, since she didn't remember that book from when she was little.

Violca noticed something when she slid the shovel back in the ground. Going down to her knees, she brushed some of the dirt off and saw something wrapped in cloth. Violca reached down picking it up, curious what her mother would have buried here. Pulling back the material, she saw it was the same book that was in her dream. Using her feet, she was able to cover the hole so the girls wouldn't fall in, and she put the shovel on the side of the porch.

Quietly walking to her room, she took off the cloth and put it on her dresser. Looking over the book, she noticed that it was written in a language she didn't recognize. Flipping through it, she noticed the writing was the same throughout and sighed. Putting the book on the nightstand, she removed her pants and crawled back in bed, then tried to fall back to sleep.

CHAPTER 26

Eryk and Chase set up the campsite close enough that they could hear the girls laughing as they played outside. Scott shifted into his cat form and went for a run around the cabin, checking out the area and looking for any signs that others had followed them.

Eryk smelled the grill and smiled. "Hey, I think I'm going to set up the little charcoal grill and cook. That smell is making me hungry."

Chase chuckled, "Yeah sounds good, I'm ready for some real food."

Scott came back right when Eryk finished the burgers. "Did you see anything?"

"No, everything looks good so far. There're some campers several miles down the river, but they sound like they're planning on leaving tomorrow."

Chase nodded at that. Since the cabin was in the woods, there were not a lot of neighbors, and only one way in, or out, by vehicle. However, by foot there were tons of ways to gain access. They were going to be keeping a close eye on the girls and the area. Chase was still trying to figure out how to approach them.

Time was running out and Viktor was not known for making empty threats.

They made a watch schedule, Chase taking the first one. He climbed up the tree near the house that gave him a good vantage point. From there, he was able to see anyone who might be walking in the woods, without making him too visible.

With all the lights out, he was surprised when Violca stepped out of the house. He watched as she dug a hole, wondering what she could be looking for. She spoke to the snow owl, who seemed curious about her actions. When she pulled something out of the dirt, he narrowed his eyes, trying hard to see it.

He watched as she covered the hole and headed back into the house. Chase knew what room hers was and watched for her light to come on. When he saw no more movement, he frowned, wondering what that was all about.

Inhaling deeply, he caught her scent still on the air and a very, very faint smell of magic. Narrowing his eyes, he swore. Whatever she dug up smelled like magic, old strong magic and just a hint of earth. Whispering on the night air, he said, "They're the ones."

Dread filled him at the thought. Chase thought he had always known, since the moment he met Violca, that she was special. However, now he knew she would always be hunted. He was not sure if he believed in the power of the stone. Some thought it only held the powers of the dragons, others that it gifted the owners with unlimited power. Whether true or not, there would always be those who wanted more power and these sisters were the key.

When it was time for Scott to take over watch, Chase jumped down from the tree, landing on his feet with a soft thud. Scott turned toward the cabin, the smell of magic still faintly in the air, before growling, "Fuck!"

Chase ran his fingers through his hair. "Violca came outside and dug something up. Whatever it was…"

Scott growled low in the back of his throat. They both knew the danger these sisters were in and trying to protect them would not be easy. But Chase knew Scott would be right by his side.

"I'm going to go get some sleep. I think tomorrow will be a long day," Chase said. Scott nodded in his direction, his eyes focused on the cabin.

Walking back to the campsite, he heard Eryk's soft snoring. Eryk and Scott were sharing a tent and Chase had one to himself. Crawling into his tent, he stripped out of his jeans and shirt and got into the sleeping bag. Chase had no idea how to talk to Violca. Based on tonight's developments, he was positive they were the ones, but still didn't know what to say. He wanted her to trust him, but had a feeling that this was going to be an uphill battle.

VIOLCA WOKE up to the smell of bacon and grits, and knew Brandon was making his special French toast. He made it every time they came to the cabin and it was to die for. AnnaBelle and Violca often joked about marrying him, just so he could cook them breakfast. Getting out of bed, Violca opened the top drawer of the nightstand. Her eyes scanned over the book. Deciding to look at it later, she closed the drawer and headed into the kitchen.

Violca saw Brandon standing in the kitchen, over the stove. He was wearing a plain shirt and a pair of blue jeans that she knew Linda would really appreciate. Brandon really was an attractive man. She wondered how different their relationship might have been if they had met now, instead of when they were in elementary school.

"Hey, you're awake!" Brandon said, with a smile that lit up his blue eyes and made his dimple stand out on his left cheek.

"The smell of bacon is better than the smell of coffee for waking me up," Violca replied, sitting on one of the bar stools.

Brandon smiled before leaning over and starting the coffee pot. "Man, I forgot how quiet it is out here. Took me a few minutes to get to sleep without the constant noise, but once I fell asleep nothing woke me up."

Violca tilted her head. "You don't sleep through the night at home?"

Brandon shrugged before saying, "There're some days that I seem to have a lot of loud people outside my apartment expressing themselves."

Violca watched as he cracked the eggs into a bowl, then mixed in the vanilla and cinnamon. They talked about his plans to buy a house, his last case, and then they started to talk about what to do while they were here. "I have some fishing poles and I was thinking, when we run into town today, we could get some bait and maybe fish tomorrow?"

Violca smiled, knowing Brandon loved to fish. "Sure, I know the younger two have never gone, and I don't know if Kati has ever fished either. She would draw pictures of us."

They both heard noises, letting them know that the other girls were waking up. Kati, the first one out of the bedroom to join them, smiled sleepily as she walked into the kitchen and grabbed a few coffee cups. She poured four cups and as if on cue, Eva came in. Violca smiled, looking over at Kati. Most of Kati's clothes were baggy and hid her body, but up here in the cabin, with just family around, she was in a pair of yoga pants and a pale pink tank top. Neither hid her body and Violca knew that once Kati gained confidence, she would give all those girls who gave her a hard time a run for their money.

"Oh, Brandon, that smells fabulous," Eva said, taking her cup from Kati before sitting on the stool next to Violca. "I still think you need to date my sister so you can cook for us in the morning."

"Nah, Angyalka is too young to date," Violca answered before Brandon could say anything.

Everyone laughed. Angyalka and Sari finally came out of their room to see what was going on. When Kati saw them, she made them two glasses of orange juice. "Why's everyone laughing?" Angyalka asked, crawling up on her own stool.

"We were just teasing Brandon," Violca replied with a wink at Brandon, who shook his head again, chuckling.

"Are all the girls coming with us to town?" Brandon asked when Violca came outside.

"No, just me and Kati. Eva's going to watch the girls. They didn't want to come."

Kati came out and they got in the van. Brandon turned the key and frowned when it made a clicking noise. "I'm going to check under the hood. V, slide over and I'll tell you when to start it, okay?"

Nodding, she shuffled over to his side and listened to him fidget. "Try it now?" Brandon said. Turning the key, she heard the engine clicking. "Hold on," Brandon called out. "Okay again." It clicked before starting right up.

There was a loud bang as he closed the hood. Crawling back over to her seat, Violca smiled at him. "Brandon, who knew you were so handy to have around."

Brandon winked at her. "Still think I'm too old for Angel?"

They all laughed, getting comfortable for the forty-minute drive into town. Violca watched the scenery, her thoughts occasionally turning to her parents, then to the book she had found. Curious as to what language it was written in, she wondered if the Wi-Fi signal was good enough that she could just look it up online.

"Hey, before we go grocery shopping, I'm going to the sporting goods store. Do you want to come with me and help me get the fishing gear?" Brandon asked with a smile.

Violca snorted. "I'm gonna go pick up a few books for Eva, actually."

When Brandon looked over at Kati, she shook her head. "Sorry, I need to get some new art supplies."

"Okay fine, what do you say we meet back here in an hour, drop off our bags, then go to the grocery store?"

"Sounds good," Violca replied before getting out of the van. Kati nodded.

Violca and Kati headed toward downtown. The sporting goods store was near where they parked, so Brandon went in the other direction. Violca smiled when Kati ignored her to go inside the small arts and crafts store.

The bookstore was just a few stores down from the craft store. Eva was big into historical romances and had given Violca a list of her favorite authors who had new books out.

Pushing open the door, a little bell chimed and she noticed the older woman behind the cash register who smiled politely in greeting. Smiling in return, Violca looked around the store for a moment before finding the romance section. She found three books that were on the list.

Heading over to the magazine section, she flipped through a couple that grabbed her attention but didn't find anything she couldn't live without, so she headed up to the cashier with the books.

When she finished paying for her books, she heard the chime of the bells on the door. Her first thought was that Kati had finished early. Turning, she stopped when she noticed that a taller guy with a shaved head was going back to the aisles. Thinking he looked out of place, she walked to the door. Before she opened it, she glanced over her shoulder and noticed that the man had a scorpion tattoo on his neck. Gasping, she quickly walked out of the store and ran down the street.

CHASE AND SCOTT decided to follow the girls and Brandon, leaving Eryk to stay by the cabin and watch the others. Following Kati into the craft store, Scott tried to keep an eye on her while not being noticed. The store was older and had mirror setups on the corners, and he found himself loving the way she ran her fingers down a paintbrush or traced her hand over a canvas. Scott noticed that, like her sister, she occasionally bit her bottom lip when she was thinking.

Kati picked up a big set of pencils and charcoals. She eyed it before putting the set down and grabbing a smaller set of pencils. Kati then looked over a few sketchpads before picking one up and heading toward the cash register.

Scott found himself looking at the deluxe set of pencils and charcoals she'd set down earlier. He could tell she wanted it by the way she ran her fingers over it. When she left, he quickly walked over to the cashier, paying for it before walking out and following Kati back to her van.

CHASE HUNG out by one of the alleys, waiting for Violca. The door flew open and Violca came rushing out. The look on her face made him think she had seen a ghost. Chase noticed that she was constantly looking over her shoulder. When the bookstore door opened again and a guy with a shaved head came out, Violca ran in Chase's direction.

Stepping out of the alley and directly into her path, Violca slammed into him, almost tripping them both. Her body trembling, he stroked her back, whispering, "Violca what's the matter?"

Violca pulled back, frowning when she saw him, then looked back over her shoulder. He looked past her shoulder and the guy he glimpsed coming out of the bookstore was now gone. Violca pulled back more, forcing him to let go of her. "I was…" her voice trailed off and she frowned. "How did you know I was here?"

Chase swallowed hard, not knowing how to explain, and decided to be honest to a point, "Actually, I'm up here for research and I think I have the proof I need." He ran his hands through his hair, trying to figure out what to say next, when he remembered how it came to be that she was standing with him. "Why were you running down the street?"

Violca shook her head and nervously looked over her shoulder again. "I've been seeing these guys with scorpion tattoos on their necks at work, and suddenly there was one here. It was probably nothing but for some reason…"

Chase fought back a growl and he could feel his dragon coming to the surface, on alert. Most scorpion tattoos were found on people that demon lords controlled. Scanning the area, he didn't see anything, nor did he smell anything in the air. "Let me walk with you, just to make sure that the guy's gone."

CHAPTER 28

Violca didn't answer him, but walked toward the van quickly. Her need to be with her sister spurred her to walk faster. Seeing Kati a few feet in front of her, she frowned when she noticed Scott behind her. "Kati!" Violca called out to her sister.

Kati turned around looking in her direction, her eyes going wide when she saw Scott between them. Violca rushed to her, making a wide circle around Scott.

"What the hell are you doing here, Scott?" Violca asked. "What the hell is going on?"

Kati looked between Scott and Violca. "V, do you know him?"

"Yeah, he works security for my office." Kati frowned at the announcement, causing Violca to look at her sister. "Do you know him?"

"That's Eryk's older brother," Kati whispered.

Violca grabbed Kati's hand, pulling her toward the van. "Stay away from us," she practically growled, looking at both of them. Violca believed in the occasional coincidences but not when two guys who knew her somehow ended up in the same small town over ten hours away. Oh, and if she had to guess, they knew each other. Yeah, right.

"Violca, wait," she heard Chase call out to her, and she pulled Kati to move faster.

Violca saw Brandon near the van and wanted nothing more than to get to him and leave. But before she could step across the street that led to the parking lot, the guy from the bookstore was suddenly before her, grabbing her around the waist. She heard Brandon and Kati both yell her name, and felt Kati pull on her arm, before a second bald guy with a scorpion tattoo came out and grabbed Kati too.

Violca screamed, struggling against the guy's hold as she tried to kick and hit him. Her back against his chest, she almost felt like she was against a brick wall, her feet about a foot off the ground. They both backed toward a white cargo van, and the side door opened. Violca could hear Kati scream and saw her trying to fight against her captor. She recognized the guy holding Kati as the first guy she had seen at her workplace.

Hearing two loud growls, Violca suddenly saw Scott grabbing Kati. Chase grabbed ahold of her arm, pulling her toward him hard. She gasped loudly, almost feeling like her shoulder was going to pop out of place. The guy's grip relaxed on her and in one smooth movement, Chase put her behind him and punched the guy in the face. Two more guys jumped out of the van and grabbed the two would-be kidnappers, pulling them back into the van before it peeled out.

Brandon reached them as the van pulled away. "Violca, Kati, are you okay? What the fuck just happened?" He reached for her first and Chase tightened his grip on her, baring his teeth. Brandon narrowed his eyes. "I don't know who you are, but you can let go of her now."

Chase slowly released his hold and she reached out, pulling Kati into her arms. A small crowd had gathered and Brandon hugged them both tight. Kati was shaking in Violca's arms as

Violca stroked her hair. "Shh, Kati, it's okay, we're okay." Violca looked up at Scott, still torn about why he was there, but too thankful to care. "Thank you," she mouthed over Kati's shoulder.

When Violca heard police sirens, she pulled back, looking at Brandon. "I don't think I can handle talking to them right now."

Brandon nodded and before he could say anything, Chase came up and touched her gently on the shoulder. "I'll take care of it, okay?" Brandon looked skeptical, but she nodded, not caring who handled it, as long as she didn't have to let go of Kati.

Violca noticed Scott staying close, his eyes on Kati. He was not looking at her like he was checking her out, but like he was afraid she might disappear. Chase spent a few minutes with the police officers and she was surprised when they got back in their squad cars and drove away.

WALKING BACK TO THE GIRLS, he noticed that the small group of bystanders that had gathered was slowly starting to move on. A few of them were still gawking, but staying away. Brandon watched him as if sizing him up. "Why don't we find a quiet place to have lunch and talk?"

Brandon nodded and stood between the two girls. Chase could feel Scott tensing up and put his hand on his friend's arm. He was fighting the urge to pull Violca back into his arms and hold her. That was too close and he wanted to kiss her, to hold her, to prove to himself that she was okay. With Scott being imprinted on Kati, his animal instinct would be a lot more intense.

Chase noticed how Brandon kept them in his vision while leading them to the small diner. Brandon led the girls to a booth in the corner. Both girls got in first and Brandon sat on the outside next to Violca, forcing Scott and Chase to sit on the opposite side.

Scott sat across from Kati, and Chase noticed that he didn't look directly at her. Kati, in turn, avoided eye contact with him and was nervously biting her lower lip. When he met Violca's eyes, he flinched, seeing the distrust. She now looked guarded and he found himself wanting to prove himself to her.

Brandon kept his eyes on them and Chase started to feel a building pressure in his head. Watching Brandon, he saw his frown deepen and the pressure build. Brandon smelled human but if he had to bet right now, he would bet Brandon was some form of a telepath. How powerful, he was not sure, but telepaths, in general, have a hard time reading other supernatural minds. It's not impossible, but very few can.

The waitress came over and took their orders, and the table stayed quiet while Chase searched for what to say. "Violca, I never did tell you the particulars about my job, did I?"

Violca shook her head, her black hair sliding over her shoulder. "No."

Chase ran his fingers through his hair. "I do a lot of different jobs, but with this one I'm looking for the last descendants of a particular family line."

Violca chewed on her lower lip, and he could see her thinking about what he had just said. He could almost see her arguing with herself. "Did you find them?"

Chase looked her straight in the eye before nodding slowly, and whispering, "I was looking for you."

CHAPTER 29

Violca didn't know what to say to that. Her heart jumped into her throat with that one statement and she felt Kati's hand squeeze hers. She opened her mouth to say something, and then closed it.

"So, what, they're royalty and have some kind of inheritance?" Brandon asked, a little edge to his voice. "And what, those guys who tried to abduct them, was that the welcome wagon?"

Violca watched Scott and Chase closely, both of them looking guilty. She wondered how they knew each other. Before they could answer Brandon, she looked at Scott. "Were you also in on this?"

Chase spoke up. "Those guys are not with us but whoever they are, I don't think they are going to quit trying."

Scott looked up at Violca and she noticed how he kept his face blank when he answered. "Yes, I work with Chase. I was sent ahead just to see if you and your sisters were possibly who we were looking for and to keep you guys safe."

The waitress headed over with their food and everyone at the table quieted down. The young waitress seemed to pick up on the nerves and, after dropping off the plates, quickly left.

"You never answered why you were looking for them. Or why those guys tried to kidnap them," Brandon pointed out, looking at Chase.

Chase picked up his burger and took a bite. He didn't think Violca was ready to hear the rest. He was afraid she would hear what he had to say, not believe him and get up and leave, refusing to see him ever again.

Right now, Chase needed to stay close to Violca; he needed to protect her and that would be easier if he could stay closer. His dragon was scratching at the surface, picking up on her unease and wanting to comfort her. Chase noticed that her hands were shaking and knew that the adrenaline was wearing off.

"I don't know who those guys were, but I think it would be a good idea if you let us help try to keep the girls safe." Brandon frowned at him and he sighed, "I promise to explain everything back at the cabin, once we're alone. We can follow you back and then Scott can pick up Eryk. If you're uncomfortable we don't need to sleep inside, but maybe camp outside, just in case."

Chase felt pressure on his head and lowered his guard just enough so he could mentally tell Brandon that he would not harm the girls.

"Fine, after lunch we need to buy some groceries for the rest of the weekend. You can follow us back, but you're not sleeping in the house," Brandon said, the tone of his voice letting Chase know he was not happy about the situation.

Chase nodded, his shoulders sagging in relief. He didn't want to fight with them, especially not here. Now, how the hell was he going to explain the rest? Even though he was pretty sure they were the girls they were looking for, he did not believe she knew, because she would have tried to use her magic to save her sister, even if she would not use it to save herself. He knew Violca would give her life for her sisters.

~

KATI INSTANTLY FELL asleep on the drive home. Brandon looked over at Violca, trying to reassure her. "The adrenaline finished wearing off, poor thing. How're you feeling?"

Violca shrugged. "I don't know," she replied truthfully. Violca glanced at the side mirror to see the SUV with Chase and Scott behind her. She was still trying to make sense of what Chase had told her. According to her mother, they had no relatives. Was he lying? Did he only spend time with her because he was researching her? Did that kiss mean nothing to him? Was it just to get close to her? Biting her lip, she leaned her head back, closing her eyes. Brandon read her too easily and she didn't want him guessing what was bothering her.

Violca felt the van stop and blinked open her eyes. She must have drifted off, too. "Sorry, I didn't mean to fall asleep on you."

Brandon smiled at her. "As long as you don't try to get out of helping me unload the van, we're okay."

Laughing, she got out, stopping when she saw Chase get out of the SUV. Scott walked around the SUV, got into the driver's seat and nodded at her before backing out. Kati got out of the back, and Violca saw her glance at the SUV warily. Frowning, she decided to talk to Kati later, when she could get her alone. She also wanted to ask Chase why Scott looked at Kati the way he did. It wasn't sexual, but it was something she couldn't put her finger on.

Chase walked up to the van. "Can I carry something?"

Brandon gave him the two biggest and heaviest bags before turning his back on him. "Most of this stuff needs to be put in the fridge."

Violca walked behind Chase, her eyes noticing how his ass flexed when he walked. Hearing the front door open, she bit her lip to try not to smile when she heard Angyalka scream as she ran out the door. "You're back!" Angyalka stopped when she spotted Chase and her smile grew. "I knew you would find us!"

Chase stopped and Violca walked around him, noticing how he smiled at Angyalka. "You did, huh?"

Angyalka nodded and turned to walk with him. "Uh huh, you have to keep the bad guys away."

Hearing her words, Violca stopped on the stairs. "What bad guys, Angel?"

Angel smiled as she skipped toward her. "The bad guys. It's okay, Chase will keep them away." With that she opened the door. Not sure what to think of what Angel had said, she walked into the house and headed to the kitchen.

Chase followed behind her and put his bags next to hers on the counter. He gently grabbed her elbow. Violca looked up at him and saw the look of regret on his face. "Violca, I'm sorry about what happened today."

Violca noticed flecks of gold in his brown eyes and shook her head. "Which part Chase, the part where I found out you were researching us, or the fact that someone almost kidnapped me and my sister?"

Before he could answer, Kati and Brandon showed up and he released her elbow, stepping away from her. Brandon looked at her as if making sure she was okay before looking at Chase. "There's a few more things in the van you can help unload." Brandon turned and Chase looked at her one more time before silently following Brandon out.

Eva smiled, walking up to her and Kati. "Did I just see Chase? What's he doing here?"

Violca handed her a bag of chips to put away. "We ran into him in town. He's going to be camping outside with some of his friends."

Obviously sensing there was more, Eva kept her mouth shut. Violca knew it was only because Angyalka and Sari were coming back in with the guys, and that the second they were alone, Eva would bombard her with questions. She only hoped she had answers.

CHAPTER 30

Chase and Scott were setting up the tents in the backyard when Sari and Angyalka ran up to Scott, and Angel said, "You're tall."

Scott smiled down at her teasingly. "Didn't Chase tell you his friend was a giant?"

Angyalka wrinkled her nose, looking him over, before shaking her head. "You're not a giant, silly, you're a kitty." She smiled brightly at him. "A big, black kitty."

Chase and Scott both stopped what they were doing and stared at her. Before either one could reply, Eryk showed up and growled at her. "That's right, he's a big, black kitty and we're going to get you!" Angyalka squealed and ran away and Eryk chased her and Sari around the backyard.

Scott raised an eyebrow looking at him. "You don't think…"

Chase shrugged. "I don't know. She was able to see me when I was shadowed."

They watched Eryk play with the girls for a moment before going back to setting up the camp. Chase looked up at the window and smiled when he saw Eva. Raising a hand, he waved at her. She waved back before walking away.

"So, we got them to invite us over. Have you figured out how to bring up the rest?" Scott asked, glancing back at the house. When his eyes lingered, he turned to see Kati standing in the window.

"No, but I think their friend Brandon might be a telepath, so be careful. I could feel him trying to probe around at the restaurant." Chase noticed Scott's eyes fixed on the window until Kati finally walked away. When Scott looked back at him, he shook his head. "Violca was watching how you looked at Kati earlier."

Scott shrugged and glanced back at the house. "I'm not going to jump the girl or anything."

Chase raised an eyebrow, trying not to smile at his friend's obvious frustration with the situation. "I'll be more careful."

Chase smiled. "Two conversations I can't wait to have, hey we believe you and your sisters are the last of the original line of Earth Witches, and oh yeah, my friend here is a panther shifter and he's imprinted on your underage sister."

Scott snorted and they both laughed, some of the tension leaving them. At the sound of the door opening, they both turned to see Eva on the porch. "Sari, Angel, time to come in and eat dinner," she called out, and both girls laughed as they ran up the stairs of the back porch. She smiled at the guys before heading inside.

Eryk walked up to them. "Want me to grill up the sausages?"

"Sure," Scott replied, "I think I'm going to check out the area."

Nodding, Chase saw his friend walk into the woods. Eryk smiled, looking at him. "It's going to be interesting watching him and Kati."

Chase grinned, picturing it. Kati was not like the girls his friend usually pursued. That was probably a good thing. When Kati finally gained her confidence, he pictured her giving Scott a merry chase and he was looking forward to watching it.

~

"SO WHY ARE we not inviting them to eat with us?" Eva asked, after calling the girls in. "Seems like we owe them for helping you out."

Brandon looked out the window, watching the guys talk for a moment before Scott walked into the woods. "I'm still trying to figure out what they were doing in town, and why the hell Chase is researching your family."

Kati looked up at him, helping Violca make the plates. "So, why'd you agree to let them stay outside our house if you don't trust them?"

Brandon smiled at her. "Partly because I owe them for helping you and your sister when I was too far away to do anything, and also so I can keep an eye on them and figure out what the hell they want."

Violca stayed quiet, listening to them talk. She went over everything that had happened since she had met Chase. The bumping into her, the times he spent with her and the girls, each kiss. Was it all just to get close to her?

She felt like the biggest idiot ever. Every guy, when he found out she was raising four girls, had bailed. Why did she think he would be any different? Her heart hurt and she blinked back tears, not wanting anyone to see her cry. "Come on guys, let's enjoy dinner and not worry about that right now."

Sari and Angyalka came out of the bathroom, having cleaned up their hands, and sat at the bar. Violca finished frying up the last of the chicken while Eva made the mashed potatoes and corn.

The younger girls ate at the bar, while the rest of them ate in the living room. Eva was brought up to date on the events in town and hugged them both, glad that Scott and Chase were close enough to help. "Did Chase ever explain why he was researching our family?" Eva asked, tucking her legs underneath her.

Violca shook her head no and Brandon frowned. "I didn't think you had any relatives. I mean, wouldn't they have come out of the woodwork after…" his voice trailed off but they all knew he meant, after their parents passed away.

"According to our mom and dad, we don't have any living relatives. At least none that were close. Maybe we have some third cousins, four times removed or something, but I doubt anyone who would come looking for us."

"Even if there was anyone, who the hell would try to kidnap you?" Eva asked, before taking a bite.

Brandon looked between the girls. "I think it's weird that two guys you knew, not only know each other, but show up after you leave town and happen to be close when someone tries to kidnap you." He stopped for a moment before continuing, "Not saying they're involved in that, but I think they know more than they're saying."

They ate in silence for a few minutes, thinking about what had happened and why. Angyalka and Sari could still be heard chatting at the bar about what they wanted to play after dinner and who would have to take a bath first.

Violca went to clean the dishes, smiling when Brandon kissed her cheek. "Hey, I got the dishes. You cooked."

Violca smiled at him. "I think I'm going to take a walk." Before Brandon could argue, she shook her head. "I need to clear my mind, but I'll stay close, I promise."

Brandon sighed and Violca bit back a grin, knowing that it was his "I can't win with you" sigh. "Don't make me go looking for you."

"I won't. I promise."

Quickly putting on her tennis shoes, she grabbed a light jacket. It wasn't cold yet but the temperature dropped fast once the sun went down. She walked out the front door, heading toward the path that ran on the side of the house that would take her away from her backyard and the men who were currently camping in it.

Chase heard the front door open and close. When he inhaled, he smelled Violca's distinctive scent. He got up and followed her. Out of the corner of his eye, he saw Eryk smirk at Scott. Scott reached into a bag and threw something at him saying, "Chase, catch."

Looking at the small item in his hand he realized it was a condom and looked at Scott who winked. "You know what they say, always be prepared."

"I don't know why you carry these around. It ain't like you're going to be needing them anytime soon." Hearing Violca get further away, he quickly put the condom in his pocket and followed her.

Chase stayed behind her as she walked on a path that led away from the cabin, heading near the direction of the river. He knew Violca was aware of him and smiled to himself, knowing she was not turning around because she was trying to ignore him.

When she stumbled, he reacted quickly and was at her side, his arms around her before she could fall. She squirmed, pushing away from him, almost falling from the effort.

Once he was sure she was okay, he carefully released her.

Standing in front of her, he looked her over and when she finally looked up at him, he noticed that her violet eyes were darker as she looked at him angrily. "I didn't ask you for your help," she snapped.

Chase knew that smiling at her right now would not help him, nor would telling her she looked beautiful when she was angry. Watching her breasts rise and fall as she breathed, her violet eyes sparkled with anger, and the straight line of her lips, he fought the urge to kiss her. "You didn't, but that doesn't mean I want to see you hurt."

She glared at him. "Why're you here? What do you want with me?"

Chase stepped closer to her and reached up to touch her cheek, dropping his hand when she seemed to flinch before he could touch her. "I'm here because I wanted to make sure you're safe."

She snorted at him and he couldn't help but smile at the unfeminine sound. "That's not what I meant and you know it." She pushed her hair back from her face and looked up at him, her voice lowering to almost a whisper, "Why did you kiss me? Was it just to get close to me?"

Chase saw a flash of hurt in her eyes and he stepped in front of her, cupping her cheek, making sure she looked at him when he answered, "I kissed you because there was no way I could be near you and not."

Violca's lips parted in surprise at his announcement and he kissed her gently. When he heard her moan, he angled her head up higher and deepened the kiss, his tongue sliding in, gently at first and dueling with hers. Violca's hands came up to his chest, her fingers curling on his shirt as if trying to hold him in place. Chase walked until Violca's back was against the tree. He slid one of his legs between hers, rubbing against her as he continued to kiss her, growling when he heard her soft moan in response.

One of his hands came up and found her breast. Massaging it, he felt her nipple harden under his touch. He felt her hands slide under his shirt, touching his chest before he broke the kiss, his mouth instantly going to her neck as her head rolled back. Gently biting and licking his way down her neck, his free hand cupped her butt, pulling her tighter against him. "You taste so good," he whispered against her neck, "I can't get enough of you."

Chase licked where he bit her, her taste intoxicating. He loved the little sounds she made. He hadn't planned on kissing her, but now that he was, Chase didn't think he could stop. When her hips began to grind on his leg, he released her hip and slid his hand under her shirt, growling when he finally touched her skin. He could feel her muscles quivering under his touch. His hand slid up under her bra and pinched her nipple a little roughly, loving the small gasp that escaped her.

Needing to touch more of her, he pulled back, his eyes meeting hers. He loved how the violet of her eyes stood out more when her pupils were dilated. He reached for the bottom of her shirt, stopping for just a second. When she licked her lips, he moaned loudly and pulled her shirt up over her head. Not wanting to bruise or scratch her skin against the trunk of the tree he laid her down gently on the grass.

Following her down, he nibbled on her lips as his hand stroked her exposed skin. When he got to her breasts, he pushed the bra up and over, growling into her mouth when she arched up and rubbed her breasts against his chest. Breaking the kiss, he looked down at her hard nipples that were a shade of brown just darker than her skin. He finished removing the bra before dipping his head and swirling his tongue around the hard nub, then sucking it into his mouth.

Violca panted, her back arching up and off the ground, offering him her breast. Her hand slid into his hair, holding him to her breast, pulling on his hair. When his mouth left her breast, she whimpered only to gasp when he bit the nipple first, before starting on the other one.

His leg slid between her thighs and her hips rocked back and forth. He could feel how wet her panties were. Each time he flicked his tongue over her sensitive nipple, her thighs tightened around his.

Chase felt Violca slide her hands up and under his shirt, her fingers roaming his chest. He could feel her fingers gently gliding over his stomach muscles and heard her low moan. She started to pull his shirt up over his head and Chase stopped playing with her breast long enough to help, throwing it in the same direction he had thrown her shirt.

Chase looked down at her, his dragon so close to the surface that he was able to see how her eyes had darkened. Violca reached up and pulled him back down, kissing him, her tongue sliding teasingly into his mouth before pulling out, causing his tongue to follow hers. She sucked on his tongue and he felt his cock harden even more in anticipation. Chase broke the kiss, panting as he began to kiss and bite gently along the column of her neck. His cock was so hard, he was afraid he was going to come without even getting inside of her. Working his way down her neck, he stopped to gently bite each of her hard nipples before kissing and licking his way down her gently rounded stomach.

When he got to the top of her jeans, he stopped. Holding onto her hips, he began to make love to her belly button, his tongue sliding in and out of her like a mini-cock. He smiled with male pride when he felt her hips buck against his tongue. The smell of Violca's need was strong in the air.

Releasing her hips, he undid her pants and pulled them down. Taking her panties with them, he removed them in one quick move. Stopping, he stared down at her. Chase loved the fact that she was smooth and almost asked her if she shaved or waxed, when he noticed her lips glistening. Meeting Violca's eyes, he licked his lips and smiled when she parted her legs more for him. The sight of her wet and needy was almost his undoing.

Bending down, he settled between her spread thighs and very slowly licked up her slit, growling loudly with approval. Violca's taste was as distinct as her smell and he wondered if he would ever get enough of it. He heard her gasp and felt her hips roll up with his tongue. Then he used his shoulder to open her wider.

CHAPTER 32

Violca's hips bucked up when he licked up her slit again and she gasped when she felt his tongue flick over her sensitive clit. Chase's lips latched onto the sensitive nub and sucked it into his mouth, his tongue still flicking over the top and her back arched as she began to make noises in the back of her throat.

She felt a finger slide into her core and her hips bucked harder against his mouth. She felt his teeth scrape against her clit and she panted, her hand going to his hair as she tried to pull his head closer to her core. He slid in a second finger and slowly moved in and out of her. When he hooked his fingers and hit her G-spot, it caused her entire body to shake in response.

He sucked harder on her clit, his free hand reaching up and grabbing one breast, squeezing gently before rolling her nipple between his fingers. Violca's entire body tightened with pleasure and she felt her orgasm building faster as he continued to tease her body until she could no longer hold out and she screamed as the first wave of pleasure hit her. Violca's hands pushed hard on his head, burying it in her core as her legs tightened around his head, trying to hold him in place. She felt his tongue come out, licking her juices.

Violca could feel his tongue busily lapping at her as wave after wave of pleasure rolled through her. Chase pulled back and quickly undid his pants. Violca saw Chase reach for something in his pocket and noticed him rolling on a condom before he settled between her thighs and kissed her roughly. Chase quickly rolled over, pulling her on top of him.

He growled softly and his cock seemed to automatically slide between her wet folds as she sucked on his tongue. Violca rocked her hips, coating him with her juices as he broke the kiss and began to bite and kiss along her neck. Violca reached between them, her hand wrapped around his hard cock and she slowly guided him into her.

He slid his hands up her thighs and his fingers found her clit, flicking it, causing her to jump and take him in deeper. Violca heard Chase growl, and her core tightened in response. She felt his entire body tense underneath hers as he let her set the pace.

Violca looked down at him, her breath coming in short little pants, and she leaned forward, resting her hand on his chest as she slowly raised herself up. Using his chest for leverage, she started a slow pace as her body adjusted to his size. She saw Chase's need in his eyes, the gold she saw earlier coming out more. "Violca, you're so tight, my love." She heard him say between gritted teeth.

Sitting up suddenly, she gasped as he captured her mouth with a kiss and his hands went to her hips to help guide her to increase the pace. He kissed his way down her neck until his mouth found one of her breasts, sucking it into his mouth.

Her hands slid from his chest to his hair as her head fell back, arching. Violca's hips rocked on him faster as her pleasure built again. Chase's hands slid from her hips to cup her butt in each hand, squeezing as they helped guide her up and down his hard cock.

Violca's hand tightened in his hair and suddenly her orgasm hit and she screamed into the air, "Chase!" as wave after wave of pleasure rolled through her.

Chase's hips thrust up when she screamed. She felt his hands tighten hard on her hips holding her tight to him. Feeling his teeth graze her neck she wondered where this urge to bite him came from. Violca rested her head in the crook of his neck, trying to catch her breath. She heard Chase breathing just as heavily. Violca almost smiled when she felt him kiss her shoulder, his hand caressing her back. Since the sun had set, the air was cooler and she shuddered. "You're cold. Let me see if I can reach your shirt."

With his arm wrapped around her, he leaned over and reached for her shirt and bra. Violca tried to get up, only to feel his hand tighten on her hip. "You're keeping me warm," Chase said with a mischievous smile.

She smiled, shaking her head and when she wiggled to put her bra on, she bit back a moan when she felt him twitch, still inside her. Chase helped her with her shirt and brushed her hair from her face.

"Do you always carry condoms around when walking in the woods?" Violca asked, and laughed when she saw him look a little uncomfortable.

"No," he replied simply before nibbling on her lips. "I should take you back to the cabin before they worry about you."

Nodding, Violca started to stand only to have him stop her with a kiss. This kiss was different than the first, gentle and sweet as his tongue slowly slid into her mouth, stroking her tongue, worshipping it with his.

When he pulled back, his cock slowly slipped from her core. He moaned softly, missing the contact. Chase had no intention of kissing her when they left the house but once he did, he couldn't stop. He couldn't remember a time when he had ever felt so satisfied or complete after sex.

Standing up slowly, he grabbed for his pants, sliding them on. Chase knew that Scott and Eryk would be able to smell her on him and debated taking a dip in the rivers after he made sure she got home okay. Chase smiled, watching Violca bend over to pull on her panties. He saw the inside of her thighs still wet from their lovemaking and licked his lips, imagining running his tongue up her thigh. His eyes were drawn to her perky butt and he smiled, wishing he could take her again.

Violca straightened up and looked at him over her shoulder. Chase winked at her when she blushed, having caught him staring at her butt. Standing up, he heard someone in the woods near them and he stood in front of Violca, his shirt in his hand. Inhaling, he smelled her friend, Brandon, and his eyes narrowed when Brandon finally came into view.

Chase heard Violca moan softly, putting her head on his back when she saw him. He chuckled softly, only to feel her reward him by hitting him.

"The girls were starting to worry about you," Brandon said, crossing his arms, his eyes meeting Chase, challenging him.

Chase put on his shirt, taking her hand and pulled Violca out from behind him, then wrapped his arm around her side, holding her next to him. "We were just heading back."

Chase swore he could almost hear Brandon growling. "I'll have her home in a few minutes."

Brandon looked over at Violca, who nodded at him before turning back and walking towards the house. Once Brandon was far enough not to overhear them, Chase turned so that he was facing Violca. "I want you to know whatever happened between us was not for my work." When she looked down, he used his hand to tilt her head up to him. "Let's get you back to the cabin before I take you again."

Violca smiled and he bent down, brushing his lips against hers before taking her hand and leading her back to the cabin. They walked in silence, Chase going over what had happened. He had never had an urge to bite a female during sex. It was the hardest thing he had ever done, not to sink his teeth into her creamy flesh.

When they got to the front of the cabin, she stopped and looked at him. Brushing her hair behind her ear, he smiled down at her. "I'll see you tomorrow." Before she could reply, he bent down to kiss her, only to hear the front door open and see Kati in the doorway. Smiling down at her, he winked, straightening without kissing her. "Sweet dreams, Violca."

"Good night, Chase," she whispered. Raising a hand, he waved to Kati before walking around the cabin to the back. Scott and Eryk were both in their tent already. Grabbing a soda from the cooler, he crawled into his tent, trying to get comfortable. He wished he were in the cabin with Violca, instead of on the hard ground outside.

CHAPTER 33

Violca blushed as she walked into the living room where Brandon glared at her. Kati and Eva both smiled, and she knew Brandon had told them that she had been walking with Chase, and that both girls had come to the same conclusion. Wanting to change the subject before it even started, she decided to tell them about the book. "I found something last night, I really want to show you guys."

Everyone stopped and looked at her and she quickly headed to her room, grabbing the book from inside the nightstand. Going to the couch, she sat between Eva and Kati. Brandon stood behind them, looking over their shoulders. "So far, I haven't figured out how to read it but," she ran her fingers over the cover and gasped when she felt something prick her finger. Bringing her finger up to her mouth, she sucked on it.

Violca's lap heated up and the book shimmered softly. The writing that she could not read before, changed to *My Darling Daughters of the Earth*. Everyone was so quiet Violca thought she might be able to hear the girls breathing in the other room. Writing suddenly appeared on the blank page in a language she couldn't read, but when Violca ran her hand over it, it shimmered and slowly changed. Violca gasped when she recognized her mother's handwriting and her signature at the bottom.

My Darling Daughters,

I am so sorry I am not with you, but I know you will not be alone for long. I wish I had time to explain everything to you, but unfortunately my time in this world was limited, but very treasured.

I don't know how to tell you this, but you, my darlings come from a long line of Earth Witches. My dear Violca, you will recognize a few of these stories as the bedtime stories we told you when you were very little. We wanted to raise you, telling you all about your family's history and watch you develop your powers. But once the hunters came trying to take you, we knew we had to hide.

This book will tell you about your history and what that means. Each one of you has a special gift. Have faith in yourselves and in each other. You are all strong on your own but together, you five hold the balance of the world.

Trust your instincts, my darlings, and know that your father and I love you very much and will be watching over you.

All my love,

Mom

VIOLCA READ, then re-read the message from her mother. She recognized her mother's handwriting, but she couldn't believe what she had read. Witches, Earth Witches, weren't real. There was a group of women who call themselves Wiccans nowadays, but they had no powers and cast no spells. Violca didn't believe in witches or magic, but found she couldn't explain how the writing on the book changed, or why her mother would write such a thing. When her mother wrote this, she seemed to know she would die soon.

Violca was very aware of Brandon behind her, and her two sisters next to her. None of them said a word as the tension filled the air. Kati finally broke the silence, "Earth Witches?"

Violca shook her head and closed the book, not sure what to say. Brandon cleared his throat. "I think it's been a very long day. Maybe we should all go to bed and deal with this tomorrow morning."

Eva reached out and ran her hand over the cover gently, and Violca could see her eyes brimming with tears. She blinked them back and Eva reached up and squeezed her hand. "I think Brandon might be right, let's talk about this in the morning."

Violca got up and held the book close to her chest. Eva and Kati stood up too, both giving her a small hug before going to their room. Brandon met Violca's eyes and she could see small lines around his mouth as he frowned. "Good night, V." With that, he turned and walked down the hall to his room.

Violca headed to her room and put the book back in the nightstand. Changing into a tank top and pajama pants, she turned off the light before crawling into her bed. She didn't know if she would be able to sleep, so much had happened. The stuff her mother had written in her book, could it be...

Violca's eyes closed almost as soon as she laid her head on the pillow. Falling into a deep sleep, she found herself standing in the woods again. She looked up to see the cabin in front of her. She quickly walked up the stairs, wanting so badly to talk to her mother.

CHASE FOUND his eyes constantly going to the cabin, as he wondered what they were doing in the living room. Chase could feel his dragon itching, just below the skin, wanting to shift and break the door down and drag Violca to his bed. After every kiss they had shared, his hunger for her had grown and now that he had tasted her, he wanted more.

Chase saw the light go off in the living room and watched the different bedroom lights go on. He imagined her lying in bed, her dark hair framing her face, her lips parted, her violet eyes growing darker in need. Growling softly, he squeezed his cock to try and relieve some of the pressure.

Deciding he wouldn't be getting to sleep anytime soon, he unzipped his tent and crawled out. Chase heard the other tent unzip and saw Scott pop out. "I'm going to take the first watch tonight."

Chase knew his friend could smell the lingering scent of sex and Violca on him. Scott raised an eyebrow and a grin lit up his face. "Wake me up when it's my turn," Scott smirked before crawling back into his tent.

Chase growled in the back of his throat as he walked toward the river. The property the girls owned was large and had several trails running along it. It wasn't fenced in, but it was clearly marked in several areas, and for the most part, it looked like people went around it. So far, only Eryk had said he ran into a guy who appeared to be trying to find his way to the river.

Seeing a fresh set of tracks, Chase inhaled, detecting the scent of several males. He followed the trail across the river determined to see where they went. The hum of voices drew his attention. Careful to avoid anyone walking alone, Chase kept a safe distance as he went to see what they were up to. There were several guys in their early twenties drinking beer and telling jokes around a bonfire. Not detecting any scent of anything supernatural, Chase watched for a few minutes before slowly sliding back into the woods and heading back across the river.

Once he crossed the river to the girls' property, he checked out the rest of the perimeter and didn't see any other signs of trespassers. Chase headed back to the house. Circling it, he went to the window where Violca's smell was the strongest. He could smell the scent of magic in the air.

Violca's window was cracked and he knew he shouldn't, but he needed to know where the scent was coming from. His skin tingled before he turned into his shadow and slid through the crack. Gliding across the floor he went to her bed. In shadow form he couldn't quite touch her, but he glided his hand over her cheek.

Violca was lying on her side, one bent leg sticking out from under the blanket. He smiled, noticing the pillow was turned sideways and she was holding it like a lover. Watching her, he found himself wondering what it would be like to hold her all night, her head on his chest, her legs thrown over his.

The scent of magic was strong in the air near her bed. Allowing his hand to materialize he reached out and opened the nightstand. There he saw a very old book. Running his hand over the book, he felt his palm heat up. Frowning, he wrapped his fingers around the spine to pick it up and felt a sudden blast of heat go through him.

Letting go, he shook his hand before looking at it. Despite the pain, there was no mark on his skin. He wondered what the book was and why he was not allowed to touch it. He was pretty sure this was what Violca had dug up from the yard last night, and it hadn't burned her. Closing the drawer, he shifted back into a shadow and slowly glided back to the window to slide out.

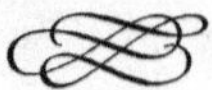

CHAPTER 34

Violca woke up, slowly stretching out. The dream she had of her mother did not help her. Her mother told her she needed to read the book with her sisters and that it would explain it all. The world was full of magic, some good and some bad. Violca had to just open her eyes and look around her to see it. With a secret smile, her mother also told her that witches were not the only magical creatures out there.

Violca felt like she had woken up with more questions than answers. She smiled, realizing she easily believed her mother was talking to her in her dreams, but the thought of witches made her roll her eyes. Trying to keep an open mind, she got up and headed to the kitchen, smiling when she saw Brandon already making sausage.

"If you keep making us breakfast, I might not object to you dating Angel," Violca said, teasingly.

Brandon chuckled. "I don't know if she's my type, and I'm pretty sure there's a law out there about not dating a girl if you can vividly remember changing her diapers."

Violca laughed. "Since you're the cop, I'll have to take your word for it." Violca looked outside and noticed Eryk walking around their little makeshift campsite in the backyard. "I wonder what they're having for breakfast."

Brandon raised an eyebrow. Violca blushed and Brandon grinned. "Go ahead and invite them in. We have enough food for everyone." Violca looked at him a little surprised, especially when Brandon smiled at her. "I think it's time I get to know Chase, don't you think?"

Violca groaned, causing Brandon to smile more. "Oh God, you're going to go all big brother cop like, aren't you?"

Brandon turned back to flipping the sausage. "I need to find out why they were looking for you," he smirked before adding, "and let him know if he plays with your heart, I'll make his life a living hell."

Violca rolled her eyes at him, causing him to laugh before she went to the back door. Part of the reason she wanted them to come in and eat, was so Kati could spend more time with Eryk. She genuinely seemed to like him, and Violca was determined to encourage it.

Opening the door, she stepped onto the patio and smiled at Eryk. Her eyes were drawn to some movement behind him and she looked up to see Chase walking in from the woods. He was wearing his pants low on his hips and no shirt. Her breath caught as she noticed his rippling muscles and the light traces of a six pack on his abs. When her eyes finally roamed up to his face, she felt her cheeks heat up. His self-satisfied smile told her he had seen her checking him out.

Eryk cleared his throat, "Good morning."

Violca swore she must be beet red. She smiled at Eryk. "Morning. I just wanted to invite you guys in for eggs and sausage."

Scott peeked his head out of the tent, "Did you say sausage?"

"Yep, do you wanna join us?"

"Hell yeah!" Scott replied, crawling out from the tent.

Violca's eyes widened. Scott was also in a pair of jeans and no shirt, and Violca smiled, thinking Linda and the girls would be mad to find out that she was the first to see him with his shirt off. She heard a growl and turned to see Chase watching her. "Be careful, I think there's an animal close by," she said, wondering where that sound came from. "It shouldn't be too much longer."

Violca turned to go in the house and saw Kati in the doorway, her eyes on Scott. Violca noticed a blush on Kati's cheek and smiled at her when Kati finally noticed her watching her. Grinning, she took her sister by the arm, leading her into the house, leaving the door slightly ajar for the guys when they came in.

CHASE WAITED for Violca and her sister to go in before looking over at Scott. Scott grinned and Chase growled at him again, only to hear him laughing.

Eryk laughed. "Hey, be careful man, there's an animal in the woods."

Chase headed over to his bag, grabbed a shirt, and pulled it over his head. "Put your shirt on Scott, before you scare the kids."

Scott chuckled, flexing. "You're just worried that Violca will have a hard time keeping her hands off the guns."

Chase snorted. "Guns, really?"

He walked up to the porch, taking a few stairs at a time. Eryk followed him in. The smell of sausage and fresh coffee caused Chase's stomach to growl. Eva, sitting at the bar, turned and looked at them. "Hey guys, there're cups next to the coffee pot if you want some coffee. Breakfast should be done in a few."

Brandon looked over at them and leveled Chase with a look that let him know he didn't trust him as far as he could throw him. Chase raised an eyebrow and walked to the counter, making himself a cup of coffee. Pouring two more, he handed one to Eryk.

Sari and Angyalka came out of their room, laughing and

giggling. When they saw him, they both hugged him tightly and he picked up Sari, as Angyalka jumped on Eryk, who picked her up. "Can we play kitty again?"

Eryk smiled, tweaking her nose. "Sure, we can play later."

She giggled before squirming out of his arms. Sari and Angyalka both took their seats at the bar. Hearing a door open down the hall, Chase looked up to see Violca. She had changed into a pair of denim shorts that showed off her legs, and a blue tank top. Looking up, their eyes met and he saw her tongue come out and lick her lips.

Remembering the taste of her lips and how she responded to his kiss, he fought the urge to go over to her and kiss her good morning. Scott came in and she looked away, smiling politely in his direction.

"All right guys, breakfast's done," Brandon announced. "Eva made the toast, and the sausage and eggs are on the stove, everyone make your plates." He winked at Sari and Angel, handing them both their plates. "Except you two."

CHAPTER 35

Scott watched how the girls interacted with each other and Brandon. Brandon, he could tell, was close to the family. He knew that Chase was a little jealous, but the way Brandon and Violca treated each other, he would've thought they were brother and sister. There was a connection there, but nothing sexual.

Feeling like he was being watched, he turned his head and saw Kati sitting on the chair watching him out of the corner of her eye. Scott noticed that in the few pictures he'd seen of her at the school, she was always wearing clothes that were baggy and didn't fit her well. Here at the cabin, surrounded by her family, she was wearing a pair of black yoga pants and a yellow top.

He knew that she would grow up to be a beauty. The only issue he had was that she seemed to be almost scared of her own shadow. When Kati noticed him looking in her direction, she blushed brightly before turning her head.

Scott turned to see Eryk watching him, a small smile on his lips. Narrowing his eyes, he almost growled before catching himself. Eryk shook his head, and Scott had a feeling that if they were alone, his younger brother would be laughing at him.

Once the girls all finished making their plates, the guys went and made theirs. Kati and Eva sat at the bar with the younger two, while the rest of them sat around the living room. The cabin was cozy, despite the tension coming off everyone. Scott knew that Brandon did not trust them and wondered if they had been invited in because Brandon had stumbled upon Violca and Chase in the woods.

Chase chose to sit on the chair near Violca, instead of on the couch next to her. He could see Brandon watching him. Violca, for the most part, seemed to be concentrating on her food, not really looking at either of them. When she finally looked up at him, Chase winked at her, smiling when he saw her blush.

Looking up, his eyes met Brandon's, as Brandon looked at him fiercely. Chase felt the corner of his lip go up in a bit of a smile. He was still a little jealous of how close they were, but he knew Violca would have never made love to him if there had been anything going on between them.

Angel came running from the kitchen area and stood before Chase. "Will you help me fish today?"

Chase looked up at Violca, then at Brandon. Brandon shrugged. "Since you guys are staying here, you might as well help us catch dinner."

"Sure, Angel," Chase replied before tweaking her nose.

Angyalka beamed up at him, then ran back to the bar. "Chase is coming, he's going to help me catch the biggest fish!"

They all laughed at her loud statement. Violca looked up at him. "Well, you better not fail or she'll never let you live it down."

Chase winked at her. "I'll do my best."

Brandon rolled his eyes at the statement and Violca elbowed him in the side, causing him to grunt. Brandon chuckled. "What?"

Violca raised an eyebrow and Chase noticed that Brandon's smile widened. Brandon pretended to rub his side as Violca went back to eating to her breakfast.

"When're we going fishing?" Eryk asked as he finished his last bite.

"Depending on how long it takes the girls to get ready, about an hour," Brandon answered, looking over at the bar where the rest of the girls were eating.

"If you guys don't mind, I'm going to stay here and read while you go fishing," Violca announced, looking over at Brandon.

Brandon sighed and Chase saw the look that passed between them before he finally nodded. After everyone finished eating, the girls cleaned up. Scott and Eryk both went in to help, but Eva shooed them away, telling them that the boys would get to clean up after dinner.

Violca helped the little girls get ready while Brandon packed up the cooler with Eva and Kati. The guys went out to their tents to change. Once everything was packed up, Kati and Eva found Violca, Eva asked, "Are you staying to read the book?"

"Yeah, I want to read while I have a chance to be alone. I hope you don't mind."

Both girls shook their heads and Violca released a breath she didn't realize she had been holding. "You guys can share the book tonight and I'll let you know if I read anything interesting."

The girls smiled before heading out. Violca saw Angyalka run up to Chase and grab his hand, leading him toward the river.

Violca went to her room and grabbed the book from the nightstand. Taking it into the living room, she curled up on the couch to re-read the note her mother had left them. Smiling, she turned the page. The handwriting and language was unfamiliar. Biting her lip, she thought about how the writing had changed when she had run her fingers over the paper. Deciding to try it again, she ran her fingers lightly over the page. The paper felt a little different, thicker, older. It warmed slightly under her fingers, then shimmered as the writing slowly changed.

This book is for those that come after me. A place for us to share our stories for those that will follow.

I think the best place to start is at the beginning. Our great grandmother was kicked out of her family's house after she got pregnant without being wed. She went into labor while passing through a small town and gave birth to a beautiful baby girl who had the most unusual violet eyes. When this girl was born, the innkeeper's wife, who had helped birth her, fell head over heels for the little angelic child and talked her husband into letting them stay and work there.

As the child grew, she won over the entire town. She was born with a natural ability to heal others and her touch was so special that even the plants would grow. Her mother never admitted to it, but the town firmly believed that the violet-eyed child was a child of the gods. Believing she was a blessing to them, the town did their best to keep her a secret.

One day, a lord came through. At this time, the child had almost reached adulthood and was of marrying age. He stuck around, bribing the people, and when he found out about her abilities, he decided he wanted her for himself.

He tried to buy her from her mother, who refused. She could see the greed in him and wanted more for her daughter than a man who would use her. When his guards physically tried to take her daughter, she fought to take her back. The man's guards stabbed her mother. The girl's cry was so loud, and so heartbreaking that several ladies in the town came running. They instantly tried to rescue the girl. The man wielded his knife, but before he could attack any of them, the girl screamed, putting both her hands on his face.

The rumor of the town was that the man went blind and released her. Grandmother just smiled and shook her head when I asked her. She ran to her mother, crying. The girl put her hands over the wound, and slowly it magically healed.

According to my great grandmother, the sound of her heartbreak was what caused the gods to bless them and give the beautiful child the gifts she had. The females that came to help her also suddenly had smaller gifts. Some were able to heal. The others had a special power over the earth. Only grandmother was blessed with the ability to call the earth and heal.

If you can read this, then you my dear, are also related to the beautiful child who was rumored to be a daughter to one of the gods. Our gifts are many and varied, but one thing is for sure, our power comes from the earth.

Violca paused there to think about what she had read so far. The story did not embellish anything, but she still got stuck on things like powers and gods. She enjoyed reading about mythology in school, but believed it was only a myth…right?

CHAPTER 36

Angyalka held one of Chase's hands while the other one held the small cooler of drinks. "Do you like my sister?"

Chase almost tripped at her question and he heard Scott and Eryk both coughing to suppress their laughter. "I think your sister is very nice."

Angyalka frowned at that, as if thinking about what he said. "You kissed my sister. Doesn't that mean you have to love her?"

This time Scott coughed and Chase saw Eryk's shoulders shaking in laughter. His eyes narrowed and he thought about how he would like to roast them. Maybe a little fire under their asses would make him feel better. "Well…umm," Chase stuttered, not sure how to answer the question.

"If you don't love her, you shouldn't kiss her," Angyalka stated before continuing, "When you marry her, I don't want to wear pink, okay?"

Chase closed his eyes, trying not to smile at her words. "I promise if I marry your sister, you won't have to wear a pink dress."

Nodding at that, Angyalka let go of his hand and skipped

ahead to Sari. Chase shook his head, wondering what that had been about. He saw Eryk and Scott looking back at him, both smiling before Scott finally said, "I don't think you should have agreed, after all, aren't colors something the bride gets to pick?"

Looking around, making sure no one was watching, he flipped them both off. Both of them laughed as they turned back around.

The trail Brandon led them down took them to the lake at the end of the river. There was a small pier that Brandon was leading the girls onto. "All right guys, let's fish before all the other people come out and scare the fish away."

Sari gave Eryk her fishing rod, asking him to help her, while Angyalka ran up to Chase, reminding him of his promise to help her catch the biggest fish. Scott set down the big cooler, watching as the girls set up. He smiled when he saw Eryk and Chase having a hard time trying to help the younger ones fish.

SCOTT WATCHED FOR A MOMENT, noticing that Kati was off by herself, frowning in frustration. Taking a deep breath, he walked over to her. "Would you like some help?"

He flinched when she jumped. Nodding, she bit her lower lip before whispering, "Sure."

Before baiting her hook, he held her fishing pole. "Okay, when you cast out, it's a flick of a wrist, like this, see?" he said, showing her how to flick her wrist while holding the pole. Handing her the pole, he stood back before telling her, "Here, you try it."

Kati flicked her wrist a few times, almost getting the movement right, but still a little jerky. "Hold on," he said and when she stopped, he moved in behind her. His large hand enfolded hers, and his panther almost purred being that close to her. "Like this, one fluid movement."

Kati repeated the movement with his help. When she had it down, he moved back and Scott baited her hook. "Okay, now you're ready."

Scott watched as she cast out. When she cast correctly, she turned to him with a smile on her lips. His breath caught. It was rare to see Kati smile, and at this moment she looked truly happy. "Good job. You'll probably catch a fish before anybody else."

KATI LOOKED AROUND and smiled when she looked at Chase and Eryk, both still trying to show her younger sisters what to do. Eva and Brandon were both smiling as well. She knew he was trying to hold back his laughter at the constant questions the girls were asking them.

Scott baited his hook and took a few steps away from her before casting. Kati found herself watching him from the corner of her eye. Scott had made her nervous since the first time they met. He had scared her when he came at Eryk. Every other time since then, Scott had both terrified her and fascinated her.

Kati's reaction to him was unexpected. Eryk was the first guy in a long time to be nice to her and stand up for her. She knew her sister, Violca, might hope she had a crush on him, but it was Scott who constantly drew her attention. Scott turned, his eyes meeting hers, and she felt her cheeks heat up at being caught staring at him. Quickly turning her attention back to her fishing rod, she jumped when she felt a tug.

"Let the line up a little," she heard Scott say, suddenly near her. "Okay, now slowly start to reel it in." The first few spins around were easy, but it quickly got harder and she frowned, using her muscle. She felt Scott rest his hands on her, and he guided her to pull it back before reeling it in. His hands worked on steadying hers, as he let her do the work, but added his support. She could feel his breath on her ear. "That's it, you've got it."

When the fish jumped up above the water, she was surprised to see how big it was. Kati took a deep breath, not wanting to let Scott down. When they finally got the fish close, Brandon appeared with the net, capturing it for her. Unhooking it, Brandon smiled. "Good job Kati, you caught the first fish of the day!"

Kati's chest swelled with pride and she turned to look at Scott. Scott grinned at her. "Good job!"

"Thank you," Kati replied before turning back to Brandon. Sari and Angyalka ran past her, each with a worm in their hand, chasing each other, squealing. Brandon put the fish in the cooler he had brought.

"Do you need help baiting your hook again, or do you have it?" Scott asked.

"I want to try it," Kati said, biting her lip when she grabbed a worm from the container. Concentrating, she baited her hook and cast out like Scott had showed her. Looking over, she saw Scott watching her. Smiling politely, she turned back to the lake, wondering if anyone else could hear her heart beating.

CHAPTER 37

Violca put the book away. She had flipped through it and come across a section that talked about the other women who had the healing touch. Reading the passage triggered memories of her sisters, and AnnaBelle always telling her that she had a magic touch.

Violca also read about times they had run into other people who had different abilities and gifts. Some of them were good; others were bad. Her ancestors learned to be wary of others and trust their instincts. Everyone had the potential to be good or bad, but her ancestors believed that individuals should be judged on their own actions, not the group or race.

Smiling, she could hear Angyalka's high-pitched squeal, and she looked out the window. Sari was the first one she saw, followed quickly by Angyalka. Slowly, one by one, they all appeared. Going out on to the porch, she smiled. "So, did you guys catch dinner?"

Brandon snorted, "Of course."

Eva winked, "Kati caught the biggest fish."

Raising an eyebrow, she looked over at Kati, who blushed.

"She did, did she?" Looking over at Chase, she smiled. "I thought you were going to help Angel catch the biggest fish?"

Chase grinned. "Well, apparently Kati had better skills."

Brandon came up the stairs with the cooler of fish. Violca grinned at them. "I made you potato salad and baked some brownies for dessert tonight."

"How about I cook the fish, since you cooked breakfast?" Scott asked.

Brandon shrugged, "Are you a good cook?"

Scott grinned, "I know my way around fish."

Violca headed back in the house, quickly followed by Eva and Kati. "So, did you read the book?" Eva asked quietly, once they were away from everyone.

Looking over her shoulder, noticing how the guys were all outside drinking the last of the beer from one of the coolers, Violca replied, "I read some of it. It seems so unbelievable, but..." her voice trailed off, now wondering what her sisters would think when she admitted that a part of her believed in what she was reading.

Eva seemed to sense her thoughts and smiled at her. "It's hard to believe, and I know some of my memories are clouded, but I don't ever remember Mom lying to us. She just always seemed to be..."

"More," Kati finished for her.

CHASE LISTENED FROM THE PORCH. Scott and Eryk already guessed at what he was doing, and kept most of the conversation going. A part of him wondered what was unbelievable. What was in that book he could not read? Did they not know what they were? Could it be possible that the Earth Witches who were expected to be able to find and unleash the power of the Dragon Ruby, did not even know what they were?

There was a faint smell of magic coming from inside the house. Chase could tell that Scott and Eryk could also smell it. While Scott prepped the fish for dinner, Eryk announced he was going to take a quick walk. Chase nodded at him, knowing he was going to do a quick perimeter check, since they had not done one since early that morning.

When he saw Violca was in the kitchen by herself, he smiled and walked over to her. Wrapping his arms around her, he put his head in the crook of her neck and inhaled deeply, loving the way she smelled. He could feel her tense up, but she looked around and realized that they were alone and then he could feel her relax against him. "Did you have fun with Sari and Angyalka while fishing?"

Chase snorted and he could feel her shoulders shaking with silent laughter. "Oh, you find that funny, do you?" When she nodded, he tickled her sides, biting back a moan when she twisted and turned in his arms, the sound of her laughter filling the air.

When Violca finally freed herself from his arms, she turned and looked at him. Her violet eyes sparkled up at him as her lips curved in a smile. Chase wrapped his arms around her, pulling her close. Giving in to temptation, he kissed her gently.

Violca pulled back, blushing. Chase saw her bite her lower lip, and said, "I think your sisters are still in their rooms."

Violca looked a little sheepish. "Sorry, since my parents passed away I…"

Chase grinned, bringing his hand up to push a stray hair back behind her ear. "Don't apologize. I think it's amazing you kept your sisters together."

Hearing a throat clear behind him, Violca jumped and Chase looked over his shoulder to see Brandon in the doorway. "Scott says the fish is almost done. V, would you mind bringing out a plate?"

~

Violca smiled at Brandon when she saw him raise his eyebrow. She knew he was probably watching from the outside. She couldn't tell if Brandon was happy or not by the development, but she knew they would talk about it later. "Sure, I'll be right out."

Reaching in the cabinet, Violca went to take the plate outside and felt Chase walking right behind her. "So, what's the story between you and Brandon, if you don't mind my asking?"

Violca looked at him over her shoulder. "Are you asking if he's seen me naked?"

Chase smiled at her, and Eva came outside with them, having obviously heard her answer. "Oh, Brandon and Violca both played, 'I'll show you mine, if you show me yours.'"

Kati laughed and Violca was suddenly aware of everyone's eyes on her. She glanced at Chase and noticed that out of everyone, he was the only one who didn't look amused. Brandon laughed. "Violca, you told your sisters about that?"

Violca rolled her eyes, bringing the plate to Scott, smiling politely at him when he took it. "We were almost nine years old, and we did not play that game, despite the many times he begged." Looking over at Brandon, she said, "I didn't tell her, by the way, they probably have some weird memory of hearing you."

Brandon laughed hard. "Quit lying, V."

Everyone laughed and she noticed even Chase was chuckling. Eryk grinned. "So, how long have you two known each other?"

Violca grinned when Brandon answered, "Forever."

Scott, piling up the fish, asked, "How did you meet?"

Violca spoke up before Brandon could answer. "He rode his bike back and forth in front of our house until my mom finally took pity on him and invited him inside to eat cookies."

Brandon gave her a serious look. "The entire neighborhood

could smell your mom baking cookies. I was just the only one smart enough to make sure I got some."

Laughing, Violca headed back into the house, Eva and Kati following her to get the rest of the items for dinner. Calling out for the two younger girls, they took everything outside. Violca smiled, watching how the two younger ones inserted themselves around the guys. They all laughed throughout dinner, the girls keeping them all entertained as they ate.

CHAPTER 38

After everyone finished eating, Violca smiled as the guys helped clean off the outside table, while Eva and Kati did the dishes. Violca sat on the floor with Sari and Angyalka while Brandon grabbed a few of the board games for them to play. Eryk and Chase joined them around the coffee table, and Violca smiled when Sari and Angyalka sat next to them and instantly gave them their version of how to play.

Scott sat back in one of the window seats, watching everyone. A small smile appeared on his lips when Angyalka told Chase he was doing something wrong. He glanced back toward the kitchen, watching Eva and Kati as they cleaned the dishes. Scott didn't have a ton of interaction with teenagers outside of Eryk and his friends, but the few girls that occasionally hung out with them always seemed spoiled and he doubted they would help out so easily.

Noticing that they were almost done with the dishes, Scott got up and walked out the back door to his tent. He reached into his bag, pulling out the deluxe set of pencils and charcoals. Not sure if Kati would take it or not, he ran his fingers through his hair. Scott couldn't understand why he was so nervous. She was a kid still. He shouldn't be nervous. He had plenty of experience with girls. Definitely more experience than she'd had with boys.

Walking back into the house, he saw Kati putting away the last of the dishes. Taking a deep breath, he headed toward the kitchen and stood on the other side of the bar from her. When Kati turned and looked at him, her eyes widened in surprise before a small blush spread on her cheeks.

For a moment Scott debated about what to say to her. "Eryk said you like to draw." Kati nodded and he saw the confusion on her face. Putting the pencil and charcoal set on the bar top, he slid it over to her, noticing her eyes growing wide in surprise before she smiled at him. "I thought you might like these," he finished lamely, wondering where all his experience with the opposite sex had gone.

Kati picked them up, at first not saying anything. When he started to get nervous, she suddenly came around the bar and gave him a quick hug. "Thank you so much. I was looking at some just like these the other day. How'd you know?"

Scott heard some chuckling behind him and knew Chase was there. He stammered before answering, "Just a lucky guess," and walked back toward the window seat.

Scott noticed Chase watching him. He could still feel Kati standing exactly where he'd left her. Scott felt like a giant ass, but couldn't figure out what to say to her. What the hell did one say to a teenage girl? Since interacting with the girls, they were under the impression that none of the sisters knew about shifters. How was he supposed to explain about imprinting? That fate had chosen this young girl to be his mate and she had the choice to accept him or not? Whether or not she chose him, this young girl would be the only one for him.

VIOLCA SAW Kati head to her bedroom shortly after Scott walked back to the window seat. Sari picked a card and jumped up and down when she ended up winning. Clapping her hands, and telling her good job, she saw Kati come out of her room with her sketchpad before curling up on the corner of the couch. Looking at the clock she smiled. "Okay girls, why don't you go change your clothes so I can tuck you both into bed?"

Both girls began to pout, but instantly went around the room, hugging everyone. Violca tried not to laugh as she watched the surprise on the guys' faces as the girls hugged them before heading toward their room.

Giving the girls a few minutes, she went into their room and tucked them both in, kissing each girl. "Do you want to read in bed before going to sleep?"

"Yes," they both answered in unison. Turning on the lamp between the bunk beds, she went to the bookshelf and grabbed a few books that she knew they both loved and let them pick which one they wanted to read.

"Don't stay up too late," Violca said as she turned off the overhead light.

Going back into the living room, she noticed that Eryk and Scott had already gone back outside. Kati was lost in her drawing on one side of the couch, while Eva was curled up with one of her new books on the other side. Brandon stood up from his chair and kissed her on the cheek. "I think I'm going to turn in."

"Night, Brandon," Violca replied, watching him as he said good night to the other two girls and nodded at Chase.

Chase slowly got up and walked over toward her. "How would you like to go out for a walk?"

Violca nodded. "Let me just put on my tennis shoes and grab a jacket."

Going into her room, she put on her tennis shoes, then ran her brush through her hair before pulling it back into a ponytail. Grabbing her light jacket, she headed back to the living room.

Eva looked up and smiled. "Be back before it gets too dark."

Rolling her eyes at her sister, Violca joined Chase at the front door. She blushed when he put his hand on the small of her back and led her outside.

"Did you want to go grab a jacket?" Violca asked him, looking up at him.

"No, I'll be fine. I'm usually a little warm." They walked in silence. Violca was aware of the last time they were in the woods together, and her cheeks began to heat up.

CHAPTER 39

Chase enjoyed the feel of Violca's hand in his and the comfortable silence as they walked into the woods. Looking down at her, he saw a small blush on her cheeks and realized where Violca's mind must have wandered. His body hardened, remembering how she responded to his touch. Clearing his throat, he said, "Brandon seems like a nice guy."

Violca smiled and he felt a stab of jealousy as her face softened. "He is. I've known him forever. I can't even count the times he's helped me while growing up, or after our parents died."

Chase squeezed her hand. Despite his twinge of jealousy, he was glad she had someone she could lean on.

"How long have you known Scott and Eryk?"

"Since Eryk was two, so almost sixteen years." Chase left out the part where he found them in the woods, fighting off some humans who had found out what they were and decided to go hunting. Scott had gotten there too late to save his parents and sister. When Chase came upon them, following the strong scent of blood, he found Scott severely outnumbered and Eryk cowering behind him.

"When I met Scott, he told me he was raising his brother." Violca looked up at him as if she was trying to see if he was telling the truth.

"Their parents and sister had just passed away when I met him, actually." Violca squeezed his hand and he saw a look of sympathy cross her face. The wind blew and Chase reached up, brushing a stray hair back behind her ear, caressing her cheek as he did. He saw her blush a little, her breath catching, and he smiled down at her. "I think it's amazing how both of you stepped up to raise your siblings." Chase saw her bite her lip and he smiled more at her, thinking that little habit of hers was adorable. "You're amazing with them. You should be very proud."

"Thank you. I don't think they'd always agree, but overall I think they're happy." Violca's eyes brightened and he saw a mischievous look on her face. Unable to help himself, he bent down and brushed his lips against her, moaning softly when she leaned into him.

Violca's lips parted under his and he deepened the kiss, his tongue slowly sliding between her lips. Chase felt her arms slide around his neck, pulling him closer as her tongue slowly dueled with his. Breaking the kiss, he put his forehead against hers, panting.

Chase moaned softly when Violca's tongue came out and slowly licked her lips. Her violet eyes were a little darker as she slowly opened them, meeting his gaze. He could smell her desire for him, and it took all his effort not to take her again in the woods.

Violca smiled up at him before taking his hand, turning, and walking back toward the house. She led him back to the cabin and almost sighed in relief when she saw that only a small light was left on in the living room, with each of the different bedroom lights on.

When they got to the stairs, Violca kept ahold of Chase's hand and slowly led him up to the door. Pausing before she opened it, she glanced up at him, suddenly feeling nervous. Chase looked down at her and his golden-brown eyes softened as he brushed her hair back. "You know we don't have to, right?"

Violca's heart swelled at his thoughtfulness. Turning the handle, she grabbed his hand and led him into the house. She locked the door behind them and the sound of the click seemed to echo. Stopping to turn off the lamp that was left on, she easily led him through the dark to her room. Closing the door behind them, she let out a breath she didn't realize she had been holding, as relief washed over her that nobody had come out of their rooms.

Violca could see Chase smile and she blushed, knowing he had guessed that she was relieved. She knew they all had guessed, but having it confirmed was something else entirely.

Violca walked to her window to close the curtain, but Chase grabbed her hand and pulled her to him. "Leave it open," he whispered against her lips. She felt his hand sliding under her jaw, angling her head up. "You look beautiful in the moonlight," Chase whispered before his mouth finally met hers. Violca felt her body melt against his, as his tongue slowly slid into her mouth.

Violca's hand glided up his chest and wrapped around his neck as the kiss deepened. She sucked his tongue into her mouth and heard him growl in response, causing her body to shudder with need. Chase broke the kiss, kissing down her neck while his hands slid up her sides to cup her breasts. Her fingers tightened in his hair as she felt his teeth lightly scrape her neck and she moaned loudly, arching her back and pressing her breasts deeper into his hands.

Chase's thumb slid back and forth over her nipples, causing Violca to feel them harden and press even harder against the material of her bra. Chase released her breasts, moving back just enough to quickly pull her shirt up and over her head before claiming her mouth in another kiss. Violca sucked on his tongue and she felt his hand slide around her back to unhook her bra.

Violca felt her bra slide off and it was quickly replaced with his hands. She moaned into his mouth, deepening the kiss. The back of her legs hit the bed and she realized that he had been slowly moving her back. Chase lowered her, never breaking the kiss. Violca began to slide her hands down his chest, grabbing the bottom of his shirt. Breaking the kiss, she quickly pulled it up and over his head, tossing it onto the floor.

CHASE SLID his arms around her and pulled her in tight. When her breast touched his chest, they both moaned. Chase nibbled on her lips, before his tongue came out and gently licked where he had bitten her. When her lips parted in a soft moan, his tongue eagerly slid into her waiting mouth. His hands slid along her chest and cupped her breasts again. Violca's breasts were more than a handful, and he gently squeezed them, loving how each time he squeezed, her breath caught.

Kissing his way down her neck, he dipped his head until his mouth found one of her breasts. She moaned when he finally took her nipple into his mouth and sucked eagerly. His fingers gently pinched and teased her other nipple as he teasingly bit on the hard nub. Chase chuckled when he felt her hand tighten in his hair and the long moan that escaped her. Releasing her nipple, he kissed his way to her other breast and teased it with his mouth. Listening to her breath increase, he growled encouragingly when her hips rocked and bumped up against him.

CHAPTER 40

Chase slid one leg between hers as he continued to tease her breasts. One hand moved down her side to cup her ass firmly, before guiding her to rock against him. He could feel her heat through their clothes and he used his teeth to bite gently on her nipple, loving how her fingers tightened in his hair.

His cock was hard and pulsing against his zipper. He wouldn't be surprised if he had the imprint of his zipper on it for a few days. Chase's mouth left Violca's breast and made its way down her belly, stopping on occasion to gently nip at her skin then trail his tongue along where his teeth had bitten. When he got to her belly button, his tongue came out, making love to it. In and out, in and out, he felt her hips arch up against his mouth, the sounds coming louder and louder as her fingers pulled on his hair.

Chase unbuttoned the top of her shorts, the sound of him unzipping Violca's shorts filled the air. His fingers hooked into the sides of her shorts as he removed them and her panties in one move and tossed them off the bed. He moaned when he looked down. Her lips glistening with her juices in the moonlight, made his mouth water. Chase put his hand on her hips, holding her still as he settled between her thighs. His shoulders pushed her legs further apart, opening her more to his view and his tongue licked up her wet folds. Chase growled loudly when he tasted her on his tongue.

Violca bucked up against his hands, causing him to moan loudly, and her entire body arched into his touch. His hands tightened on her, and his tongue flicked against her sensitive nub. Looking up he saw her biting her lip to keep from being too loud, as her head rolled from side to side.

Chase glided his finger into her core as his mouth latched onto her clit and sucked hard, causing her to buck harder against his face. Chase hooked his fingers in her core and hit her G-spot. She bucked harder against his mouth and began to shudder under him as her pleasure built. He heard her scream, as her pleasure hit her core, spasming hard around his fingers.

Before Violca could come down, Chase quickly undid his pants. Grabbing the condom in his pocket that he had taken from Scott earlier, he removed his pants and kicked them away. As he came up her body, Chase captured her mouth in a rough kiss. Putting the condom on quickly, he thrust into her. He captured Violca's moan in his mouth. Taking one leg by the knee, he pulled it up to rest high up on his hip and moaned into her mouth as he slid in a little deeper.

Trying to give her a moment to adjust to him, his tongue gently dueled with hers. Chase felt her hips roll up, bumping him and he smiled against her lips as he moved inside her in long, slow strokes. Violca's hands wrapped around his back, her nails digging in as she scratched downward. He grunted against her neck, kissing and licking every inch of skin he could find. When her nails dug into his ass, encouraging him to go faster, he was helpless to do anything but comply.

Violca turned her head, kissing and licking along the column of his neck, her breath coming in short little pants. He felt her teeth as she scraped them along his neck and down his shoulder.

Chase growled, picking up the pace as she moaned, biting a little harder. He heard her gasp when he bit her in return. He felt her body tighten around him and he growled loudly.

Chase grunted when he felt Violca contract around him. Violca's teeth on his skin caused his dragon to come up right below the surface, and he could feel his dragon's pleasure mixing with his. Violca's nails dug deeper into his skin, her face buried in the crook of his neck. He could feel her breathing hard against his skin. Her core tightened and he knew he was close, so he slid his hand from her hip up to her breast and pinched her hard nipple, sending her over the edge, her hips bucking as her core spasmed around his thrusting cock. He tried to hold back to delay her pleasure, when suddenly her teeth sank deep into the crook of his neck, piercing his skin.

The pleasure was so intense it caused his own orgasm to hit and his teeth sank into her shoulder. When he tasted something metallic on his tongue, he realized he had broken the skin. He worried when he felt her buck against him. Violca's teeth were still locked onto him, and he heard her muffled scream, as her core tightened harder around him.

When he finally came down, he felt her body lightly shuddering around him and her tongue licking where she had bitten him. Chase pulled back, seeing his teeth marks in her skin and a little blood. He dipped his head, licking along the mark and felt her shudder with pleasure. Rolling to his side, he pulled her with him. Chase's hand slid up and down her back, holding her near him, sighing happily when she cuddled closer to him.

After a few moments of them catching their breath, Violca looked up at him, a light, satisfied smile playing on her lips. She glanced at his neck where he could still feel tingling from where she had bitten him. She looked almost sheepish and he grinned down at her. "You know, I never would've pegged you for a biter."

Chase's grin turned into a big smile as he watched her. There wasn't enough life to see her clearly, but he was sure he would see her blushing. "I…" she stammered.

Brushing the hair back from her face, he smiled. "I liked it." Bending down, he kissed her gently, then playfully nibbled at her bottom lip. He felt her sigh against him and he looked down at her. "I didn't hurt you when…" his voice trailed off when she shook her head no and kissed his palm, which was still cupping her cheek.

Violca laid her head down on his chest and kissed him right above his heart. Closing his eyes, his hand gently caressed her back until he felt her body relax and her breathing even out. Once she was asleep, he let himself drift off.

CHAPTER 41

Violca woke up to the sound of a loud crash and the feel of the bed shaking so much she almost fell off. She heard Sari and Angyalka crying as her room filled with smoke. Chase jumped up, grabbing his pants and throwing his shirt at her. Taking her hand, he pulled her behind him as they headed out of the room.

Violca saw her sisters and Brandon coming out of the rooms, everyone coughing and covering their mouths. The smoke was coming from the living room. Turning to look, she gasped, seeing a hole where the door used to be.

"Everyone okay?" Chase asked as they joined in the middle of the hall next to the living room.

Everyone mumbled something in the affirmative and Sari and Angyalka both threw themselves against Violca's legs. The back door slid open and Scott came in, his eyes instantly going to Kati before looking at everyone else. "Where's Eryk?"

Scott shook his head. "He went out on patrol after you guys got back and hasn't come back yet."

Through the hole in the wall came several shadows. Chase and Brandon both stiffened. Turning, Chase took Violca's hands in his. "Whatever happens, stay inside, keep your sisters close." He brushed his lips against hers, quickly whispering, "Go lock yourselves in the back room and stay there. No matter what you see or hear, please trust me."

Chase turned, looking at Scott. "I'll take the back, you get the ones in the front." He pointed to Brandon. "Get your gun, make sure no one gets inside that room." Violca ushered the girls into the room, turning to look at Chase, fear for him rising. He turned, his face looking solemn. "Stay away from the windows."

Violca closed the door, telling Angyalka and Sari to sit on the chair away from the window. With the moonlight coming in she realized that Brandon had the blinds open and quickly closed them. Stopping, she saw Chase standing outside and several men coming out from the woods.

Violca could only make out their shapes, but they were all tall and thick. It looked like Chase was about to be surrounded by a group of linebackers. She blinked several times, not believing her eyes as she watched a black shimmery cloud surround Chase and a moment later, a black dragon stood in his place before giving a roar that shook the house. Moonlight shimmered off the black dragon as it stood on all fours, panting heavily, small puffs of smoke in front of his face. The dragon turned, looking at her and their eyes met. Violca could actually see the dragon's golden eyes staring at her, and she quickly closed the blinds, backing up to the bed.

"What was that?" Eva asked, looking at her intently.

Violca opened her mouth to say something before closing it again. She didn't know if she even believed what she saw. No way was she saying she saw a dragon. Eva walked toward the window.

"Stay away from the window. We don't need anyone to see that we're in here."

Eva frowned and went back to standing by Sari. Angyalka had curled up on Kati's lap and Violca heard Kati making soothing noises. They jumped when they heard a thud against the wall.

She wanted to check to see if the dragon was still outside. She wanted to see if Brandon was okay. Violca knew she had to protect her sisters, but wished she could be more help.

~

CHASE'S MUSCLES STRETCHED, and he let out a loud roar at the end of his change. Aware that eyes were on him, he turned to see Violca in the window. When she closed the blinds quickly, he felt his dragon's hurt and wondered if she would be able to accept this side of him.

Changing was painful when they first learned how, but Chase was old enough that he barely felt it this time. He knew Violca could not see much. The few that had seen them change never could describe more than a shimmer or a cloud around them.

Focusing back on the men coming out of the woods, he growled and scratched the ground, ready to attack. From the scent, he could smell that some of them were human. They were marked by a demon, the smell of the sulfur lingering on them. The other ones were demon halflings, demons that were born from human females that had been tortured and raped. They were not as strong as demons, but stronger than humans. Some of them even had special abilities they received from the women who were picked.

Six of them circled him. Chase resisted the urge to blow fire, knowing that if he did, there was a chance he could set the entire forest on fire. Four of them attacked at once. Swinging out his arm, he swiped at one, causing him to hit the side of the house near the girls' room.

Chase hissed and bit the one near his right arm when he felt a blade slicing into his skin. He saw two of them trying to circle behind him, heading to the house and he used his long tail to swat them away, knocking them over. Out of the corner of his eye, he saw several more men coming out of the woods, heading toward the house. Grabbing two of the humans, he swung them up and over the woods. He felt several more knives trying to slice him, so he used his paw to hold one of them down.

STANDING in the backyard Scott's eyes narrowed, he heard Chase roar and smiled. He was worried about his brother, but focused on the shadows he saw coming closer. The smell of sulfur was strong and he narrowed his eyes. Fucking demons. It figures they would join against Viktor, siding to help his brother Dmitri.

Three men came out of the trees into the clearing. As if on silent command, they all rushed at him and he smiled, running at them. This was his element, fighting, protecting others. He was not built for sitting by and watching. He clotheslined the first guy, knocking him on the ground before dodging the punch of the second. Scott came up with an uppercut, hitting the guy on the jaw.

The third attacked him only to be knocked to the ground when Eryk came out of the woods. Scott growled, "Good to see you, little brother," before swinging at the guy in front of him.

"Sorry, was a little tied up, brother. Hope you didn't have too much fun without me," Eryk said, and Scott fought the urge not to grin.

CHAPTER 42

Violca could hear Brandon fighting outside her door and Chase fighting in the front. Each time they heard a thud from any direction, the girls jumped. "Do you think they're going to be okay?" Kati asked, looking at the door, biting her lower lip.

Violca smiled reassuringly at Kati, "Of course, you know how strong Brandon is, and I bet Chase and Scott are just as strong."

Kati nodded, biting her lower lip. The room began to shake and the girls cuddled together in the corner, away from the door and the windows. It felt like someone was shaking the room, until the boards broke in half and the wall was flung at the dragon that was surrounded by men.

Violca stood in front of Eva and Kati, who were guarding the younger two girls as they whimpered. Violca heard Eva whisper, "Is that a dragon?"

Violca's eyes were drawn to the group of men heading toward her room. All of them looked to stand well over six foot. The one in the center seemed to be leading. His pale white hair reflected the moonlight as he approached, his eyes almost seemed to be glowing and were red in color. When he was close, she noticed how his smile was predatory. When he spoke, his voice was deep, rich, alluring. "Come with me, my dears. Let me take you from these *shifters* and save you."

Angyalka whimpered, her voice barely heard over the fighting, "He's not a nice man."

Even though Violca could barely hear her sister, the guy tsk'd at her comment. "I promise, I'm a very nice man."

The roar from the dragon caused Violca to look in its direction. She could see smoke coming from its mouth. The dragon came at them. The man made a motion with his hand, and more people came out of the woods to attack the dragon.

"Come with me before someone gets hurt." His voice sounded impatient as his eyes narrowed.

The door flew open and Brandon stood in the doorway. He looked at the missing wall, his eyes rounding in surprise. Aiming his gun, he shot at the guy trying to come in. The silver-haired man put his hand up, and the bullet froze in the air before it dropped.

Violca was frozen, until she felt Brandon grab her arm. "Violca, come."

Turning, she grabbed Angyalka, but before they could get anywhere, two of them grabbed Sari and Angyalka away from them. Before Brandon could help, two more guys appeared in the doorway, distracting him.

Fear rising, Violca tried to fight them. Her arms went up to push the guy in front of her, and she felt a blast, almost like electricity, shooting from her fingers and into the one trying to take Angyalka, knocking him out of the room.

Angyalka ran to Eva and Violca reached out, feeling a pulsing power coming from the crook of her neck. That same power left her fingertips and shot at the second guy. When he flew backwards, she quickly grabbed Sari, pulling her behind her, backing them toward the door.

Not sure what had happened, she kept her hands in front of

her. Violca could still feel a light pulsing of power in the crook of her neck. Looking up, she saw the man with the white hair watching intently. When he smiled, she swore his teeth all looked like they were shaved into points. "Until later, my Earth Witch."

The words were barely past his lips when he was suddenly gone. Not just him, but all his men had disappeared as well. Even the ones who had been fighting Brandon in the doorway were gone. Violca turned to look outside and saw the dragon standing just outside her room.

Slowly walking toward him, his chest heaving and small puffs of smoke coming out with each breath. The dragon itself was probably just slightly smaller than her house. Violca could feel him watching her, the eyes so familiar to Chase's, but different. The moonlight glittered off his obsidian black body and she hesitantly stepped closer.

Brandon tried to grab her arm to stop her from stepping out of the hole in the wall. "Violca?"

She heard the question in his voice and she shook him off, continuing to walk to the dragon.

Violca swore she could hear her mother's voice in her head encouraging her. When she stood just in front of the dragon, Chase, he lowered his head. She walked around him, noticing the wings on his back and wondered if he could fly, how his scales were so black and reflected the moonlight. When she came back around to the front of him, she reached out and touched his arm. Violca thought it would be rough, but instead it was smooth, and the muscles under her hand contracted.

Looking up, she saw him watching her. "Chase?" His name came out like a question and his head came down, nudging her. Closing her eyes, she rubbed her cheek on the dragon's nose. Hearing someone clearing his throat, she looked up to see Scott and Eryk coming around the house.

"Eryk, we were worried about you."

Eryk blushed, running his hand along the back of his neck.

"Sorry, they lured me away before I realized what was happening."

Brandon cleared his throat, his eyes narrowing, his voice sounding rough when he finally spoke. "We need to get away from here, and you need to explain what the fuck is going on."

Scott nodded. "You're right. Let's hurry up and get everyone's stuff together and get out of here before they decide to come back."

Brandon looked at the girls. "Grab what you need. We can replace your clothes."

Violca grabbed her mother's book from the nightstand, then her purse and her phone, before following Sari and Angyalka to their room. Collecting a few books that their mother had written in, she helped them put the stuffed animals they'd brought into their backpacks. Noticing the look on their faces, Violca stopped, going to her knees to look at them. "Hey, it's going to be okay, I promise."

Angyalka sniffled, using her arm to wipe her nose, while Sari nodded, biting her lip. "Are they going to come back?"

Violca brushed her hair back. "I don't know, sweetie, but just in case, we're going to go somewhere else, okay?" Both girls nodded and she smiled at them. "Okay, have we gotten all your stuffed animals? Do you need anything else?"

Both girls looked around, grabbing one or two more items, then putting them in their backpacks as they headed into the living room, where they found everyone waiting on them.

Chase and Brandon eyed each other with mistrust before Chase finally spoke up, "It's a long drive home. I think we should head in that direction and find a hotel about an hour or two from here. Get some sleep and then talk in the morning after every-one's had a good rest."

Brandon nodded. Looking away, he grabbed his bag and Angyalka. "Follow us. I think I know of a good place."

CHAPTER 43

Violca watched out the window. When she heard the sound of gentle snoring, she turned to see the younger two girls had fallen asleep. She looked over at Brandon, who was still gripping the steering wheel tightly. "How much farther?" she whispered, hoping Eva and Kati, who were sitting in the back, didn't hear her.

Brandon glanced at her, then ran his hand through his hair. "About an hour." She nodded, sitting back in her seat. When Brandon finally looked over at her, his voice was a hushed angry whisper, "What were you thinking walking up to that…that…"

Violca winced before saying, "Dragon."

"Dragons don't exist," Brandon said between gritted teeth, shaking his head before whispering, "Neither do guys who disappear into thin air."

Violca closed her eyes and whispered, "Neither do witches."

Brandon reached out and squeezed her hand. She tried to smile at him as she took a deep breath and let it out slowly. If she told anyone about what happened tonight, they would put her in a straitjacket and throw away the key. She would not believe anyone. She barely believed it and she was there.

Brandon drove for another hour before pulling off at a hotel that had a view of the highway and took cash. Telling her to stay in the van, he got out and talked to Chase. When they disappeared into the office, she heard Kati from the back whispering, "V, who were those guys?"

Violca turned in her seat, seeing Kati and Eva both watching her. "I don't know," she answered truthfully, "but we'll find out."

Brandon came back, opening the door and getting in. "We got the two rooms at the end." Starting the van, he drove around to the closest spot to their room and looked back at the sleeping girls in the middle. "Our rooms are adjoining, figured we could sleep in one and the girls in the other." He pointed toward the SUV. "They're in the room next to us."

Nodding, she got out, and opened the side door to the van. She reached in and picked up Sari. "Eva, can you carry Angyalka for me?"

Laying her sister down on the bed furthest from the window, Violca removed Sari's shoes. Once Eva laid Angyalka down, she adjusted her in the bed, and Violca covered the two. The adjoining door opened. "Eva and Kati, I hope you don't mind, but I thought you two could sleep in here with your sisters and share the other bed. Your sister and I will sleep in this room. The door will stay open just in case."

Eva and Kati both nodded and he smiled at them. "I know it'll be hard, but let's get some sleep."

Violca followed Brandon into the other room, sighing when she sat on the bed. "Try to get some sleep," Brandon said, lying on top of his blankets. Kicking off her shoes before lying down, Violca closed her eyes. She did not think she would be able to fall asleep, but soon her eyes grew heavy and sleep took hold of her.

Scott paced in the room. His cat wanted out as soon as Kati

was in danger. His skin was itchy with his desire to change. Even though he had not claimed Kati as his own, his desire to protect her was just as strong as if he had. Scott realized that even though his human half might not have fully accepted her as his, his animal half had no such reservations.

"How long do you think until they try again?" Eryk asked, drawing everyone's attention.

Chase shrugged. "Not long. I messaged Viktor on the way here. He said to take the girls to the house. They have reports on where Dmitri is hiding, and Viktor went with some of his guards to see if they can capture him."

Scott watched Chase glance at the window. "I'm going to go for a run and check the surrounding area."

Not waiting for an answer, Scott headed outside. At this exit, there was only the hotel, a mom-and-pop restaurant and a gas station. There was also a service road that ran between the highways and connected small towns. Scott walked around the hotel. Heading off so he was out of sight, he stripped and stacked his clothes neatly where he could find them later and quickly shifted into his panther. Turning his head, he could smell Kati in her room and his cat let out a low whine. Staying in the long grass, he ran along the highway for several miles on alert for anything out of the ordinary.

CHASE WATCHED his friend from the window before turning to Eryk. "Get some sleep, I have a funny feeling it won't be long before they try again."

Eryk kicked off his shoes, crawling under the blankets, still dressed. Chase sighed, leaning his head against the window frame. The relief his dragon felt when Violca approached him and touched him, almost made him roar, he was so happy.

Chase rubbed the side of his neck where Violca had bitten

him earlier. He was surprised when she broke the skin, but the surge of pleasure that went through him called to his animal instinct and he had bitten her in kind.

Chase felt so much fear when he saw the side of the house ripped away and the demon, Micah, approaching the girls. He was so outnumbered all he could do was watch from the corner of his eye. If needed, he would have lit the entire forest on fire to keep her safe. It was ingrained in them early on, to always be careful with their flame and only in rare circumstances were they allowed to use it.

Chase rubbed his neck again. The superficial wounds he received during the fight had healed during the attack, but he could still feel her teeth marks in his skin. Through it, he was able to feel Violca using her power. It was a pulsing sensation he felt even as he assumed his dragon shape. At this moment, he felt like they were connected and that she was drawing power from him.

He found that he liked feeling connected. Even with a wall between them, he could feel her. Sighing, he crawled into the other bed, knowing that when Scott got back, he would wake him up to take the next watch.

CHAPTER 44

Violca woke up to the sound of voices and stretched. Recognizing Chase and Brandon's voices, she smiled and looked toward the door. Brandon was standing in the doorway and before she could make out what they were saying, he closed the door.

"They're going to get breakfast and will come over with it so we can talk in private," Brandon told her, seeing the curious look on her face.

Nodding, she looked around the room and realized she didn't have a toothbrush or toothpaste. In her haste, she had only grabbed a few things. Getting up, she headed to the girls' room to see if Kati or Eva were smart enough to bring one.

Walking into the adjoining room, she saw Kati was the only one really awake and whispered, "Hey, did any of you think to grab a toothbrush and toothpaste?"

Kati reached over into Eva's backpack and pulled them out.

"I'll bring them right back. The guys are going to bring us breakfast so we can talk."

Kati looked around the room. "I'll wake up the girls when you come back with the toothbrush."

Violca headed back to her room, brushed her teeth and ran her fingers through her hair. Feeling better, she brought the toothbrush and toothpaste back and helped wake up the little ones.

"Ugh, I hope we go home and grab clothes. I understand why we wanted to hurry, but I hate sleeping in my clothes and then wearing them the next day," Eva said, straightening her shirt.

"I'll ask Brandon. If not, then we'll have to find a store," Violca told her, looking up when she heard a knock on the other door. "That should be our food."

Violca stood between the two rooms watching Chase, Scott, and Eryk come in, carrying several bags of food. Eryk smiled at her. "We decided to get everyone French toast, sausage, and orange juice."

"Sounds good," Violca said.

"Hey Sari, Angel, do you want to eat breakfast with me?" Eryk asked, approaching the table and unpacking the plastic containers. The two girls eagerly ran to him.

Eva and Kati followed Violca into the other room and Brandon pushed the door around so they could keep an eye on the girls, but keep them from hearing too much. Violca looked up at Chase to feel him watching her. An image of him transforming into the dragon last night played in her head. She knew she should be afraid of him, but she realized that she was not. When she finally smiled at him, she saw his shoulders relax and his eyes light up as he smiled back. "We figured Eryk could keep the girls busy while we talk."

"Good idea," Brandon said, helping Scott unpack the bags he'd brought in. Once everyone was settled, all eyes turned to Chase as if silently, everyone had decided he was the one who should start. Chase cleared his throat, looking at Violca, his golden-brown eyes appearing more golden this morning. "There is a legend that says the gods made dragons to help destroy the titans. They were so big, that when they stood on their back legs and stretched their wings, they could touch the sky." He paused for a second before continuing, "Once the titans were destroyed, the story goes that the gods killed all the dragons and they were never seen again. Although the story ends there, it's just the start of the story of my people.

"When the dragons fought the titans, one was wounded. As he lay in a field, a farm girl came out and she healed him. When the gods came to kill the dragon, she stood in front of him and cried, telling the gods she loved him. The farm girl's plea touched the gods and they gave the dragon a choice. He could stay and live among the humans, but he would never be as strong. He would be given a human form and the dragon would share the body. The gods made the dragons smaller and took away some of their powers. The powers the gods took from the dragon went into a stone that is called the Dragon Ruby. This stone is believed to be buried deep inside a mountain, hidden from the world."

The room was silent and Violca and her sisters listened intently. When Chase paused, Violca frowned. "I don't understand what any of this has to do with us."

Chase smiled. "When the gods buried the Dragon Ruby, we were given the warning that we could live among humans as long as we never tried to find it. Over a hundred years ago our king's younger brother, Dmitri, decided it was time for all supernaturals to come out. To rule the world, so to speak. In his quest, he found a prophecy that stated there would be a time when the earth would try to balance itself and for the first time five Earth Witches from the original line would be born and save him, giving him what he desired most." He looked between her and her sisters. "You and your sisters are the last of her line."

Violca sat back in the chair, her eyes going to her sisters. There was a part of her that wanted to tell Chase to leave. How could he make up such a huge story? It was the craziest pickup line ever.

But deep down, Violca knew he was telling the truth. She had seen him change into a dragon, the dreams of her mother, the book, and the message written on the inside. The parts of the book she'd flipped through and read stuck with her and made what he said seem very possible. Reaching up, she rubbed the side of her neck where her skin itched, and she frowned when she felt the marks still there from where Chase had bitten her last night. When she moved her hand, she saw Chase rubbing his neck as well, his eyes meeting hers.

"You're all shape-shifting dragons?" Kati asked, looking at Scott then lowering her eyes when he looked at her.

Scott paused for a moment before finally replying, "No, my brother and I are were-panthers. We shift into black panthers."

"So, you're trying to tell us that some shape-shifting dragons are after Violca and her sisters in order to become stronger, and you're just here to... protect them out of the goodness of your hearts?" Brandon asked, not even trying to keep the skepticism from his voice.

"When the gods made the Dragon Ruby, we had a warning that if we went looking for it or if we uncovered it, we would be made to pay. Since Dmitri's been looking for it, many of our kind have gotten sick and are dying."

Violca chewed on her bottom lip before finally asking, "So Scott got a job in my office, and you and I met so you could make sure we were these sisters."

Chase looked across the room at her. The room was silent as if everyone was holding their breath as they waited for his answer. Violca almost wished she could take it back, but found she needed to know. "Part of my job was to meet you and your sisters."

Violca nodded, looking down at her partially eaten breakfast. Her stomach cramped at the idea of eating anymore and she closed the box. The room was quiet and she felt all eyes on her as she looked around. "So, what're we going to do now, about the people who're trying to capture us?"

Scott answered, "Our king, Viktor, wants us to take you to our house and he'll join us there in a few days and then we can discuss options."

"What about school? Violca only pulled us out for the trip and we're only excused for a few more days," Eva asked, looking back and forth between Violca and the guys.

"Don't worry about that," Brandon answered calmly. "V, you need to call your work and I'll call mine, come up with some kind of family emergency." Violca nodded at him. "Look, it shouldn't take long to get ready to go. Meet us outside in thirty minutes. Then we'll follow you."

The guys nodded and Violca could feel Chase come up behind her. He lightly touched her lower back, and Violca fought the urge to lean back into his touch.

"Chase, you don't have to be nice to me anymore. You already got what you wanted," she whispered before he moved away from her and she heard the door click.

CHAPTER 45

Chase let Scott drive the entire way back to their place. He wondered how long until they could expect the next attack. Sighing, he put his head back, thinking about the look on Violca's face when he confessed he met her because he needed to verify who she was.

He fought the urge to tell her that he had slept with her because he wanted to. Chase didn't think that confessing to her that he was drawn to her before he even met her was appropriate. But the first chance he had to get her alone, he would explain it to her. If he could get her alone.

Looking in the side mirror, he saw Violca in the van behind them. She was looking out the window, her lips moving and he wondered if she was singing to the radio or talking. He reached up to his neck, rubbing it, still feeling her teeth marks, and he saw her doing the same. He wondered if she could still feel his bite too and then wondered, with his healing ability, why it hadn't healed yet.

They stopped a few times along the way to get gas and food. During lunch, everyone was mostly quiet except for Angyalka and Sari, who were very excited to spend the night at a boy's house. By the time they pulled up to Scott and Eryk's, the sun had started to go down.

Scott and Eryk led everyone in and Chase stayed behind. When Violca walked up the stairs, he grabbed her by the hand. Startled, she looked up and he saw doubt cross her face before she masked it. "Take a walk with me." When she paused, he squeezed her hand, trying to be reassuring. "Please, the guys will take care of the girls."

His heart almost stopped as she paused before she nodded and let him lead her around the house. Chase wanted to go far enough away, so no matter what was said, Scott and Eryk wouldn't be able to hear, but close enough that if anything happened, they could get back fast.

When they reached the tree line behind the house, he stopped. Chase turned to look at her and waited for her to look up at him. Chase reached up to tuck a stray hair behind her ear, and he fought the urge to kiss her, when he noticed her biting her lip nervously. Before he could say anything, Violca interrupted him. "Was it all an act?"

Chase shook his head, taking a deep breath, running his fingers through his hair. "Violca, I won't lie and say I didn't orchestrate meeting you." The look on her face showed him how much his words hurt before she looked down. His hand came up and he made her look up. "I've been drawn to you since seeing your picture. I volunteered to come out here because I couldn't stand the idea that someone else would. I needed to meet you, to be near you and everything that has happened since meeting you has been about my desire to be near you."

Chase couldn't help but smile as he thought about how content he had been since meeting her, and his hands came up to cup her cheek, his thumb brushing across her cheek. "I promise, nothing I've done since meeting you was what I was sent here to do."

~

VIOLCA FOUGHT the urge to lean into his touch. Her eyes closed as she thought about what he'd said. The whole drive, she couldn't help thinking about everything that had happened. Not only did she find out that there are witches, but that she was, in fact, one of them. Violca was also trying to wrap her mind around the fact that dragons, animal shifters and other things that go bump in the night were real.

Opening her eyes, she saw Chase was watching her. "Did you put those nails in my…" The look on his face told her he did. "You should have told me the truth before we…" Taking a deep breath, she shuddered. "I can't focus on that now, I need to make sure my sisters are safe first and figure out what's going on." She pulled away from him, needing to create a little space.

The look that crossed Chase's face said he noticed her reaction. "I get it. It's a lot to take in at once." He frowned. "Can I ask you why you decided to suddenly go up to your mom's cabin?"

Violca bit her lip, thinking of what exactly to tell him. After everything that had happened, could she really trust him? Realizing at this point, she had no choice, she decided she must. "I've been having dreams of my mother. The cabin was one of those places where I could feel close to her."

Chase nodded in understanding. "Can I ask what you dug up in the yard?"

Violca frowned, angry that he had been spying on her. After everything that came out, she should have realized it. "It was a book of my mom's. I…" she paused, chewing on her lip. "I didn't know anything about any of this, and suddenly I have a book, declaring us *Earth Witches*, people hunting us, and a group of guys who were sent to spy on us to make sure we're the right ones."

Chase winced at her words before nodding. "I hope you don't see everything that has happened as bad." He brushed his thumb back and forth against her hand, and Violca shivered in response.

Needing to think about everything that had happened, she turned to look at the house, "We should head back. I want to check on the girls." She felt Chase walking beside her. "I need to go to the house and get some clean clothes for us. Brandon made us pack in a hurry, and I'm afraid I left pretty much all of our clothes."

"I don't think that's a good idea. They'll probably be watching." Chase paused for a moment. "It would probably be best if Scott and I go out to a store, we can buy what you need for a few days, until Viktor is able to get out here."

Stopping, Violca waited for him to stop and look at her. "No, my sisters have gone through a lot and right now, they aren't even allowed to go home. I've agreed to stay here for a few days, but they need some normalcy. You can go with us if you'd like, or I can go by myself."

Chase sighed loudly, running his fingers through his hair before finally agreeing. "Fine, give me and Scott a chance to make sure it's okay, and tomorrow night we'll take you, and if needed, one of your sisters can come with us." He held up one finger. "Only one to help you figure out what you need, and if there's a hint of danger, we leave, understand?"

Knowing he was not at all happy about the situation, she simply whispered, "Thank you." Turning, she continued to walk back to the house, her step a little lighter. She knew it shouldn't, but winning that little fight made her feel better. When she entered the house, she smelled food cooking in the kitchen. Her stomach growled and she heard Chase chuckle.

Brandon stepped out from the kitchen, his eyes instantly looking over Violca. She appreciated that he was fighting his protective urge so he could get along with everyone and keep them safe. "You okay?"

"Just hungry and ready for a long, hot shower."

Brandon smiled at her. "Well, I can help with one. I already started dinner."

Brandon went back into the kitchen. Hearing her sisters squealing as they ran from room to room, she walked upstairs to see what they were doing. When she got to the top, she turned to see Chase watching her, still standing where she'd left him. She nodded at him before turning and following the sounds of her sisters.

CHAPTER 46

Kati and Eva shared Scott's room. The guys, having decided that they were going to take turns patrolling the area, would sleep in the living room. The girls all took different rooms. Kati sat in the chair near the window with a small light, finishing up her picture of a panther fighting a man. She'd started the picture last week and was just finishing up the details. The man's body was covered in tattoos. Even his bald head had a tattoo. The tattoo was of a snake wrapped around his chest and around part of his neck, so the snake looked like it was going to come out and bite you from the back of his skull.

Eva lay snoring softly in bed and Kati got up quietly, putting her sketchpad away. Hearing a noise outside, she went to the window and parted the blinds. Seeing a movement in the yard below, she found Scott standing up after removing his pants. Her eyes caressed his naked back, widening when she saw his butt. The moonlight shone on his body and she gasped when he glanced up at her. Her cheeks heated as she dropped the blinds, praying he hadn't seen her. Taking several deep breaths, she parted the blinds again to see a black panther looking up at her window. The panther seemed to bow its head at her before turning and quickly dashing off into the woods behind the house.

Kati watched, unable to look away. The moonlight shining on his black fur looked amazing, and Kati tried to put the image to memory to draw later. She wished she were closer to take a better look at him in this form. For the last year, several of her drawings had been of a panther. Not that anyone had seen those drawings. For some reason, they always felt too personal to share with anyone.

When Kati was no longer able to see him, she slowly made her way to the bed. Curling up on her side, she held the pillow tightly. Breathing in Scott's scent, she smiled to herself. Realizing she was developing a crush on him, she bit her lip and held her pillow more tightly as she drifted into a deep sleep.

CHASE AND SCOTT spent the better part of the next afternoon checking out Violca's house and the neighborhood, looking for anything out of place. A person, a smell, anything that would tell them if the demon and his minions were watching the place, but found nothing. Having decided that the best time to take the girls would be after the sun went down, they went back to the house.

Since Scott would be the one to go with them, Chase suggested Kati go as well. Chase understood Scott's need to be near her.

Telling the others the plan, he suggested everyone rest since it would be a long night. When he proposed Kati go, Brandon spoke up, "Why don't I go instead?"

Chase shook his head. "Kati knows where everything is, so it'll be faster. Plus, that way you're here with Eryk to help protect everyone else."

Nodding at his words, Chase turned to look at Eva. "If you

want something in particular, make sure one of them knows, and we'll pick it up."

Eva nodded and Chase saw the look on her face. He could tell she wanted to say something, but held herself back. The rest of the day, the house was surprisingly quiet despite the large number of people and the two younger girls.

Chase stood on the porch, watching as the sun started to set. Feeling a small hand slide into his, he looked down to see Angyalka standing next to him. "Hey sweetie," he said when she looked up at him.

Angyalka's usual sparkling blue eyes appeared almost solemn. "Don't be sad, Chase. Violca will be ok."

Chase frowned at her. "What do you mean?"

Angyalka smiled up at him. "You'll save her, don't worry." With those words she released his hand and ran back into the house.

Shaking his head, he followed, wanting to ask her what she meant. Walking into the living room, he saw Kati coming down the stairs. At the same time, Scott came out of the kitchen. When she almost ran into him, her cheeks turned several shades of red before she quickly turned and headed down the hall. Chase raised an eyebrow at his friend, who just shrugged.

Wondering what that was about, Chase headed upstairs, deciding to take a shower, then make a pot of coffee to help him stay awake for the long night ahead.

Violca spent most of the day bored. She wasn't used to spending the day with nothing to do. With so many adults in the house, she barely had to lift a finger. By the time the sun set, she was more than ready to go. She wanted to go home, to sleep in her own bed, but she knew that being here was the safest place to be.

She saw Scott standing in the doorway of the room she was using and smiled at him. "Time to go?" she asked.

"Yep, would you mind letting Kati know?"

Violca nodded, getting up from the chair by the window. Kati was in the other room with Eva. The door was open and she saw Kati drawing, curled up in the chair while Eva was on the bed reading.

Watching Kati's pencil fly over the paper, she wondered what her sister was working on. Violca could always tell by the expression on Kati's face what she was thinking or feeling. If she was working on something, she found difficult, her brow would scrunch up. If she was not happy with something, she looked mad enough to spit. But her favorite was when Kati closed her eyes, as if picturing something only she could see.

When she cleared her throat, both Eva and Kati looked up. Violca glanced over at Kati. "Hey, it's time to go."

She then looked down at Eva, smiling and kissing her on the forehead. "I love you brat. Stay safe."

Eva's blue eyes met hers. "Love you too, come back quickly okay?"

"Yes ma'am." Violca felt better when Eva smiled back at her. Violca might have parental custody of all the girls, but she knew she never would've been able to manage this without the help of her friends and Eva and Kati. Their relationship wasn't traditional, but Violca would not have it any other way.

Heading downstairs with Kati, Violca saw Scott and Chase waiting for them. She felt Kati tighten up next to her. Looking at her sister, she saw her blushing. Looking back at Chase and Scott, she raised an eyebrow. Chase shrugged and Scott just smiled. "Remember in and out, we didn't see anyone earlier, but we don't want to take any chances."

CHAPTER 47

Scott pulled up to the house and stopped Violca before she could open the door. "Wait in here while we check the inside of the house, just in case."

Violca handed him the keys, then watched Chase and Scott go inside. Once they were inside, Violca looked at Kati. "Is everything okay? Did something happen that I don't know about?"

Kati's blue eyes widened as she shook her head. "No, nothing happened. Why?"

Violca watched her for a minute, thinking she was hiding something. "Are you sure?"

"Why? Why do you ask?"

Kati bit her lower lip and Violca sighed before finally replying, "Nothing, you just seem a little nervous."

Before Kati could reply, they saw Scott in the doorway, waving them in. "If you need to talk about anything, Kati, please know I'm here for you."

Kati nodded and they headed into the house. Kati was going to pack up what she and Eva needed, both clothes and a few things to keep them busy, while Violca packed up what she and the two younger girls needed. When they got to the front door,

Scott smiled. "All clear, ladies. Chase is in the backyard, and I'm going to keep an eye out here. Get whatever you need for a few days, but try not to take too long."

Both girls nodded before walking down the hall to their separate rooms. Searching through her closet, Violca found a small bag. She first headed to the bathroom to get a toothbrush and hairbrush and other toiletries. She grabbed a few of the books by her nightstand before heading back into her closet to find some clothes.

Stepping out of the closet with a few shirts on her arm, she felt the air change around her. Violca looked up to see a man standing in front of her. He stood over six feet tall with a shaved head and shoulders that didn't look like they would fit through her doorway. Before she could scream, he was suddenly in front of her, chanting some words that she couldn't make out. Her world was suddenly black as she felt her legs go out from under her.

CHASE STOOD IN THE BACKYARD, walking around, listening to the sounds of the night. He looked at his watch. It had been a little over ten minutes. Looking back at the house, he wondered how he was going to be able get Violca to understand that, yes, he met her because of his job, but his feelings for her were only about her and had nothing to do with the mission.

Chase glanced at his watch again, knowing that every minute they stayed there was dangerous. Inhaling, Chase suddenly smelled traces of magic tainted by sulfur. He heard Scott yell from the front and he ran to the sliding glass door. Entering, he saw Scott in the front door and they both ran down the hall, Scott following Kati's smell to her room, Chase running to Violca's.

When he got there, Chase saw a pile of clothes on the floor by the dresser, and the smell of sulfur and magic overwhelmingly assaulted his senses from the corner of the room. Walking toward it, he inhaled deeply the scent centered in one area. "Fuck, a portal," he growled.

He heard a loud growl coming from Kati's room before something loud crashed against the wall. Walking into the hall, he saw Scott coming out of the other room. "Demon portal," Chase announced.

"Fuck," Scott said between gritted teeth, and Chase could see his friend's fist at his side.

Knowing Scott was as upset as he was, he nodded. "Grab what Kati packed, I'll get what Violca started to pack and a few things for Sari and Angyalka. They still need clothes, and then we need to figure out where he took them."

They quickly threw a few things in the bag. Chase had Scott sit in the passenger seat, afraid that his friend wouldn't be able to drive home safely. His hands were holding the wheel so tightly, his knuckles turned white as his thoughts turned to figuring out how to find the demon, Micah. Micah had a few different aliases, making it hard to track him. When they pulled up to the house, he saw Angyalka on the porch.

Getting out of the SUV, he walked over to her, letting her jump into his arms. "What are you doing awake, little one?"

Yawning, she put her head on Chase's shoulders as she snuggled closer to him. "I couldn't sleep. I forgot to tell you that Brandon can help you."

Chase frowned, looking down at her. "What do you mean Brandon can help us, Angel?"

Angyalka pulled back. "To help save my sisters, silly."

Brandon heard those last words as he walked down the stairs. "What do you mean save her sisters, where're Violca and Kati?"

Chase looked up, his eyes meeting Brandon's. He could see the fierce look on Violca's friend's face and winced, knowing Brandon would blame him. Not that he shouldn't. Chase blamed himself. He should have stayed in the room with Violca. He should have realized that the demon would have done something like that. "The house was empty when we got there. I didn't realize that the demon, Micah, was strong enough to make portals, let alone ones that he could pull others through."

Chase watched Brandon's reaction as his hands turned into fists at his sides. Putting Angyalka down, he kissed the top of her head. "Hey Angel, why don't you go back to bed while Brandon and I talk?"

Nodding, she started to go upstairs. When she got about halfway up, she stopped and ran down, running into Scott's leg and looking up at him. "Kati will be okay, I promise," she whispered, before she ran to Brandon, hugging him tightly.

When she released him, Brandon looked down at her with a small smile on his lips. "Go back to bed, little troublemaker." She nodded and headed back up the stairs. Everyone was quiet until they heard the door to her bedroom close.

"Brandon, I'm sorry. I never should have left her alone in the room." The words were barely louder than a whisper.

Brandon stood, his shoulders rigid, and Chase let down his mental guard enough for Brandon to feel his pain. "Give me the information you have on this demon," Brandon said.

Chase walked into the house and headed to the back room. The room was small and had a tiny desk that barely fit the laptop on it. Bending down, he went through one of the boxes and pulled out a file. "Kassandra, a woman who works with us, was able to find several of his aliases and some information about him, but not much."

Brandon nodded, going through it, looking over the information on the file. "Can I use this computer?"

Chase nodded and Brandon sat down. "This could take a little while. Would you mind making me a pot of coffee?"

Chase raised an eyebrow, and biting back a reply, headed to the kitchen to start a pot of coffee. Knowing that Brandon wouldn't like him watching over his shoulder, he ran his fingers through his hair, sighing in frustration. Walking to the living room, he saw, through the screen door, Scott standing on the porch. Deciding to leave him alone, he paced in the living room, trying to be patient, while he fought the urge to shift into shadow form and look for her.

CHAPTER 48

Violca moaned. Her stomach felt queasy as she blinked open her eyes. Confused, she sat up in the strange bed and saw Kati in another bed, lying on her side. Getting up quickly, she went to her sister, gently shaking her shoulder. "Kati, Kati sweetie, wake up."

Violca sighed in relief when Kati's hand came up to her head. "Kati, are you okay?"

Kati's eyes slowly blinked open and she winced as she tried to sit up. "What happened?" she asked.

"I don't know. The last thing I remember was grabbing some shirts from my closet. All of a sudden, there was a guy there and… everything went black."

Kati nodded, rubbing the back of her neck. "Yeah, there was a guy who just suddenly appeared in my room, too."

Beside the two beds, there was a table with two chairs, a dresser, and French doors. Kati slowly got up, looking around. Everything in the room was high quality and looked very expensive. Red with gold strings ran through everything.

Both girls looked at the French doors and Kati slowly stood up. They walked to the doors together. Violca put her hand on the gold handle, looking at Kati before shrugging, "It's worth a shot."

Opening the door, the girls stepped onto the balcony. The room faced a huge, immaculate yard surrounded by a tall brick wall. Walking to the edge of the banister, they looked down to see two very big men below. "Shit," Violca mumbled. One turned his head up and looked at her, his eyes red as he smirked, daring her to jump.

Stepping away from the banister, she chewed on her lower lip, her eyes meeting Kati's, as she fought the urge to flip off the guy below. Walking back into the room, Violca closed the doors, not wanting the men below to hear anything they said.

"What do you think the odds are that there are people at that door too?" Kati asked, as she eyed the bedroom door.

Taking a deep breath, then letting it out slowly, Violca squared her shoulders. "Only one way to find out." She walked straight to the door, and grabbing the knob, she tugged. Realizing it was locked, she kicked it hard, wincing as pain shot through her toe.

"Guess it doesn't matter unless you know how to pick a lock," Violca said with a grin. When Kati made a face Violca replied, "Guess I should've encouraged you to hang out more with the wrong crowd at school."

Kati laughed and Violca felt some of the tension ease from the room. Violca sat on the edge of the bed, trying to think of possible escape routes. Kati pulled her from her thoughts, "What do you think they want with us?"

Playing with the edge of the comforter, Violca shrugged. "I'm not sure. I don't know how they expect us to find some dragon stone. I wouldn't even know where to look." Sighing, she ran her fingers through her hair, then her hand slid to the part of her neck where she could still feel Chase's bite. It tingled under her fingertips. "Mom said we're important and that we each have special gifts. I kind of thought she was doing her motherly, 'God made you special, you can do anything' speech she used to give us, but maybe she meant something else."

Kati shrugged, rubbing the back of her head again.

"Does your head still hurt?"

Kati nodded and Violca patted the bed next to her. "Come here, I want to try something."

Kati got up, a skeptical look on her face. "You're not going to zap me like you did that guy, are you?"

"Maybe, now sit down and be quiet while I think," Violca said with a smile, glad her sister's spirit was up enough to tease her.

Motioning for her to turn, Violca ran her fingers over her sister's scalp. In the beginning of the book, the girl's gift was healing people and plants. It reminded her of when she first met AnnaBelle and the plants that she'd touched. Not sure what exactly to do, she concentrated on taking her sister's pain and almost cried out when the back of her head started to pound.

Kati jumped up, looking at her, her eyes wide in surprise. "My head doesn't hurt anymore," she whispered.

The pounding in Violca's head slowly eased and she nodded. "Good."

"We always teased you about having the healing touch, but it was never…" Kati's voice trailed off as she chewed on her lower lip, before she looked back at Violca. "What did you do?"

Violca shrugged. "I don't know. The little bit of the book I've read so far mentioned that the person they considered to be the first, could heal people, and plants would grow at her touch. It reminded me of when AnnaBelle and I first met, and a few plants I touched recently seemed to grow when I touched them, so I thought I would try."

Kati smiled at her before taking her hand, squeezing it. "Well it's pretty cool, thank you."

Violca grinned back, the moment ending quite abruptly when they heard someone outside the door. The nob turned slowly and in walked the man with the shoulder-length, silver hair. He was again surrounded by men who were all muscular. Violca thought they looked like skinheads who were converted into bodyguards. Most of them appeared to have that same scorpion tattoo on their necks, except for one, whose neck looked to be part of a snake.

Hearing a small gasp, Violca looked to Kati to see her eyes focused on the man with the snake tattoo who was standing to the right of the silver-haired man. Violca grabbed her hand and squeezed it tightly, turning her attention to the men in front of them.

The silver-haired man, unlike his bodyguards, was wearing a suit that she would bet was tailored just for him. He carried himself like a man who was used to getting his way. She noticed his eyes were a dark brown and a small smile played on his lips. When he finally spoke, he did so with a hint of a French accent. "Violca, my dear, it's a pleasure to finally meet you and your sister, Kati. My name's Micah. I was hoping to be able to meet you under different circumstances, but alas, some things are beyond our control, yes?"

Violca glared at him, feeling her sister's hand tighten. "Why have you kidnapped us?"

Micah chuckled softly. "Why, to get you away from the dragons and the panther shifters, of course. Your telepathic friend, I think, would have been more reasonable, but I could not be sure, so this seemed the best way to get you alone, chérie."

Violca heard the word telepathic friend, and she stored that bit of information for later. "If you want to talk to me, fine; then let my sister go. I'll talk to you all you like."

Micah's eyes flashed red before returning brown. "I don't think so my dear, Violca. I know as long as I have your sister here, you'll be cooperative. I've watched you with them and know you'll do anything to protect them." His smile became almost predatory as he stepped closer to her and ran his finger down her cheek. Violca fought the urge to shudder as he stared at her mouth, his eyes going red again. "Family's important to you, as it should be. I'll do my best to reunite you with the rest of your sisters and keep you together."

Violca gasped, but before she could say anything Kati got up and slapped his arm away. "Do not touch my sister."

Violca was almost frozen in place, surprised by her sister's sudden protectiveness and bravery, until the man with the snake tattoo smacked Kati so hard she flew across the room. Violca's anger rose and she felt that weird current building. Her hand went up and the energy left, like a bolt of lightning, and shocked him. When he fell, she glimpsed the head of a snake on the back of his skull before she ran to Kati.

"Are you okay?" Violca kneeled at her sister's side, seeing that a bruise had formed on her cheek as she moaned.

The man with the snake tattoo snarled and stepped toward them, but Micah suddenly grabbed him by the shoulder, flinging him back behind him with a growl, "I told you not to touch them." Micah's eyes were red and flashed as he smacked him across the face, causing him to fly out of the room.

Kati opened her eyes. Violca sighed in relief, wishing she knew how she'd managed to get that energy in her hand and how to control it. Would it be enough to get them out of this house? As if reading her mind, Micah, in a very calm, quiet voice said, "There're men everywhere, my dear, Violca, and your power is new and unpredictable. You cannot escape." He looked behind her to her sister. "I'm sorry, my dear, Kati. He never should've touched you. I'll arrange some food for you both. You have my assurance, no one else will harm you while you're here." He looked toward Violca. "But they will not let you leave, so if you try to escape, I'll separate you and your sister. I would rather not hurt her, but don't tempt me."

CHAPTER 49

Chase woke up in the living room. Rubbing the back of his neck, he was surprised by how much light was coming in. Wondering how long he had slept, he glanced at the clock, realizing it was just past ten in the morning. Smelling bacon, he heard Eva's voice in the kitchen as she talked to her little sisters and Eryk.

Stretching, he got up and headed to the kitchen. Chase tried to go to sleep in his own bed, but found the scent of Violca that clung to the pillows and sheets, was too much to bear. The more he smelled her, the more his dragon wanted to come out. His dragon missed her as much as he did. It should bother him how much both he and his dragon felt the pull of her, but instead, he found it settling. The restlessness he was feeling had eased since being with her.

Walking into the kitchen, he went to the coffee pot, making himself a cup. Chase leaned against the counter as he took his first sip, sighing in relief that this was a fresh pot and not the same one he'd made last night. "Where's Scott?" Chase asked Eryk.

"He turned into a kitty and went for a run. I asked him if I could ride on his back, but he said maybe next time," Angyalka answered, smiling at the thought of riding a big cat.

He winked at her and Eva handed him a plate with bacon and eggs. "Thank you."

Chase listened to the girls chat about what they were going to do that day. Hearing someone in the hall, he inhaled softly and knew it was Brandon. When Brandon stepped into the kitchen, he walked to the coffee pot and Chase stepped aside. Eva made him a plate, handing it to him. "Eat."

Brandon smiled at the command. "Yes, ma'am." He took a sip of his coffee before setting the cup down to take a bite of his food.

The room got quiet and Eryk ruffled Sari's hair. "Hey girls, why don't we go outside and play?" Both girls yelled in agreement. Eva slowly followed them out, stopping in the doorway. "I'm going to go outside while you two talk, but I expect you to tell me how the hell you plan on saving my sisters." The look Eva gave them let them all know she expected a full report when she got back.

The sliding door opened and they heard Scott tell the kids to stay in sight of the house. They waited until Scott joined them in the kitchen before Brandon started, "Your friend did a great job finding aliases that the demon used. I was able to track a company that's local after some digging. The company owns several houses."

Scott whistled, looking at Brandon. "Kassandra's a whiz at finding information, but she couldn't find any of this. How did you?"

Brandon shrugged and Chase could smell the tiniest hint of deception in the air before he continued, "Out of the houses, only two would offer him the privacy to keep Violca and Kati without having to worry about other people seeing or hearing them. One of them has a high-end security system. That's the one they'll most likely be at."

Chase nodded. "We can drive by both just in case, but I'm pretty sure you're right. Then we can make a plan to get the girls back."

Brandon took a few more bites of his breakfast and another sip of his coffee. "I need to take a quick shower, then whenever you guys are ready, we can head out."

Brandon cleaned his plate and placed it in the sink before heading upstairs to take a shower. Once they heard the shower running, Chase looked at Scott. "I wonder what he was hiding a minute ago."

Scott nodded, gripping the edge of the counter. "If I didn't know how much he cared about Violca and her sisters, I'd make him cough it up. But right now, all I care about, is if he's right and how soon we can go."

Chase shrugged. "You're right, but after…" He looked at Scott and they both nodded. Violca and Kati were their priority, but later, he would find out what Brandon was hiding, besides being telepathic.

Chase heard Eva come down the stairs a few minutes later. Walking into the living room, she asked, "So, what's going on? Have you found my sisters?"

Chase felt a small smile tug at his lips. This girl, who was several inches shorter than he, and had seen him in his dragon form, walked into the room and demanded answers from him with no fear. He was glad she was that comfortable with him and thought one day she was going to make some lucky guy one hell of a partner, if he was able to get past her sisters. "Brandon thinks he found a house where they might be keeping them. We're going to drive by it and do some surveillance to see what we can find."

Eva put her hands on her hips, "I want to go," she declared, looking at him like she was daring him to argue.

Chase ran his fingers through his hair. "Eva, if it wasn't for Sari and Angyalka, I'd take you, I promise. But right now, I think it's important that you and Eryk stay here and watch them while we go and check out the house." He could see Eva's mouth open and put his hand up, stopping her. "Your sister would kick both mine and your ass, if I let you go and something happened to the younger two. He wants all of you."

Eva glared at him and the look on her face told him she was thinking about his words. Her shoulders sagged and she nodded. "Fine." Looking down at her, he could see the worry in her eyes. "Please, save my sisters, Chase."

He nodded, trying to smile at her reassuringly. Turning, Eva went to leave. Pausing in the doorway she looked over her shoulder at him, and said, "Violca hasn't let a guy close to her since her boyfriend dumped her when she took custody of all of us. When you find her and save her, you better let her know she means more to you than a job."

Chase smiled, realizing Eva had just given him her blessing. His urge to get to Violca was stronger than ever. "Yes ma'am." When she took a step out of the room, he stopped her. "Eva, you're going to give some guy one hell of a hard time someday. I hope to be there when you do."

Eva smirked. "Don't mess things up with my sister, and I'm sure you will be."

Chase laughed, unable to help himself as she walked away. Shaking his head, he went to the closet, grabbed a few items and headed down the hall. With the younger girls around, they were being extra careful with the weapons. They had given each of the girls a huge talk about them, but to be safe, they had made sure to keep them locked away.

When he walked into the room, Scott handed him two guns. The bullets were laced with pure silver and holy water. These bullets wouldn't kill a strong demon, but would incapacitate most supernaturals. Based on the group of people that attacked the cabin, not all of Micah's men were demons, so lacing the bullets with both, they should be able to wound almost anything they came across.

Eva and Eryk joined them in the dining room. "We're going to check out the house. If everything goes well, we'll be back late tonight with Violca and Kati. If anything happens, Eryk, you're to make sure the girls get out safe. If you can't get to the SUV, take the trail through the woods. At the end of the trail is a garage. The keys are in the car. Call Kassandra and she'll arrange a pickup, do you understand?"

Eryk nodded and Scott patted him on the back. "Both vehicles have untraceable cell phones in the console. Use them and ditch your phones." Scott looked at Eva. "Both of you."

She nodded. "Be safe," Eva said, looking at all of them. "Violca will kick your ass if you get hurt saving them."

Brandon chuckled, shaking his head, whispering, "She would, too."

Eva and Eryk stood on the porch, watching them as they drove away, both looking very serious. Brandon had printed out copies of the floor plan and brought one of the wireless laptops. He was hoping to be able to break into the security system when they got close enough, at least long enough to help them get into the house.

CHAPTER 50

Kati sat on the bed while Violca paced, trying to think about how she was going to get them out of there. She wanted to heal her sister, but Kati pointed out that Violca might need her power and they weren't sure whether she could use it later if she used it now.

When the door opened again, Violca gasped at the sight of her friend AnnaBelle striding in with three of Micah's men. Anna-Belle smiled at them. "Come on you two, let's go downstairs and talk before they serve lunch."

With that, she turned but stopped and looked over her shoulder. "Come on, I'm hungry."

Violca walked over to Kati and helped her up from the bed. Seeing her wince, Violca held her hand. The men surrounded them as they walked downstairs. "AnnaBelle, what're you doing here?" Violca asked, between clenched teeth.

AnnaBelle ignored her, leading them down a hall to a very large, formal dining room. When the girls walked in, the guys remained outside, closing the door. Violca walked up to her friend, grabbing her arm. "AnnaBelle, what the hell?"

AnnaBelle turned and looked at her, pulling her arm back before sitting in one of the high back chairs at the table. "V, do you remember when you met my grandmother? How she used to fawn all over you, but refused to meet your mother?"

"What does your grandmother have to do with anything?"

"She knew exactly what you were when she met you. Every time you did anything, she would compare us. She was so angry that you, as a child, had more power than she ever would."

"Your grandmother was an Earth Witch?" Violca asked, her voice rising. "Why didn't you ever tell me, Belle?"

"I…I didn't tell you because I didn't want you to have the same low opinion of me my grandmother did. But all you have to do is help them find what they need, and you can help unleash my power too. Wouldn't that be amazing, V?"

Violca shook her head, unable to believe her friend would have ever agreed to let her be kidnapped. "Belle, there's no guarantee if we help that anything will change with you or with your grandmother. We don't know what will happen, if anything. I can't believe you would be okay with them hunting us down, almost kidnapping Kati and me on the street, destroying my family's cabin and for what? Just to get to us? What if someone was hurt? How could you, Belle?"

AnnaBelle frowned, standing up. "They were never going to hurt her, V. They need you, Kati was never in any danger. They just needed to get you away from those guys so they could talk to you and explain." AnnaBelle took her free hand, looking at her pleadingly. "Don't you understand? We can finally be sisters, for real. My family will finally quit comparing me to you and both our lives will be complete."

Violca yanked her hand back from AnnaBelle, shaking her head. "I have always loved you like a sister, and I never would have put you in danger. I'm sorry about your family, but you can't destroy mine to make yours better."

Before AnnaBelle could respond, a door opened and several

different servants came in with trays of food. Despite herself, Violca heard her stomach grumble in response. She had been so worried, she hadn't realized exactly how long it had been since they had last eaten.

AnnaBelle stepped back, her face hardening. When she turned, Violca noticed something on her neck. It almost looked like a small tattoo, like the ones she had seen on some of the men who attacked them. Letting go of Kati's hand, she went to pick up her friend's hair, only to have AnnaBelle pull back.

"Don't touch me, I thought you would understand. You were always so selfish. You never even noticed how cruel my family was. Shit, even Brandon stayed at your house more than his own to escape his family and all you would do was complain because no one liked you in high school, or how your boyfriend dumped you because he couldn't handle you suddenly taking care of your sisters. At least you weren't alone. I was always there for you, and you won't do this for me."

Violca felt a stab of guilt for not realizing how unhappy her friend was, but she knew in her heart that this was wrong. Her eyes filled with unshed tears as she shook her head. "I can't Belle, I'm sorry, but I can't."

AnnaBelle squared her shoulders, giving her one last look before heading toward the door. Violca watched as she left. AnnaBelle paused, her hand on the doorknob. "Violca, in the end, you and your sisters will help them with what they want. Don't do anything you'll regret." With that, AnnaBelle opened the door and left them in the room by themselves.

Violca sat down, feeling numb, still not believing the part her best friend had played in all this. Kati came up beside her and put her hand on her sister's shoulder. Violca looked up and saw the hurt in Kati's eyes, realizing that not only had her friend betrayed her, but Kati and her sisters as well.

"It'll be okay, Kati." Smiling at her, trying to be reassuring, she heard Kati's stomach grumble. "Come on, we need to eat something and keep our strength up."

Kati sat next to her and they ate in silence, both lost in their own thoughts. Sighing, Violca looked out the window, only to see another guard standing in front of it. She went back to her food, more determined than ever to get out.

The gates opened and Brandon frowned as a car drove past them. Chase glanced up to see what had Brandon's attention and thought he recognized the driver. "Who's that?"

Brandon shook his head. "That looked like AnnaBelle, but it couldn't be. What would she be doing here?"

Letting the matter drop, Chase went back to looking at the schematics of the property. From where the cameras were placed, there were only two blind spots. One in the back of the property, and one closer to the side of the house. "I'll plant the explosives here, toward the back of the house. It looks like we might be able to draw most of the guards to the back, which might give you both enough time to get over the wall, here, to save the girls."

Brandon looked it over. "You said there are about six guards in the back and four in the front, not counting the two at the gate. We have no way of knowing how many there are inside the house."

Frowning, Chase nodded. "I know, let's hope that a big enough explosion will get their attention." Chase inserted the earbud into his ear. "I don't know how long we'll have until the cops show up, so I can't change, but we have enough guns that I should be able to create quite a distraction."

Scott shook his head. "I wish we knew exactly what room the girls are in and how many guards they have inside."

Chase looked at Scott, making eye contact. "I trust you'll be able to easily find Kati. Let's cross our fingers that they have them together." His tone got serious. "No matter what happens, I'm trusting you both to get them out of here."

Brandon frowned. "What do you mean, he can easily find Kati?"

Chase glanced at him. "Her scent is easier for him to detect."

Brandon looked at him for a moment, an uncomfortable silence lingered before he shrugged, deciding that their first obligation was to rescue the girls.

Scott and Brandon put in their earbuds and double-checked to make sure all their guns were loaded, and that they had plenty of extra ammo, just in case. Gathering the backpack that Scott prepared for him, and with the detonator in his pocket, Chase pulled the hoodie over his head to hide his face when he walked by the cameras.

"Give me a few minutes to set up before you guys get out, just in case they're watching for you. I'm going to go around on the other side of the street and cross when I get near the blind spot."

When he opened the side of the van to step out, Brandon grabbed his arm stopping him. "Be careful. Violca seems to like having you around."

He chuckled at that. "Just make sure you save her. We'll worry about her being mad at us later."

Chase nodded to Scott, knowing that he could trust his friend to save Violca and Kati. Besides his need to protect his mate, Scott would never leave a woman in need. Taking a deep breath, he said a silent prayer that this would all work out and that he would be able to get out of the situation with Violca. The moment he saw her picture, he had wanted her, but since the first time he had met her, he had needed to touch her and once he did touch her, he never wanted to stop. His need for her grew with each passing moment, and he would do anything to keep her safe.

VIOLCA AND KATI sat in their chairs after they finished eating. Kati grudgingly admitted that the food was amazing. The servants came and took their plates as soon as they'd finished.

When the door opened, they both stood up, Kati standing close to Violca, grabbed her hand. Kati was scared, especially when she saw the man with the snake tattoo. He looked so much like her drawing. Since finding out that Eryk and Scott both turned into black panthers, she found herself afraid that one of them would fight him. Kati also wanted to know what it meant that she had drawn him, having no memory of seeing him before.

Micah smiled at Violca, his eyes traveling over her. Kati felt her sister stiffen when he walked toward her. "I hope your meal was acceptable." He reached out and gently touched Violca's cheek, his smile almost predatory. She flinched, pulling back as he pushed her dark hair behind her shoulder. His eyes narrowed on her neck and flashed red as his voice hardened. "You shared your blood with the dragon." His voice barely a growl, Kati took a step back as he stepped closer to Violca, who stood her ground. Kati admired her sister's defiance as she looked up at him. "You let the dragon mark you as his, did you finish the mating process?"

Micah bent down, inhaling the scent of Violca's neck as if searching for the answer. When he pulled back, he had a small smile on his face as if finding the answer, he needed. Violca pushed Kati behind her. "What I have and have not done with Chase is none of your business."

Standing at his full height as he looked down at her, "You're wrong, Violca. You're very much my business."

Kati could feel her sister's anger and she squeezed her hand, afraid that if Violca reacted, he might lash out and hurt her. "Violca," Kati whispered and suddenly there was a loud boom from outside.

"Take the girl back upstairs and guard her," Micah said as he grabbed Violca by the upper arm and tried to pull her. "Kill anyone you see."

When he pulled Violca, Kati felt her sister's hold tighten. "No, I won't leave my sister."

Micah pulled harder on Violca, dragging her with him. Kati kept a grip on her hand but the man with the snake tattoo grabbed her by the waist, pulling her so hard she was forced to finally let go. Kati screamed and fought the man whose arm was around her like a band of iron.

Kati watched Violca continue to fight Micah, he stopped and his hand smacked her across the face so hard, Kati could see an imprint of his hand on her sister's cheek. When they got to the base of the stairs, the man carrying her headed back up to the room, while Micah pulled Violca down another hall. Kati scratched the man's face as he carried her. She heard him growl loudly in her ear, "Stay still, bitch. There're many ways for me to hurt you without killing you."

CHAPTER 52

Violca tried to fight Micah as he dragged her down the hall. "Why can't I go with Kati?" Micah kept pulling on her arm, forcing her to go with him through a door that led to the basement.

"It's safer to keep you and your sister apart. You my chérie, are going to stay close to me. I'll not lose you. You're promised to me, and I'll not let you go."

Violca almost tripped at his words, pulling harder to get free. Micah turned his flashing red eyes down at her. Violca forced herself to stand her ground. "I'm not yours, and we'll never help you with anything."

Micah's canines lengthened, showing over his lower lip. "You will." His fingers traced along where Chase bit her. "I'll take care of the dragon that tried to mark you as his, and then I'll take you and make you mine. And unlike your dragon, I'll finish the mating."

Violca tried to focus on what he was saying and how he would take care of the dragon. She felt her heart clench, knowing that whatever was going on involved Chase. Struggling more, she tried to pull herself free.

CHASE RUSHED toward the hole in the wall, shooting at the guards before he ducked behind a tree for cover. From the number of guards coming at him, he wondered how many men were in the house. Peeking around the tree, he shot the guard closest to him, then without really aiming, he shot across the yard, hitting another in the leg.

Glancing around the tree again, he saw he was going to be surrounded quickly. Taking a deep breath, he hoped that Brandon and Scott had made it over the wall and were in the house. Chase's goal was to cause a big enough distraction to give them a head start. When he saw a statue, he sprinted out from behind the tree trying to aim and fire. As he ran, he only saw two of the guards go down. Most of his shots missing, he felt the sting of a bullet hit him in the thigh, causing him to fall right when he reached the statue.

Wincing in pain, he looked down noticing that the bullet went straight through and hadn't hit any major arteries. Wishing he could shift into his dragon so he could heal, he heard the distinct sound of a gun cocking next to his head. "Well, if it isn't the dragon shifter. My boss has been waiting for you."

Chase slowly stood up, wincing slightly when he put his weight on his injured leg. Looking around he smirked. "Well, who am I to tell your boss no."

There were five men surrounding him and several more standing back, their weapons drawn. The two closest to him grabbed his arms. The guy in front of him smiled, showing his long canines before hitting him with the butt of the gun hard on his temple, causing him to see black as his body went limp.

THE GUY with Kati shoved her back into the room upstairs and she pounded on the door. "Where did he take my sister?" she sobbed, pounding harder. Screaming in frustration, she hit it one more time before turning her back on the door.

Hearing a noise from the balcony, Kati's eyes glanced up, scared. When the door opened, she saw Brandon. Running to him, her arms went around his neck, holding him tightly. Kati jumped when she heard a loud growl and felt someone pulling her from him. She tried to pull her arm from his grasp and was surprised when she saw Scott was the one who'd grabbed her. She flinched when his hand came up to her face. "Are you okay, Kati? Who hurt you?"

Kati realized that it was not anger on his face but concern. "I'm okay, but they took V. We have to find her."

Kati heard her voice quivering. She looked at Brandon, who was glaring at Scott before turning to her. "We'll get her Kati. I promise."

The door opened and the guard with the snake tattoo appeared in the doorway. He looked at Kati, smiling wickedly. "Well aren't you full of surprises." He smirked, "I hope you don't mind if I and my friends join the party." The snake guy stepped back and three of the other guards came in.

Scott pushed Kati behind him and growled low in his throat. Brandon and Scott stood in front of her and Kati felt frustrated with herself. She was tired of cowering.

Scott and Brandon lunged at the first three guys. Three more rushed in the room, joining the fray.

Kati looked up to the door and saw the man with the snake tattoo smiling at her. He circled around the group, his eyes focused on Kati. Keeping her back to the wall, she circled around until her legs hit the bed. The loud crash caught her attention and she looked up to see Brandon lying on his back, the table in the room broken and two of the guards standing over him.

Hearing a noise close to her, Kati glanced over as the snake man grabbed ahold of her ankle. Trying to kick and scramble, she screamed in frustration, but he easily pulled her up between the two beds. Grabbing her by the arm, he dragged her over the other bed. At the door she heard a loud growl. Looking over her shoulder, Kati saw Scott and the rage on his face was undeniable. Scott's hand sliced the throat of the guy he was fighting, and Kati noticed that at the end of his hands, claws had appeared.

"Interesting." At the deep sound of tattoo man in her ear, she turned and saw him smiling at Scott before yanking her out of the room. The fierce sound of an animal growl followed them and the tattoo man chuckled. "Well little witch, who would've thought you have your own personal cat body guard."

CHAPTER 53

Micah took Violca to a room at the end of the hall and pushed her into a chair. Picking up his phone with one hand, his other stayed on her shoulder. She couldn't hear what the voice was saying, only his reply, "Good, bring him down to me."

Micah looked down at her, his eyes red, his teeth poking out from his lips as they curved in a wicked smile. "Your lover will be here any minute." His smile broadened. "Looks like we'll be able to take care of your little dragon shifter before we leave."

He gestured toward her and she gasped when ropes suddenly tied her at her wrists to the arms of the chair. She felt ropes sliding around her legs. "One day soon, you'll be mine, and I'll be able to trust you but today…" His voice trailed off and he winked. "I look forward to winning you over, mon amour." He traced his finger down her jaw and she shook her head, pulling away. His eyes narrowed and his arm came up as if to smack her before he collected himself. "You will learn to crave my touch."

Violca gave him a look that let him know she would never be that girl. When he stepped away, she looked around. If she had to guess, she would say this used to be some old-fashioned torture room. There were chains hanging almost everywhere, along with a wall of different kinds of whips, some weird looking sticks, and some different types of knives.

In the center of the room, hanging from the ceiling, were two chains with wrist restraints. A small shudder ran up her spine. Micah looked at her, his canines showing again. "I can teach you and your sisters how to use your magic, Violca. Once you learn how to use your powers, there will be no stopping what we can do together."

Before she could reply, the door opened behind her. Violca tried to look over her shoulder. After the first guy walked through, she was able to see two other guys dragging Chase between them. Gasping when she saw him, she whispered, "Chase," but he didn't even move.

They dragged him to the middle of the room and put his wrists in the restraints. He groaned as he hung awkwardly from his arms. Hearing his groans, Violca found herself blinking back tears.

Chase moaned, his head coming up slowly. His eyes looked her over as if reassuring himself she was okay. Micah growled at him when he saw him checking out Violca and punched him in the stomach, causing the chains to rattle as he swung to the side. Chase grunted in response. Chase's eye color turned more of a golden color and Micah smiled at him. "You can't shift as long you are in my home, dragon shifter."

Chase growled, pulling slightly on the chains. From the angle his arms were at, Violca knew he must be in pain. Micah looked at the guards. "Go find out what's going on upstairs. Make sure the other girl is well guarded and anyone who's trying to take her is killed."

~

SCOTT GROWLED LOUDLY when he saw the man with the snake

tattoo pull Kati out of the room. His claws came out and he sliced the throat of the man he was currently fighting. Picking up the other guy in the room, he threw him against the dresser. The guy groaned as he hit the wall and passed out. The third guy charged at him, and Scott punched him quickly, pushing through him as he ran toward the door.

Scott saw Kati being pulled down the stairs. Growling, he caught up with them at the bottom of the stairs. The guy pulled out a knife and held it up to Kati's throat. "Care to try me, cat man?"

Tattoo man pushed the knife hard enough against her throat that he broke the skin. Scott could see and smell the blood. His hands clenched into fists at his sides as he took deep breaths to calm himself. His cat was just below the surface, fighting to get out, wanting to protect her. "Let her go, and I promise to kill you swiftly."

Kati whimpered and he growled at the back of his throat. Scott felt something holding him back and wondered what was keeping him from shifting completely.

Scott heard Brandon behind him. "Kati, down!" Brandon shouted a split second before he raised his hand as if he was reaching for the knife. The knife seemed to get yanked out of the tattooed guy's hand and went flying across the room into a wall, as if on its own. His hold on Kati loosened and she dropped to the floor. With Kati out of the way, Scott punched him in the face.

Scott grabbed Kati by the arm and pushed her in Brandon's direction, before the tattoo man lunged at him, knocking him to the ground. The tattoo man punched him in the face and Scott bucked his hips up, forcing the guy off him. "Get her out of here," he growled to Brandon as he and the tattoo man traded blows.

Scott heard Brandon hurry outside as the tattoo man taunted him. "You seem a little old to be lusting after some young girl, don't you think?" He smirked, "You know it's illegal right? Do her sisters know?"

Scott swung and connected with his jaw, a growl escaping him. The man was part demon and stronger than the average human, and he found himself wishing he could shift. The only part of him that changed was his claws, which lengthened as he swiped across the man's stomach. The man grunted, his head going down, and Scott uppercut him, slicing across the demon's jugular. The tattoo man fell at his feet, grabbing his neck. Scott could hear the man's heartbeat slow as he lay there dying.

Breathing heavily, he went down the hall trying to find out where Violca was being kept. Inhaling deeply, he smelled her scent. One of the doors opened and three guys stepped out. They stopped when they saw him. Grabbing his gun, no longer having to worry about Kati being in the crosshairs, he shot the first two guys, killing them instantly. The third guy lunged at him and Scott threw him against the wall before hitting him in the back of the head, knocking him out. The third guy crumbled, and Scott headed down the stairs.

CHAPTER 54

With another punch to Chase's gut, Violca bit her lip, having figured out that when she cried out, Micah seemed to enjoy it more. Micah's voice was growly when he spoke, "Stupid dragon shifter. I can't believe you thought were worthy enough to mate with someone as unique as her. She's way above you, and you'll pay for daring to touch what is mine."

Violca noticed Micah's arm changing. His skin was turning black, almost reptilian, while his fingers turned more into yellow claws. Pulling back, Micah sliced across Chase's stomach, and Violca couldn't help but cry out. Seeing blood, she called out to Micah, "Please, stop. Please, Micah, leave him alone and I'll stay with you."

"Violca, no!" Chase said, before he was interrupted with a punch to his jaw.

Micah pulled back as if to punch him again and Violca whimpered, "Please." Micah paused a second, and Violca found herself praying that he would listen to her. When he turned and finally looked at her, she swallowed hard before straightening as best as she could, determined not to give an edge. Micah's skin almost looked to be crawling, his eyes glowing red, as he walked toward her, his movements predatory.

When he stood in front of her, Micah reached up, his yellow claw-like hand touching her cheek, tracing it until he reached her neck. She could still feel where Chase had bitten her. It pulsed just under her skin. Micah's claw traced the mark and she shuddered.

Micah's hand wrapped around the back of her neck, pulling her up higher as he bent down, claiming her mouth with a rough kiss that felt like he was bruising her lips. She could hear the sounds of the chains rattling and a growl coming from Chase. Looking over Micah's shoulder, she saw Chase's eyes flashing gold as he pulled harder on the chains.

Micah pulled back and a long, forked tongue came out to lick her lips. Turning her head, she kept her lips pressed together as she whimpered. Micah's voice was harsh as he leaned into her. "He will die for touching you, trying to mark you as his. No one touches what is promised to me."

Violca turned and spit in his face, her fingers curling around the edge of the chair. She could feel the hair on her arms stick up as the energy pulsing in her body got stronger. "No one," she said between gritted teeth, "can promise me to someone else."

Micah threw back his head and laughed. "For you, my dear witch, I'll kill him quickly."

The door was kicked open and Violca looked over her shoulder just in time to see Scott shoot Micah in the chest. Picking up Micah, Scott threw him to the far side of the room. He easily cut through the bindings at her wrists and her legs. "Run, V. Go outside, your sister and Brandon are waiting for you."

She snorted, following him as he went over to help Chase. He was not able to cut his bindings like he had Violca's. Violca hurried over to Chase and wrapped her arms around his waist.

Scott growled at her. "I told you to run," he said, before reaching up and using his strength to pull the chains out from the ceiling.

"Too bad, I'm not leaving him." Parts of the ceiling fell on her head as Chase suddenly sagged against her.

Hearing a noise behind them, Violca turned and saw Micah heading toward them. Her whimper caused Scott to turn in time to see Micah swing at him before grabbing Chase from her and flinging him across the room. Grabbing her arm roughly, his face next to hers, she could almost see a beast under his skin. "Mine!" he growled, his face so close to her she could feel his breath on her lips.

"Never yours," Violca said, her hands going to his chest. The power she felt earlier, built up, and shot from her fingertips into his chest, causing him to fall back. She saw Scott getting up as she turned to help Chase. "Come on, get up, we need to get out of here."

Chase moaned, "V, run."

Violca shook her head, blinking back tears. "Not without you."

Violca felt the wind brushing past her and her mother's whisper in her ear, *I bind my life with yours. My power and strength belong to you. I am yours, from now to eternity.* The words repeated in her ears again and Violca looked into his eyes and repeated her mother's words. "I bind my life with yours. My power and strength belong to you. I am yours, now to eternity." Her teeth throbbed. Violca followed her instincts and leaned forward, biting him in the crook of his neck, somehow knowing instinctively it was the same place she had bitten him last time. She could taste the metallic taste of his blood on her mouth and heard him moan.

Chase's deep voice whispered in her ear, repeating her words, "I bind my life with yours. My power and strength belong to you. I am yours, now to eternity." Chase bit her neck and she whimpered when she felt his teeth cut her skin. His tongue came out, licking where he bit and she did the same to him.

Violca could feel both Chase and his dragon. Her eyes widened as she looked at him. Before she could ask him, there was a growl so loud that it shook the room, causing her to jump. Turning, she saw Micah charging at them. Scott tried to stop him, only to be knocked away. He grabbed her by her shirt, pulling her up off her feet. She heard Chase trying to get up, only to have Micah pin him in place with a blast of power that Violca could feel.

"What the fuck did you just do?" he shouted at her. "You are mine, I will break your bond and make you watch as I kill him slowly. You will learn not to defy me!"

Feeling Chase's pain behind her, her breathing picked up and she felt her strength building. She could feel and see her mother with her. Micah's eyes widened as Violca felt herself being picked up off the floor by an unseen force. Violca raised her hand and pointed at Micah, not recognizing her own voice as she began to speak, "I bind you, I bind you back to the hell from which you came, never to return. With the power of the earth, the power of my ancestors, I bind you. Return back to hell, Micah." She heard him scream and smelled smoke before her world went black.

CHAPTER 55

Chase watched, unable to move at first when Violca slowly levitated above the ground. When she spoke, her voice sounded like there were several women's voices coming from her. When Micah screamed, Chase was suddenly able to move again. Whatever hold Micah had on him was gone. Suddenly Violca dropped. Chase quickly reached out for her, catching her before she could hit the ground.

Looking up, Chase saw a flame surrounding Micah before he was gone. A small burn mark on the floor was the only sign of where he had been. Looking down at Violca, he brushed her hair back, worried because she looked so pale. He could feel her pulse within him. Scott moaned, working his way over to them, holding his side.

"What the hell was that?" Scott asked, looking down at her. Chase could see the worry on his friend's face.

"I don't know," Chase whispered, feeling her pulse get stronger. He felt his dragon's worry for her as well.

Scott reached down to take Violca from him and Chase growled. "I'm just going to help you. You're in no shape to carry her."

Chase nodded. He didn't quite understand what had happened between him and Violca, but both he and his dragon could feel her heart beating, as well as her power. While she was banishing Micah, he could not only feel her power, but also felt her using his, and felt her using her ancestral power as well.

Scott carefully scooped Violca into his arms. Chase heard her moan softly and felt her pulse pick up. He used the broken chair next to him to help raise himself. Wrapping his arm around his own waist, he felt his body healing itself. Walking behind Scott, he asked, "Did you find Kati?"

Scott nodded, "Yeah, I sent her with Brandon and told him to keep her safe." Chase raised an eyebrow, surprised by his friend. "I think there's more to Brandon than we guessed."

Before Chase could reply, he heard Violca moan. "She was amazing," Scott whispered, adjusting her in his arms.

Chase smiled, feeling very proud of her. "Yeah, she is." He chuckled, "Don't think she needed us at all."

When they got outside, they saw a few guards and Brandon at the front gate with the van. "Come on, guys, we have about three minutes before the cops get here and I would rather not lose my job because they don't believe me when I say I had to save my witch best friend from a demon."

Chase went to the passenger seat, Scott hopped in via the sliding door, Kati gasped when she saw her sister. "Is she okay?"

Scott got in, carefully laying Violca on the bench seat next to Kati. "We think so."

Kati looked up at Scott, who closed the door behind him. "What do you mean you think so? What happened to her?"

"We're not a hundred percent sure exactly what happened. Let's get you both back to the house," Chase said, wincing slightly as he turned to Kati.

Right before they pulled into the driveway, Violca stirred.

"V! V, wake up, please?"

Chase turned. The cut in his side felt like it was mostly healed.

He watched as she slowly opened her eyes. She smiled when she saw Kati looking down at her.

"You're awake," Kati said.

Violca smiled, and slowly sat up, hugging her sister. "Kati, I was so worried when they took you away."

Violca pulled back and looked over at Chase. "Are you okay?"

Chase nodded. "I'll heal. How about you?"

Violca frowned and he sensed her confusion. "Yeah, I'm fine, thanks." She looked at Brandon, smiling softly at him and he could feel her affection for him. She turned, looking at Scott. "All of you, thank you so much."

The mood was lighter with her awake. Everyone was quiet as they pulled up to the house. Before the van was even in park, Eva, Angyalka and Sari ran out of the house and threw themselves into Violca and Kati's arms. Chase shook his head, a smile on his lips. He couldn't quite make out exactly what they were saying as they all talked to each other at the same time. Normally he didn't like chaos, but the sounds of them happy, and feeling Violca's joy at being reunited with her sisters, gave him a peace he didn't ever remember feeling before.

Eryk came out of the house and hugged Scott. He glanced at Kati and Violca. "You saved them."

Scott shook his head. "We helped, Violca did most of the hard work."

Eva heard him and looked at Violca, her eyes wide. "Really?" When Violca bit her lip and blushed, Eva grinned. "You guys have to tell me everything that happened."

The girls headed upstairs. When they got to the door, Angyalka turned and ran back down the stairs, jumping at Chase, who smiled as he picked her up. "I told you she'd be okay." She smiled, her blue eyes twinkling as she gave him a big kiss on the cheek. "Thank you for going to get her. I knew you could bring her home."

Chase kissed her cheek. "Yes, you did." When he looked up, he saw Violca standing in the doorway looking back at him. His heart skipped a beat when she smiled, winking at him before following the other girls in.

Carrying Angyalka in his arms, Chase and the guys followed them up. Scott paused for a second, shaking his head, muttering, "Who would've thought the sounds of female chatter in the house would be so..."

Chase grinned, "...Soothing."

The guys laughed and Brandon grinned, taking Angyalka from Chase. "The Grey sisters have a way of wiggling into your life and changing it forever."

Angyalka smiled at him, a secret smile that seemed way older than her ten years and all the guys smiled, thinking how true it was. Looking around, he realized that none of them would have it any other way. Joining the girls in the living room, he sat next to Violca on the couch, putting his arm around the back of the couch, smiling when she leaned on him.

CHAPTER 56

Avoiding questions about what happened, Violca shook her head when she noticed Eva frowning. "Tomorrow," Violca said, looking at Kati, smiling at her sister. "We'll tell you about everything that happened. Tomorrow, I promise." She leaned into Chase, who was lightly stroking her shoulder with his thumb. "Tonight, I just want to take a shower, eat some food and get some sleep."

Eva smiled, giving her a hug. "You're right, tomorrow's soon enough. Go take a shower, we'll order some pizza so when you get out you can eat."

"Sounds like a plan." She smiled at Chase before getting up. Kati followed her upstairs. When they got to the top, Violca hugged Kati. "You were so brave, sweetie. I love you very much. You do know that, right?"

Kati nodded, her eyes filling with tears. "I was so scared."

Violca hugged her again, whispering, "So was I, sweetie, so was I."

Kati smiled, pulling back and biting her lower lip. "Brandon somehow made a knife fly through the air…"

"We've known him forever. I'm sure he will explain it tomorrow. Tonight, tonight, I just want to celebrate us all being together."

Kati smiled, "Sounds like a good idea."

Violca used the bathroom that adjoined Chase and Eryk's room, letting Kati use Scott's shower. Standing under the shower, letting the water run down her body, she sighed happily.

Feeling better after her shower, she slipped into a pair of yoga pants and a tank top. Walking downstairs, she smelled pizza and smiled, hearing Sari and Angyalka giggling as they talked to Eryk. Walking into the kitchen, she saw Kati quietly sitting, and Violca noticed that the bruise under her eye was starting to fade.

Violca saw Brandon leaning against the counter, watching Scott intently. Not seeing Chase, but aware of him, she turned and headed into the living room. Chase was standing by the window and looked at her over his shoulder. Turning, leaning against the window frame, he watched her.

Violca walked over to him, feeling nervous. She thought about what the demon Micah had said about the bite marks, and about Chase marking her as his, but how it wasn't complete. Was that what she did? Was that why she could feel him and his dragon? She now knew they were two parts of the same person. "Thank you for coming after us."

Chase smiled and when she was close enough, he reached out and took her hand, pulling her toward him. "Did you really think I wouldn't?" Violca thought for a moment and realized that she knew he would. She had always known. "Besides, it was you who saved us. I was just there to back you up."

Violca blushed, looking down at his chest, biting her lower lip. Feeling his finger slide under her chin, he gently raised her face so she was looking at him. Violca saw the flash of gold in his brown eyes. "How did you save us?" he asked her quietly, before brushing his lips against hers. "How is it I can feel you and your power, even when you're in the other room?"

Violca looked down. "I don't know," she answered truthfully.

"The demon, Micah, said you tried to mark me as yours, but hadn't finished yet."

Looking up, she saw a small grin on his face. Chase stepped closer to her before asking her, "So you marked me as yours?" Violca felt her cheeks heat up and wished the floor would swallow her, when he started to laugh. He wrapped his arms around her waist, pulling her hard against him, then whispered in her ear, "Does that mean you've forgiven for me for not coming clean when we first met?"

Looking up at him, his lips so close, she could feel his breath on her lips. Before she could reply, he leaned in and captured her lips with a soft kiss. Moaning, her lips parted and she felt Chase pulling her more tightly against him, as his tongue slid into her mouth and began to gently duel with hers. Violca felt herself melting against him, her hands going around his neck, sliding into his hair. Chase broke the kiss, putting his forehead against hers. "Come, let's go get some pizza before they eat it all."

Taking her hand, Chase led her out of the living room and back into the kitchen. Everyone turned and Violca blushed when she saw Eva's big grin, when she noticed Chase holding her hand. "Well it's about time," Eva said. "We were trying to save you some, but we weren't sure if you'd be joining us any time soon."

Violca rolled her eyes. Finding a paper plate, she grabbed a slice of pizza and stood next to Brandon, wondering what had him so uptight. Nudging him with her arm, she smiled at him.

He turned and asked, "Feel better?"

"Yeah, I do, thanks. I don't know if I thanked you both for coming for us."

Brandon shook his head. "V, you guys are the sisters I never, ever, wanted. You should know by now, I always have your back."

"I love you," she said and grinned when he put his arm around her and pulled her in for a hug, whispering he loved her too.

When he released her, she looked over at Chase, who was standing across the room eating his pizza. He smiled at her affectionately and Violca smiled at him. As they all finished eating, Violca quietly enjoyed the sounds of her sisters' chatter. Even though this was not how she'd pictured her life when she was younger, she couldn't think of a single thing she would have done differently.

The two younger girls went to bed early, in Eryk's room, while everyone else sat in the living room. Everyone was tired from the events of the past few days, and Eva made a point of reminding them of their promise to tell her about what had happened, in the morning. "I promise." Violca kissed her sister on the cheek and hugged Kati, watching them both go up the stairs.

Turning, she saw Chase leaning against the door frame of the living room, watching her. Chase's golden-brown eyes looked more golden than brown, causing her to shiver in response. Feeling a little shy, she nodded at him before heading up the stairs.

CHAPTER 57

Chase followed Violca up the stairs, watching the way her hips swayed with each step. He could feel the fact that she was a little nervous. When she looked at him over her shoulder, at the top of the stairs, he looked up from her butt to her face and caught her blushing when she noticed what he was staring at. He shrugged, not at all embarrassed about being caught admiring the view.

Chase followed her to the room he was using. Tomorrow, they would probably go back home, but tonight they were staying here. She opened the door, holding it open for him and he followed her. Stepping in, he heard the soft click of the door as she closed it.

Turning, he watched her as she leaned back against the door, watching him warily. He reached out and pulled her into his arms. "Why do you look so serious?"

Violca bit her lower lip and he bent down, kissing it gently. When he felt her relax, he pulled back and brushed her hair from her face. "So, are you going to tell me what you're thinking about?"

Violca nodded, tilting her head to look up at him. "I was wondering how I can suddenly feel you and…"

He smiled, putting his head against hers, "My dragon." She nodded, and he smiled bigger. "I don't know exactly, to be honest." Cupping her cheek, he pulled back, making her look up at him. "Before Dmitri started a civil war, when dragons found their mate, they would mark them as theirs for the world to know. After the division, not one dragon has been able to find his mate. I was drawn to you long before I met you, Violca, and when you cast that spell that got rid of Micah, I could feel your power like it was mine and felt you using my strength when you bound him back to hell."

Violca took a step back, thinking about his words. Did that mean what she thought it did? Were they now bound? What did that mean exactly? "What do you mean exactly by mate?"

Chase leaned against the wall. "It means that for me, there's no one else." Her eyes widened, and she wondered if this meant she somehow just tricked him into being hers. "Violca, I don't understand all that's happened between us, but I don't regret any of it. Since the day I saw your picture, I wanted to meet you, then I wanted to be near you, and when I thought I'd lost you…" Chase stepped forward, wrapping his arms around her. "For me, it's you Violca. But if you need more time, then you have…"

Before he could finish that last sentence, Violca reached up and kissed him, and he realized that she didn't need more time. She only wanted him. Chase growled low in his throat, holding her tighter as he deepened the kiss, his tongue sliding into her mouth, dueling with hers.

Lost in the kiss, she barely realized that he was lowering her to the bed and smiled against his lips when he broke the kiss long enough to pull his shirt over his head. Sitting up and grabbing the bottom of her shirt, she felt Chase's hands pushing hers away. Chase pulled her shirt off and threw it across the room. Pushing her back down, he kissed her, his hand sliding up her stomach before cupping her breast.

Violca moaned loudly into his mouth and her nipple hardened against his hand as he squeezed her breast gently over her bra, before pushing it up to touch her soft skin. Her back arched up, pressing harder into his hand and she heard him moan, as if in approval. Kissing his way down her neck, he nipped gently at his mark on her skin. She shuddered under him and he nipped it again. When she moaned loudly, he responded with a growl.

Chase pulled back just enough to see the little clip between her breasts and unhooked it as his mouth found her nipple, biting it gently before sucking it into his mouth, licking away the sting of his bite. Violca's hand slid to his hair, holding him tight to her breast as he continued to tease first one nipple, then the other. When Violca pulled harder on his hair, he bit her nipple a little harder.

When he slid lower, kissing her chest just below her breast, she slid her hands to his chest and pushed him gently onto his back. Violca followed him over and straddled his lap. Licking her lips, she saw his eyes turn gold with pleasure as she looked him over. Violca's fingers were feather light, as they traced the contours of his chest.

Leaning down, she began to kiss and lick his chest. Chase moaned lightly when she bit his nipple, before flicking it with her tongue. His hand came up to her head, brushing her hair back as she continued to tease him with her tongue and mouth as she scooted lower down his body. Chase hissed in pleasure when Violca nipped at his belly button, before her tongue came out and began to make love to it.

Violca's fingers moved lower, tracing the muscles of his stomach. She felt them quiver slightly under her touch, before she moved to his pants. The sound of her undoing his zipper was loud in the quiet room. When her fingers hooked into the sides of his jeans, he raised his hips, helping her as she removed the remaining clothes, tossing them behind her. Violca slid her hands up his legs until she got to his hips. Her lips hovering just above his cock, she could feel his hips tense under her hand.

Chase hissed softly when she ran her tongue up his length, before swirling around the head of his cock. Looking up at him, she saw him watching her as she teased his hard cock with her mouth. Chase brought one hand down, resting it on her head. When she moaned around his cock, she smiled to herself as his head went back and he hissed with pleasure.

Violca felt Chase's hip moving as the vein on his cock throbbed. Violca touched him everywhere she could. Her hands slowly sliding up his thighs, one hand wrapped around the base of his cock, while the other cupped his balls, massaging them gently.

When his hips moved faster, he growled, pulling her up and kissing her hard as he rolled her to her back. Reaching down, he yanked off her yoga pants and panties in one swift movement. Quickly coming up her body, he claimed her lips again in a deep kiss. His hand went to the nightstand and fumbled around looking for a condom. He broke the kiss long enough to rip open the package and slide it on before claiming her mouth again. She slid one of her legs up his and Chase grabbed it, putting it high on his hip. Rocking against her, he moaned into her mouth and slid inside her with one hard thrust, swallowing her moan.

Breaking the kiss, Chase put his forehead against hers before slowly moving his hips, his pace slow and gentle as he moved in and out of her. Violca wrapped her arms around his back, holding him tightly. Her nails dug into his back, and when he growled in response, she shuddered, dragging her nails downward. When she got to his ass, her nails dug in and she felt him pick up the pace.

With every moan and whimper, Violca felt Chase's body respond to her. Chase growled before biting her neck, causing her to shudder under him.

Violca's entire body shook in pleasure, her core tightening around him. She barely recognized the sounds coming from her. Her nails dug into his back, and she whimpered when he pulled his head away from her neck. His eyes were golden when she saw them, before he bent down and bit her hardened nipple.

Screaming into his shoulder when her orgasm hit, her core tightened hard around his thrusting cock. She bit her mark in the crook of his neck, and his hips thrust harder, faster into her and she heard him grunt in pleasure. He bit his mark on her and she screamed into his neck as another orgasm hit, her body shuddering in pleasure.

Violca felt Chase breathing hard on her neck and shoulder. Her entire body tingled in the aftermath. Sighing happily, she licked where she had bitten him, more from instinct than anything else. When Chase pulled back, his eyes met hers and Violca noticed that they were still more golden than brown and she smiled, feeling his dragon just below the surface. Reaching up, she cupped his cheek and Chase's chest rumbled, almost like a purr, and she smiled at feeling them both in that one touch.

When Chase softened and slipped from her core, she moaned and he nuzzled her neck in response, before lying on his back and pulling her into his arms. Listening to his heartbeat under her head, she sighed happily when she felt his hand stroking her back. He kissed the top of her head and Violca fell asleep.

CHAPTER 58

Waking up the next morning, Violca smiled as she felt Chase's hands gently sliding up and down her back. Stretching slightly, his arms tightened around her and she looked up at him. Chase kissed the top of her head, smiling at her. "Good morning, beautiful."

Violca could feel her cheeks heat up. "Good morning."

Violca glanced at the nightstand and the clock and was surprised to see that it was already after nine. When she started to sit up, he tightened his hold on her. "The girls are okay. Eryk and Brandon made them breakfast this morning, and right now they're watching cartoons." When Violca frowned, he shrugged. "What? I have good hearing."

Violca shook her head. "So, you have amazing hearing and turn into a dragon." He nodded, and she took a deep breath before continuing, "So what other things can you do that I should know about?"

Chase looked at her thoughtfully and she could feel his dragon shift as if it was pacing. "Well, most of us have a special gift or ability. Besides shifting into a dragon, I can also turn into a mist or shadow."

"Can you go through walls?"

"Not exactly, but I can slide through little cracks. So as long as a room isn't airtight or magically enforced, I can usually escape."

"Anything else I should know? Do you live forever? Eat anything weird? Do I have to worry that one day you'll sneeze and our house will go up in flames?"

Chase's hand paused on her back, laughing at her last question. "I don't live forever, although I do live for a very long time. I don't think I eat anything weird, and I've never sneezed and caught a house on fire."

Before Violca could ask him any more questions, she heard footsteps on the stairs and Sari and Angyalka laughing. She started to stand up, but Chase stopped her. He leaned down and brushed his lips against hers. "I promise to answer more questions later, but right now, I think your sisters are coming to find out why you're still in bed."

Grinning, she got up, found her clothes and called out to her sisters, whom she could hear right outside her door. "I'll be right out."

Sliding into her clothes, she ran her brush quickly through her hair. Looking back to the bed, she saw Chase leaning back against the headboard watching her, a small smile on his lips. "Are you getting up?"

Chase smirked, looking down and she noticed a small tent forming under the blanket. Violca felt her cheeks heating up, and clearing her throat, she tried to hide her embarrassment when he announced, "As you can see, I'm already up. But if you'd like, I'll join you downstairs in a few minutes."

Shaking her head, she opened the door, pushing Sari and Angyalka away from it. "Come on, let's go downstairs. I'm hungry."

Violca heard Chase chuckle as she closed the door. The girls took her hands and led her downstairs. They took her into the kitchen and she smiled as she poured a bowl of cereal.

Angyalka hugged her tight. "I told them you'd be safe, but I missed you."

Sari hugged her too, and Violca kissed the tops of both of their heads, smiling when Sari piped up, "I missed you so much, V."

Hugging them both, she smiled down at her two sisters. "I missed you guys, too." Pulling back, she looked at them both. "Were you good for everyone, or did you give them a hard time?"

Sari grinned and said, "We were good!" at the same time as Angyalka said, "Gave them a hard time!"

Laughing as she ate the rest of her cereal, she smiled at Chase when he walked into the kitchen. He ruffled the girls' hair and kissed Violca on the cheek as he reached for the bowl just past her. Sari and Angyalka both giggled and whispered to each other. Violca shook her head, her cheeks heating up, but she couldn't keep the smile from her face.

Chase made his bowl of cereal, winking at her, leaving them alone. Eva and Kati walked in a few minutes later. The smile on Eva's face let Violca know that her sisters both knew where Chase had slept last night. Sari grinned hugely. "Eva, Kati, guess what happened?"

Violca closed her eyes, knowing what was coming, but before either one could answer, Angyalka popped up, "Chase kissed Violca!"

"I wanted to tell them," Sari pouted, right before Eva and Kati burst into laughter.

Violca bit her lip, shaking her head. She grinned when she heard Chase and the boys laughing in the living room. Eva and Kati smiled at her, and she realized that they both approved.

Walking to the living room, she glanced at Scott and Eryk, who both made little kissing noises, copying the younger girls. Rolling her eyes, they both started laughing in response. Chase smiled at her as she sat next to him on the couch. "Are the girls giving you a hard time?" Chase asked, and Violca couldn't help but notice the big grin on his face.

"No more than usual. I think they love the fact that they can now tease me over a boy."

Chase puffed up his chest. "A boy?"

Violca tried to suppress her laughter, but when Eryk and Scott began to laugh, she couldn't hold back and started laughing so hard she ended up putting her head on his chest. When she was done laughing, she wiped away the tears that had formed in the corners of her eyes.

Chase smirked at her. "I'm used to those two laughing at me, but if I wasn't so happy that you're safe, I think I'd be offended that you called me a boy and then laughed at me."

Violca smiled up at him and heard the boys make woo-hoo noises when he bent down and kissed her gently. Chase put his arm around her and his hand slid up and down her arm. She heard Brandon in the hall talking to the girls in the kitchen before he came in and sat on the chair opposite her.

The look that Brandon gave Scott made her wonder what the hell was going on and she frowned, looking back and forth between the two. If she wasn't so confused at what was going on between the two, she would find it funny, but instead she was wondering why Brandon was watching Scott so intently and why Scott was pretending he didn't notice.

Looking between the two, she asked, "Should I ask what the hell happened between you two?"

Scott shrugged and Brandon looked over at her. "I asked Eva and Kati if they wouldn't mind playing outside with the girls for a bit so we could talk about what happened before I take you home. Eva wanted me to remind you that you promised to fill her in, but she'll take the girls out for now."

CHAPTER 59

Violca felt Chase tense up next to her and she nodded, leaning forward. She started with telling them about how she woke up in the room upstairs with Kati. She mentioned healing Kati, mainly because she was still surprised. Pausing for a moment, she looked up at Brandon. "AnnaBelle showed up to, umm, *eat* with us. She left shortly before you arrived."

Brandon swore and rubbed his hand on his face, "Shit, I thought I saw her leave. What the hell was she doing there?"

Violca bit her lip, trying to think of everything her friend said when she felt Chase's hand slide up and down her back reassuringly. "She said she's also a witch, a demi-Earth Witch, and that if I helped Micah, I could help release her and her family's powers."

Brandon frowned. "I don't understand exactly how you could help with that."

Chase cleared his throat before speaking, "The rumor is that Violca's ancestors always had one daughter who inherited their powers from the original Earth Witch. Like Violca, they all had these incredible violet eyes. The rest of the kids were always born boys. Occasionally, one might have a gift, but their daughters always had limited magic. This is the first time an Earth Witch is known for giving birth to more than one girl. The fates foresaw this and each sister is predicted to be very powerful. The five of them are very important to all of us. Unfortunately, the prediction is vague and some people see the balance you'll bring as a power play and a chance to rule over the heavens and the earth."

Everyone got quiet, thinking about what he'd said, until Scott looked at Brandon. "Since we're all talking, would you like to explain how you were able to move the knife that was held up to Kati's throat across the room?"

Violca looked over at Brandon, and her eyes widened when Brandon swore under his breath before saying, "Why don't you tell me why you yanked Kati from me like some jealous boyfriend?"

Violca raised an eyebrow, looking between them both. She heard Scott growl, his eyes changing slightly. "Both of you are going to chill out and tell me what's going on. Brandon, you start."

Brandon looked at her nervously, glancing at Chase and Scott before looking back at Violca. "Your mother told me once, I was a special kind of telepath. One of the reasons I used to love hanging around your family, was that I couldn't hear what everyone was thinking, and your mom used to help me learn to put up walls, so I could block out most of the voices. Then, when I got older and learned to move things with my mind, your mom informed me that I must come from a rare line of telepaths who were known for having telekinetic powers along with a few other rare gifts."

"Your mom or dad had special abilities?" Violca asked, unable to keep the surprise from her voice. Brandon's parents were prudes. They were religious to the extreme. Picturing them being different in any sort of way was difficult.

Brandon looked down at his hands before looking up at her. "No, my mother apparently had an affair when my dad was away on a business trip. She swears he forced her and when I replied to something she said in her head, my parents decided that was the proof they needed. If I could read their minds as a boy, my mom pointed out that my real father could've easily tricked her into sleeping with him."

Violca gasped, everything about his family suddenly making sense. Her mother once said that Brandon was a special boy, and had always said he was gifted. Her father had also taken a special interest in Brandon, making sure to take him out for guys' time. She had thought it was because her dad had always wanted a son, but maybe it was because they knew exactly what he was going through. "Why didn't you ever tell me, Brandon?"

Brandon fidgeted. "It never came up." When she raised an eyebrow at that, he rubbed the back of his neck. "I didn't want you to treat me any differently. When my parents found out I could read their minds, they never treated me the same. Deciding I was a 'devil' child. I couldn't read you, and I didn't want to lose you as a friend."

Knowing Brandon wouldn't appreciate her hugging him right now, she reached out, squeezing his hand before turning to Scott. He squirmed under her stare before he cleared his throat.

"It's not what it sounds like," Scott started, and Violca frowned, thinking of all the times she saw him watching Kati.

"Then you better explain," Violca said, keeping her voice calm.

Scott looked toward Chase as if asking for help and Chase looked at her. "Were-panthers recognize their mates by scent. When they smell their mate, they imprint on them."

Violca frowned, getting up, agitated, and paced back and forth. "Mate, I'm guessing you don't mean friend." The look of guilt on both Chase and Scott's faces caused her anger to build and she saw Scott shifting in his seat. "So, because you smelled my sister, you think you have a claim to her. Kati, my younger sister, who has never had a serious boyfriend and is just about to get her driver's license?"

Scott looked guilty before continuing, "It's not like that exactly. I wouldn't try to have a relationship with her until she's…"

Chase interrupted his friend, and Violca guessed it was because he saw the murderous look on her face. "Right now, he'll be like a big brother to her, protecting her, and looking out for her. When Kati's old enough, she can choose to accept or reject him as her mate." Scott growled, and Violca gave him a glare that caused him to back down before Chase continued, "But when the time's right, it'll be her choice."

Violca stared at Scott. In some ways, she was glad that her sister would have a protector, but the thought of a grown man having a claim on Kati, before she had a chance to grow up and find herself, pissed her off. Brandon stood up, looking at her. "You can't be thinking about this, Kati's fifteen, for goodness sake!"

Scott stood up growling. Standing toe to toe with Brandon, his canines lengthened.

"Both of you, knock it off," Violca said, and was surprised when they both jumped back. Neither one sat down, but went to stand on opposite sides of the room.

Walking up to Scott, she looked at him. "You'll let Kati date other boys her own age?" Scott's eyes narrowed, but he nodded. "And when she's old enough, you'll give her the choice, not force yourself on her?" He nodded again, the look on his face saying he was offended she would even ask.

Violca thought about it for a moment. The idea of a guy her age, thinking that her sister was supposed to be his when she was older, would normally weird her out, but she knew deep down, Scott would never harm her sister. That feeling alone, along with her mother's whisper, *fate has a way of protecting her children* caused her to pause before replying, "You'll never tell my sister. Her life will be normal, she will date, probably fall in love and experience heartache. It'll be her decision when she's older, not yours. You'll not interfere or act like a jealous boyfriend when she goes on a date. Understand?"

"I would never do anything to hurt her, I promise."

"There has not been a whole lot of normal in Kati's life and she needs all the friends she can get, but I will not let you be around if you don't agree to let her grow up and experience the things she should. Even if you think you have some bizarre claim on her."

Scott looked down, and she could feel him fighting with his decision before looking up at her. "I promise not to stand in the way of her having a normal life, and I'll keep this from her until she has come into her own."

Violca nodded, knowing they'd come to an agreement, for now. Looking down at Chase, who smiled at her, she announced, "I think it's time the girls and I went home. Their life needs some normal in it."

Chase nodded at her and Violca turned, heading out of the living room to go upstairs. While Kati and Eva had the girls distracted, Violca packed up their stuff. Hearing someone behind her, she looked over her shoulder and saw Brandon. "I'll help you pack," he announced as he headed toward the room Angyalka and Sari had shared.

CHAPTER 60

When they first pulled up, Violca found she was a little nervous about going into her house. Looking at Kati, she saw the same flash of fear across her sister's face. Taking a deep breath, she reached out and grabbed her sister's hand and walked into the house. The fear that she had instantly left her, as once inside, she found she could breathe easily.

After the conversation with Scott, Violca suggested that he and Eryk stay home. They knew that the threat to them was not over, but Violca refused to live in a glass bubble. The school year was almost over. There was also Eva's graduation to go to. They would need to come up with a plan, but they also needed some normalcy in their lives.

Violca used the drive to read more of their mother's book. The book almost seemed to turn to what she was looking for on its own. She found the section that talked about witches finding their life mate, and how it was discovered that once the couple bonded, the witch was able to use her mate's strength to help with spells. The binding was permanent and more sacred than any marriage. There was a side note that talked about how the fates blessed them in their choice of mates and that the binding spell was never written down but whispered in their ear from ancestors of the past, when it was time.

Violca smiled when she read it. When she met Chase, she was attracted to him. When she found out he'd orchestrated their meeting she was hurt, but when she thought she might not see him or that he would die, she realized that it didn't matter. She realized that in the short amount of time she'd known him, she had fallen in love with him. He did not shy away from hanging out with her or her sisters and he risked his life to save her. Violca decided she would tell him about what she had read later that night. Mated or bound, they would need to decide how to proceed.

Brandon checked out the house before coming back to her in the living room, and kissed her cheek. "I'm going to have to work tomorrow, but I need you to promise if anything comes up, you'll call me."

Violca smiled at him, wrapping her arms around him and hugging him tightly. "I love you, you know," she whispered in his ear and smiled when he hugged her more tightly.

When they pulled apart, he grinned down at her, his blue eyes sparkling. "I love you too, brat, but if you don't call me, I'll beat your ass." His smile broadened and she watched as he said goodbye to the girls.

Locking the door behind Brandon, Violca frowned at Chase. "What're you thinking about?"

"You and Brandon." With that reply, she raised an eyebrow and he smiled, "I admit, I was jealous at first. You guys are very close and it's easy to see the affection you both have for each other. It's hard, but I'm glad to know there's someone else out there who has your back."

Violca smiled, the look on Chase's face actually appeared to be pained. "Yes, Brandon will always have my back. I treat him like a little brother and he treats me like a little sister. It makes for an interesting relationship."

Chase chuckled, pulling her into his arms. "My king, Viktor, messaged me during the drive over here."

Violca felt her heart rate pick up.

"He thinks it would be a good idea if I stayed here, just in case. I can sleep on the couch. He's worried his brother might have something up his sleeve and wants us to be prepared, just in case."

Violca nodded. "That should be fine." Hearing Angyalka call out to her, she brushed her lips to his before heading down the hall to see what was going on.

CHASE WATCHED her walk away before sitting on the couch. He didn't tell Viktor that he'd mated with Violca, or that Scott had imprinted on Kati. His king was fair, but the stress of the war with his brother was starting to wear on him. With him and Violca mating, he hoped it meant that some of the balance was being restored.

Chase smiled when Kati walked into the room. "Hey, everything okay?"

"Yeah, I just wanted to ask you a question." She bit her lip before sitting on the couch on the other side of him. "Can you teach me how to defend myself?"

Chase nodded. "I don't see why not. If you'd like, either I can teach you or we can find a class you like, or both. Classes will help you spar against other people and teach you different techniques I can't."

Kati nodded and he noticed that she was still biting her lower lip. "Is there anything else, Kati?"

Sighing, she looked at him. "Do you think I'm weak?"

Chase smiled at her, understanding her concern. "You're not

weak, Kati. You're a teenage girl who got attacked by men and demons. I can show you a few things that might help and maybe as you develop your magic, you'll develop your own ways of protecting yourself and your sisters."

Kati smiled and he saw a little doubt left in her eyes before she nodded. "Thank you."

"Anytime," he said with a grin. Taking her hand as he stood up pulling her with him.

Kati started to walk out of the living room before turning to look at him. "My sister sacrificed a lot to keep us together, although she'd never admit it. She deserves someone who sees how amazing she is. I am glad it's you."

Chase smiled at her. He noticed how different her stance was when she was defending her sister. Scott was going to have his hands full when she gained confidence and could stick up for herself. "I'm glad it's me too." He winked at her, "And I think your sister is amazing, four sisters and all."

Violca and her sisters had a bond he envied. He enjoyed being around them and knew he and Violca would need to figure out how they wanted to proceed. He knew they were mated, but since they'd just met, she might want to take things slowly. Plus, since she was living with and raising her sisters, she had to think about what kind of example to set.

CHAPTER 61

The girls' lives were pretty much back to normal. Everyone was in school and Violca was at work. Chase knew it bothered her that she hadn't heard from Anna-Belle, but he didn't think it was that big of a loss. Her friend had betrayed her.

Chase had spent the last few nights sleeping on the couch. Well not totally, he would move to the couch during the night, before the girls woke up. Eva and Kati both knew, but Violca was still trying to figure out how to talk to the two younger girls about it.

Viktor was due to come in that afternoon. Scott was going to pick him up and bring him to the house after his plane landed. Scott had stayed away for the last few days, but Chase knew it was killing his friend. Scott wanted to check in on Kati and make sure she was okay, but was trying to respect Violca's wishes. Violca had agreed that Scott could come over on the weekends to help teach the girls some self-defense techniques. All the girls were going to learn some basic ways to protect themselves physically. At night, the older girls read some of their mother's book, learning more and more about their family history while trying to learn how to use their magic.

After spending lunch with Violca, Chase swung by the younger two girls' school. Just in case, he had started picking them up, and Eryk was helping by taking Eva and Kati home. The initial threat was over, but he knew Viktor's brother was still out there, plotting something.

Chase knew Viktor well. The war had cut the number of dragon shifters in half. Most had lost someone in their family and some families were lost completely. Viktor would always do what he thought was best for his people, but he could be rough and hard, pushing people to see what they were made of. He smiled because as scary as Viktor was, he knew his mate would stand toe to toe with him when it came to her sisters. His mate was fierce and powerful in her own way. Viktor was his king, but Violca was his mate, and he would support her, always.

Hearing the bell ring, he leaned against the car, smiling when he saw Angyalka. Sari came out a few seconds later, smiling brightly and ran toward him. Chase felt his heart swell, surprised at how quickly these two little girls had wormed their way into his heart. He noticed a few of the moms checking him out, some of them whispering, obviously trying to figure out who he was and why he was picking them up.

Not even the prettiest among them held a candle to his mate and her strength and he ignored them, laughing when Angyalka and Sari practically tackled him.

"How was school, girls?" Chase asked as he took each one's hand.

"My teacher made me do a picture of my favorite animal, so I drew a dragon." Chase chuckled as Angyalka continued her story, "My teacher said they don't exist and that I should draw something else. I was going to tell her that they do, but I remember you telling me that it was a secret, so I drew a big black kitty and told her the cat's name was Uncle Scott."

Biting his lip, trying not to laugh at her story, he said, "I'm sure Uncle Scott will love to see your picture." Turning, he looked at Sari. "How about you, short stuff, anything exciting happen?"

Opening the door, they both crawled in the back, buckling themselves up while he got in the front. "A few of the girls were teasing me because their mommies think you're cute."

"Why were they teasing you?" Chase asked puzzled by kids' train of thought.

"The moms said you would leave my sister 'cause she has all of us and no guy would want her since she comes with so many bags." He glanced at her reflection, seeing she was upset before she continued, "Are you going to leave because you don't like us?"

Chase shook his head picking his words carefully, thinking that Violca and he needed to talk to the girls soon. "No, sweetie, I love you guys and I'm not going to leave your sister. They were just being mean because...well, some people are just mean."

Sari nodded, accepting his answer and the girls both began to chatter. Chase halfway listened, making the appropriate comment when needed. He found he really didn't like the idea of Sari being picked on, and really hated that the stupid moms at her school were talking about Violca. Instead of recognizing what a wonderful thing she did by keeping her family together, they talked about how they think she couldn't keep a man. Only a boy would not recognize Violca's worth and look at her raising her sisters as too much of a challenge for them.

When Chase pulled up to the house, he saw Eryk's car pull up right behind them. Heading toward the house, Eryk jogged up to him. "Hey, Scott said he and Viktor should be arriving about six."

Chase snorted. "Great. So, he should be pulling up about the same time Violca gets home."

Eryk stood outside with him as the girls headed into the house. "How's Violca feeling about Scott and Kati?"

Chase smiled, knowing Eryk was asking out of concern for

his brother. "She finds it a little weird that with one scent and one look, Scott knows Kati is the one, but as long as Scott's willing to let Kati have a normal teenage life and not interfere with that, she said she'll not interfere."

Eryk snorted. "I understand why Violca wants Kati to have a normal life, but it's going to be hard for Scott to watch Kati date."

Chase nodded. "Yeah, it will be, but when we talked about it, he didn't want to be the reason Kati missed out on something. He knows, in the end, Kati will be his. He said fate has already decided that. He might have to be patient and wait. At least he knows who she is, and he doesn't have to wait as long as I did."

Eryk chuckled, shaking his head. "Yeah, you didn't look like you were suffering," he said, opening the door to the house and going inside.

CHAPTER 62

Violca couldn't help but smile, coming home to Chase and the girls. Chase was so good with them. She was a little surprised that Scott's SUV wasn't there. She was nervous about meeting Chase's king. Chase told her that Viktor was a good man, but he was used to being obeyed. Violca had been on her own for so long, she didn't take orders well, and she wanted the girls to have as normal a life as possible.

Walking in the door, she heard voices coming from both ends of the house. Angyalka and Sari came running down the hall, stopping when they saw her. "We're going to go get pizza with Eryk," Sari announced.

Looking up, she saw Eryk coming up behind them. "We thought you could use some time with Viktor, alone, so we're all going out for pizza."

Kati and Eva came from the kitchen area, smiling at her. "Hey, we were just about to go and grab dinner."

The girls gave her a quick hug before walking out the door. Eryk smiled, nodding in her direction as he followed the girls outside. Feeling Chase, she turned to see him standing in the doorway.

"Viktor and Scott should actually be here in a few minutes," Chase said, walking over to her, wrapping his arms around her waist before brushing his lips against hers.

Violca stiffened in his arms and he brushed his lips against hers again. "Relax, just remember, he has you and your sisters' best interest at heart. And the final decision on what happens is yours."

Knowing he was trying to be supportive, she raised an eyebrow, biting her lip. "You have my back?" she asked as she heard Scott pull up.

He nodded. "You're my mate and I'll always have your back, I promise," Chase said, kissing the top of her head.

Taking a shaky breath, she smiled and Chase took her hand as she turned and walked toward the door to let them in. Seeing Scott first, she smiled at him and noticed that he looked a little uncomfortable. She wondered if it was about Viktor or about being around her. She chose to believe it was about her, because if it was about Viktor, then she would have to admit she was really nervous.

Viktor walked in behind him and Violca felt her eyes widen when she saw him. He stood taller than either Chase or Scott, stooping to get in the door. When he looked at her, she found herself almost lost in his startling, blue eyes. Chase squeezed her hand and she realized she was staring.

Viktor nodded in her direction before reaching his hand out to her. "It's a pleasure to meet you, Violca," he said with a faint English accent.

"It's nice to meet you too, Viktor," Violca replied and gestured toward the couch. "Would you like to have a seat?"

Viktor sat in one of the chairs while Chase sat next to her, putting an arm around her, in support. Violca saw Viktor stiffen and look at Chase before glancing at her, his startling blue eyes zeroing in on her neck. Chase's mark on her pulsing as Viktor's lip curled. "You marked the witch as yours?" The words were said between gritted teeth and she felt Chase stiffen beside her.

Before he could reply, Violca's eyes narrowed. "I marked Chase as mine, and I'm more than just 'the witch.'"

Viktor smiled and Violca could see his canines poking out the side of his lips. "No, you're not just the witch, you're one of five whom he was sent to protect, not to fuck."

Before Violca could say anything, Chase growled low next to her and she could feel his body vibrating. "What I did with her, Viktor, is none of your business. All you need to know is she's mine, and you will not talk to her like that."

Viktor chuckled at his words and Violca's body tensed, her hands curling into fist. Chase tensed up next to her. Viktor raised his hand in surrender. "Since you felt free to mark her, she's your mate and yours to protect. I expect you to have them all packed and moved as soon as possible."

Standing up, Violca looked down at Viktor, who raised an eyebrow. "What the hell do you mean packed and moved? This is our home."

Viktor looked at her almost sympathetically. "Violca, the fate of more than just my people rests on you and your sisters. It would be easier to protect you all, if you move to my home."

Violca paced back and forth. "I won't have my sisters locked away. They need to have as normal of a life as possible. My sister graduates next month, I can't just uproot her."

Viktor got up and in one giant step was in front of her. Violca tilted her head up, meeting his eyes, and his voice softened as he spoke to her. "Violca, I'm not trying to lock you and your sisters away. We'll come up with a way to keep you safe, while letting you live as normal a life as possible. My people have found a haven where they can hide in plain sight, and plenty of space to hide when their dragons need to shift, when Chase's dragon needs to shift."

Violca glanced toward Chase. His golden-brown eyes met

hers and he nodded at her, seeing the question on her face. He told her he would support her in every decision, regardless of what she chose. Biting her lip, she thought about what Viktor had told her. "I'd like to talk to Chase about this alone." Viktor nodded, and she looked at Scott, who was watching her intently. She knew her decision affected him too, but her priority was to her sisters.

Viktor looked toward Chase. "We'll leave you two alone to talk. My brother seems to be regrouping, according to what Kassandra has heard so far." He looked back to Violca, "I understand your need to protect your sisters, my goal is to help you, but also to protect my people, little Earth Witch. I hope we can come up with a solution, quickly."

Violca watched as Viktor and Scott left the house. Sitting down next to Chase, she felt his hand come out and squeeze her hand reassuringly. "Our lives will never be the same, will they?"

Chase shook his head. "Not exactly, but that doesn't have to be a bad thing."

Biting her lip, Violca nodded. "We're going to have to talk to Eva and Kati. I couldn't make life changes without talking to them first. It's their lives too, and it wouldn't be fair to them."

Chase nodded, pulling her against him, his hand gently stroking her arm. "I think that sounds like a good idea. You're probably the first person to stand up to Viktor in a long time. I don't think he was expecting that."

She grinned. "Well, as long as you have my back, I can do anything."

"Always, my witch, always," Chase said before kissing her. Moaning into the kiss, she smiled when she heard Chase's stomach growl and he pulled back. "Let's eat before the girls get home."

After arguing with Viktor, Chase finally got him to agree to let the girls finish up the school year before moving. Violca was sad to be leaving her childhood home, but knew her sisters' safety was more important than the house.

Viktor was going to send people to fix the cabin. They were going to sell the house, but keep the cabin under a company name so that way they could still feel a connection to her parents. Plus, once Chase told Viktor about how her mom had buried the book there for her to find, Viktor didn't want to take a chance that her mother might have hidden something else out there. There was even some debate about doing the same thing with the house, and renting it out, just in case, but that wasn't fully decided yet.

Brandon probably took them moving the hardest of all. The case he was working on blew up and some evidence came up that would have him going to Arizona. There were some bodies found that had similar wounds and a matching signature to his serial killer. This could be a career case for him. His captain told him that he couldn't believe a rookie caught the case, but since he did, he was being watched closely. Viktor was also keeping an eye on

Brandon. When they talked about his ability, Viktor mentioned that they could use a guy like him.

Chase felt bad that Violca was sad to be moving away from Brandon and knew she was still upset about AnnaBelle. Brandon went to her condo downtown, only to find it empty. Violca never brought it up, but he saw her looking at her phone sometimes, like she was waiting for a call.

Pulling up to the house, Chase noticed an envelope taped to the door. Walking to the door, he saw Violca's name on it and pulled it off. The girls were inside sitting around the table looking at old pictures and laughing. Violca looked up at him and smiled. Walking over, he brushed his lips against hers before handing her the envelope. "Hey, this was on the door for you."

Frowning, she took it, opening it carefully. Chase watched her face as she read it, seeing her eyes mist up. Before he could ask what was wrong, she handed it to him.

Dear V,

I'm sorry for everything that happened. I promise, before Micah, I was never jealous of you. I love you like a sister and I don't know what happened, or how to explain it. One day, everything was perfect then I was... I'm so sorry, I understand if you never forgive me.

All my love, AnnaBelle

P.S. Please tell Kati and your sisters I love all of you and I'm sorry.

Chase looked down at Violca. He saw relief in her eyes and was glad she had some closure before they moved. Sitting down at the table with them, Chase put his arm around Violca, who went back to going through pictures with her sisters. Chase looked around the table and realized this was what he and his dragon had been missing. Love and family. He was finally right where he belonged.

ABOUT THE AUTHOR

Leilani Love is a proud mother of two very active boys. She loves traveling to new places and meeting new people wherever she goes. Thus far, Leilani has visited Paris, DenBosch and Amsterdam and hopes to one-day return. On her next trip she hopes to be able to make stops in Scotland and Italy. Currently residing in Oregon, she has also lived in Hawaii, Florida, Alaska, Virginia, Texas, Washington and California. She loves to read books and has a passion for various genres. Her love affair with dragons began when she was young and she still dreams of having her own dragon and Black Panther. For now, she is content to write about them in her books.

Aithne couldn't believe she was stuck rescuing her sister, again. Her mother, Boudica, had found out that her oldest daughter, Ally, had been captured by the Vampire King Lazzaro. "Shit," she swore softly, as she watched two of the human guards talking. Waiting for an opening, she wondered when her sisters would ever learn. Both of her older sisters were always chasing after men who they thought were good looking and rich. Time and time again, her sisters proved that the more handsome the man, and the more money he had, the more nefarious he probably was. Not all men, of course, but well, more were than weren't.

Their mother had always been strong, and had pushed her daughters to follow in her footsteps. By the time their father had died, her older sisters, Ally and Cinnie, had already been promised for marriage and were ready to be married. The Romans had decided to attack when their mother had refused to step down as the clan leader, and had destroyed all hope of that future. Both of her older sisters resented the fact, that in one moment, the life they had been promised was taken away. Aithne was the youngest of the three, and had an easier time adjusting to the change in their lives. Because of this, she often found herself cleaning up after her sisters' messes.

Aithne watched as a tall man came around the corner and gave the two guards orders. Just by the aura around him, she knew he had to be the leader. Where the two human guards were both attractive and strong, this one stood a head taller. The way he walked, his head held high, commanded authority and respect. The three were built like linebackers, but this one, this one she was sure, was mixed with something supernatural. Once he finished giving his orders, the leader and one of the guards walked off, heading west of the compound, leaving the human guard alone.

Aithne watched him, waiting for her opening. Not sure what type of supernaturals he employed, she'd rubbed wolfsbane all over her body while preparing for this rescue. Wolfsbane was great at helping to mask one's scent. Although she was prepared, and was being cautious, she still tried to keep downwind. She had trained for hundreds of years on how to fight both humans and supernaturals. Her only goal was to get in, get her sister, and get out, with no killing, if possible.

Just then, the guard's phone began to ring. He looked at the screen before he discreetly answered. As he began to talk to the person on the other end, Aithne crept up, ducking behind a tree near him. She could hear a woman on the other end. Licking her lips, she smiled, knowing he was definitely distracted. Men are just *too* easy, she thought to herself. She heard him say he would see her later before hanging up.

Slipping out from behind the tree, she quickly wrapped an arm around his neck. Her knife skillfully pressed into his sweet spot, right between his ribs. The position was an easy one for her to achieve. Normally, she stood five feet ten inches. However, she was currently wearing heeled boots that made her just over six feet tall. This made her almost the same height as the guard. "If you move, I'll slide this knife right between your ribs and into your heart. Do you understand?"

She could feel his body tense up at the sound of her voice. Most men hated the idea of having a woman get the jump on them. The way his body tightened when he heard her speak let her know he was surely one of those types. She pressed the blade against him, hard, trying to discourage him from being stupid. She could hear him growl before asking, "What do you want?"

"You, my friend, are going to help me inside to get my sister." She needed him to let her in, but knew that once they were inside, he would cause problems by alerting the other guards nearby. Lazzaro was known to be paranoid. She knew that once she got inside, she would be dealing with his fanged friends.

"Dumb bitch, once you're inside, you know they're going to kill you," he said between gritted teeth, as she pushed him forward.

With the knife still pressed to his ribs, she whispered. "Well if I go, I'm taking you with me, so you best pray I make it out of there alive." Aithne had studied the property earlier, so she knew there was a small side door up ahead. She guessed it was most likely the servants' entrance, from when the house was originally built. Out of all the doors, this one should have the fewest guards.

When they got to the door, she pushed him forward. When he didn't move to open the door, she nudged him with the silver blade of her dagger, just enough to break the skin and heard his hiss of pain, "You seem to be going out of your way to save a girl who's probably not even here."

"I think you'll remember her. She's five foot six, waist-length black hair, green eyes, and large breasts." She heard him snicker softly to himself. Holding him the way she was, her body was pressed against him and she knew that the snicker was due to her less than formidable chest size.

Once she was inside, she knew she needed to rescue her sister quickly, before the vampires inside discovered her. "Where are they keeping her?"

When he didn't answer, she pressed the tip of her blade further into his ribs, cutting deep into his skin. She heard his sharp inhale of discomfort. "Tell me," she demanded.

"The girl is upstairs, but you'll never get that far. They'll kill you first," he retorted, his body shaking in anger.

Aithne removed the knife from his ribs and swiftly used the hilt to hit him on the side of the head. She landed right in the spot where she knew he would be out for several hours. Pulling him into the bushes that lined the perimeter of the house, she used her zip ties to bind his hands and feet. She tore off a piece of cloth from his shirt and shoved it in his mouth, then removed his belt and used it to hold the gag in place. Even though she figured he would be out for a while, it was better to tie him up and hide him, instead of taking any chances.

Taking a few steps back to the door, she listened for any sounds. Not hearing anything, she turned the handle and walked into the house. The door opened into a servants' hallway. It was long, and led to a set of stairs on the right. A little surprised that no one was visible, she wondered where they could be. She had expected to have seen at least a few guards roaming around, and she knew something was off. So far, this had been way too easy.

Carefully walking up the stairs, Aithne peeked around the corner to see two guards standing in front of one of the doors. Rolling her eyes in frustration, she could see there was no way for her to sneak up on them. Both stood well over six feet tall and were sporting broad, muscular chests. With bodies so big, she wondered how they even managed to get up the stairway.

Her sister was going to owe her big after this one. One of the other doors in the hallway stood slightly ajar. Aithne checked to see if they were looking in her direction, then quickly ducked through the door. Luckily, the room was empty, so she was able to take a moment to assess the situation. She knew she couldn't take both on at once, so it was imperative that she get them separated. Reaching into her pocket, she found a quarter and decided to flick it so it would bounce off the metal globe that sat on the desk. The sound would be just loud enough that the vampires would hear it, but not loud enough to make them both leave their post at the same time.

The guard closest to her doorway responded to the sound and walked toward the room. Hiding behind the door, she watched from the slight opening until she saw him reach the door. It creaked loudly as he pushed it open. Just as he made his way over the threshold, she unhooked her black shillelagh that was hanging from her belt. Using the wooden knob on the hilt, she hit him just hard enough in the back of his knee that he fell forward with a grunt. Aithne then slid the long, slender club around his neck and pulled back as hard as she could. He began to struggle against her, but the more he struggled, the closer he came to passing out. Suddenly, his head flew back, hitting her hard in the temple. She blinked back stars of pain, but in doing so, her grip loosened on the shillelagh. The guard turned and lunged for her. Aithne reached into the pouch on her belt and grabbed one of her poison-laced daggers. As he rushed her, she stabbed at the side of his torso, nicking just enough skin to make her happy. With a menacing smile, the guard flashed his fangs and Aithne watched as his eyes turned blood red. With his rage in full throttle, he charged at her again. Jumping out of the way, she barely managed to escape his grasp. She was enormously thankful that she had so many years of training to help her deal with these bloodsuckers.

Watching him closely, she noticed his movements had started to slow. With a grin, she signaled for him to come at her. As he reached for her, she watched his eyes began to roll back in his head. With his next step, he toppled to the floor.

Aithne heard the creak of floorboards outside the room, which let her know the second guard was headed in her direction. Grabbing another poisoned dagger from her belt, she stood in the doorway and skillfully threw it at him. Knowing he would be able to dodge the first one, without any hesitation, she threw a second, hitting him in the bicep.

He pulled the dagger from his arm and Aithne smiled. The poison would take a few minutes to kick in, and she hoped she would be able to distract him that long. She wanted to be sure that he didn't have time to call for help. But in a flash, he was right in front of her. He grabbed her by the neck, lifting her up and pinning her against the wall. Struggling against him, she kicked and scratched at him, trying to get him to loosen his grip. The fangs in his mouth began to slide into view, as she continued to fight against his stranglehold. Luckily, the poison from her dagger began to take effect, and he finally let go of her and fell to the ground with a hard thud. She thanked the gods the poison hadn't taken any longer to knock him out.

Cautiously, Aithne approached the door that they had been guarding. She pressed her ear to the door and listened, but since she didn't hear any sounds, she turned the doorknob and stepped inside. She had to blink her eyes a few times so they would adjust to the lighting as fast as possible. When they finally adjusted, she could see a figure on the bed. She started to take a step forward, then saw the shadow move, reaching toward the nightstand and turning on the light.

"Lazzaro," she whispered.

Lazzaro stood up. Aithne tensed, not sure what he was planning on doing. As tall as she was in her heeled boots, Lazzaro's height made her feel small and inferior. His shoulder-length blond hair looked soft to the touch as the light reflected off it. His icy blue eyes bore into hers as he purred her name. "Aithne," he said as he rose to stand before her. "I've been waiting for you."

Aithne flinched as he tried to run his finger along her jawline.

She instinctually smacked his hand away. Her gaze settled on his body, taking in the fact that he was fully dressed. He was wearing a pair of form-fitting black slacks that showed every twitch of every muscle in his legs. His light blue silk shirt emphasized his cold blue eyes as they observed her. She had to admit, he was definitely the type of man to turn her sister's head. He wasn't as large as his guards, but even so, she knew he was just as dangerous. If she were forced to fight him, her chances would be slim. "Lazzaro, I'm touched that you would be waiting for me. Can I ask why you decided to *honor* me so?"

Lazzaro chuckled, a wicked smile curving his lips. It made her stomach churn. "I need a favor, cara mia." He walked over to the bar he had set up and offered to pour her a brandy, then proceeded to pour one for himself.

Declining his offer with a shake of her head, she glared up at him when he handed her the glass anyway. She placed the glass on the counter before she turned back towards him, crossing her arms over her chest.

"I'm in need of your special skill set, to obtain a certain someone," Lazzaro continued.

Aithne raised an eyebrow at his request. "Why do you need me? Are your servants that unreliable?"

Lazzaro gave her the once over, then smiled. Just below his upper lip, you could see the tips of his fangs. "Your ability to blend in, without anyone knowing how dangerous you truly are, is what I need, my dear Aithne." Crossing the room in just a few steps, he backed her up against the wall. His arms pressed the wall on either side of her, effectively caging her in. Slowly, he moved his hand to her jaw, running his fingers along the edge, as he had tried to earlier. "You do this little job for me, and I'll return your sister." Pausing for a moment, his face watched hers. "She's unharmed and will stay that way, unless…"

Glaring at him, she tried to stand a bit taller. She absolutely hated being trapped in this position. She would, of course, do what she could to save her sister. However, she couldn't help but wonder who was stupid enough to earn the wrath of the vampire king. "What do I have to do?"